Dough
or Die

Books by Winnie Archer

Kneaded To Death

Crust No One

The Walking Bread

Flour in the Attic

Dough or Die

Dough
or Die

A Bread Shop Mystery

Winnie
Archer

KENSINGTON BOOKS
www.kensingtonbooks.com

KENSINGTON BOOKS are published by

Kensington Publishing Corp.
119 West 40th Street
New York, NY 10018

All Kensington titles, imprints, and distributed lines are available at special quantity discounts for bulk purchases for sales promotion, premiums, fund-raising, educational, or institutional use.

Special book excerpts or customized printings can also be created to fit specific needs. For details, write or phone the office of the Kensington Sales Manager: Attn.: Sales Department. Kensington Publishing Corp., 119 West 40th Street, New York, NY 10018. Phone: 1-800-221-2647.

Kensington and the K logo Reg. U.S. Pat. & TM Off.

First Printing: September 2020
ISBN-13: 978-1-4967-2441-0
ISBN-10: 1-4967-2441-0

ISBN-13: 978-1-4967-2442-7 (ebook)
ISBN-10: 1-4967-2442-9 (ebook)

10 9 8 7 6 5 4 3 2 1

Printed in the United States of America

For Liane MacMillan. Thank you for teaching me about keyhole gardens, the art of letter writing, and for being the kind of friend for whom time and distance will never be an obstacle.

Chapter 1

Olaya Solis, the queen of all things bread, stood at one of the stainless steel stations in her industrial baking kitchen in the back of Yeast of Eden, the heels of her hands pressing into a mound of dark dough. She moved rhythmically, folding the dough in on itself, turning it, then pressing her heel in again. Over and over and over, she kneaded it until it was a smooth ball. I scanned the ingredients sitting on the counter next to her station: bread flour, rye flour, wheat flour, cocoa powder, yeast, and water. Whatever she was creating, it wasn't one of the standard doughs she baked for the bread shop.

"What are you making?" I asked as I wound my ginger curls into a topknot.

"It is bread for the steakhouse."

"What steakhouse?"

"The new restaurant that opened up on

Broadway. Sofia's Chophouse. Apparently, they do not like their bread supplier's products. The chef asked me to bake a sample of a typical steakhouse bread so he can taste. And so I oblige."

A new steakhouse in town. That was interesting. But even more interesting was the bread Olaya was baking. I'd been to restaurants that served a dark brown soft bread with whipped butter. I'd wondered what kind of bread it was, but it had never occurred to me that it had cocoa or rye in it.

"Can I help?" I asked. I'd arrived early to start the first-ever blog entry for Yeast of Eden, but if Olaya needed help baking, I was always game. She'd taught me everything I knew—which to this point, still put me on the novice scale. The breadth of bread knowledge she had in her brain, accumulated during her sixty some-odd years, was breathtaking. I couldn't begin to learn it all, but I wanted to absorb everything I could from this woman who favored the long-rise of traditional bread-baking, freshly ground flour, and a combination of herbs that made her creations rise above the rest. I'd be her apprentice forever—and I'd enjoy every second of my time learning from her.

"Tell me what to do," she said, raising her gaze to mine.

Olaya was usually the one giving me advice, not the other way around. I stared at her. "What do you mean? Tell you what to do about what?"

"Sandra Mays has a new television show. Well, her and a man. They are co-hosting. They will

travel around the country finding interesting bakeries to feature. They call this reality TV?"

I had to laugh. Olaya said those two words like
they were a brand-new concept, but reality TV
had a long and sordid history. "Sounds a little
like *Diners, Drive-Ins and Dives*, but with bakeries."

Olaya's brows pinched together. "I do not
know this *Diners, Drive-Ins and Dives*."

"It's a reality show. Guy Fieri—he's a celebrity
chef on the Food Network—goes all over the
country in search of cool greasy-spoon restaurants that make excellent food."

She drew back, not impressed by the idea of
being in the company of greasy spoons. Olaya
was about all things bread. She could give the
iconic Nancy Silverton and La Brea Bakery a
run for their money. There was no question that
La Brea made great bread, but somehow Olaya,
who came from a long line of *curanderas*—
women who healed—infused Yeast of Eden's
bread with some kind of magic. People left the
bread shop feeling happier, or more content, or
relaxed, or amorous. Whatever they needed,
those needs were met through the bread.

"They want to film me baking bread, they
want to hear my story, and they want to film the
Bread for Life program."

Goose bumps prickled my skin. "That's amazing!" Yeast of Eden was my home away from
home. I freelanced as a photographer, had finally started a website to promote that business,
but I also helped Olaya in the bread shop, including setting up the new blog that would fea-

ture up-to-date posts of her breads and the go-ings-on at the bakery. Working around her, the baking, and the yeasty aromas, fulfilled me in a way nothing else ever had. It was healing, and Olaya was like family to me. Sharing that all with the world via reality TV meant other people could experience the magic of Olaya and Yeast of Eden, too.

"But I do not know if I should do this." She shook her head, sighing. "No, I do not know," she repeated with a frown. "Yeast of Eden will be the pilot, they said. What is this, a pilot?"

Olaya had been in the United States for a long time and her English was nearly perfect, but there were still a few words that were not in her vernacular. "A pilot is the launch show for the series," I said.

"Ah, right. Yes. It will be a long episode be-cause it is the pilot. They told me that means three different days of filming. More, if neces-sary. The women, they may not like this. Our classes, they are personal. The women, they have gone through so much. Surely they do not want their lives broadcast on television."

"But what you're doing—the program—it's uplifting. The Bread for Life women *should* be celebrated."

"*Pero* would *you* want your life exposed for everyone to see?"

She was being a little dramatic—which was out of character for Olaya. Usually, she was com-pletely in control of everything she did, from the moment she woke up and began the day's baking to the second she laid her head down to go to sleep at night, and everything in between. Seeing her unsettled was unusual. She wore a paisley printed headband at her hairline, holding back the short strands of her iron-gray hair. Her white apron made her look like a baker, but the rest of her flowing clothes revealed her free-spirit nature. She was one-of-a-kind and had a gypsy heart, but succumbing to drama was not part of who she was.

Still, I considered her question. "I don't think I'd mind. The women are all incredible, with amazing stories. Maybe it'll help them to be featured."

She peered at me. "Help them in what way?"

I could think of lots of ways. "To gain confidence, to get jobs, to just feel good about where they are and what they're doing. People can be very supportive and everyone loves a feel-good story." I paused before adding, "Plus, it would be great publicity for the bread shop."

She shook her head at that. "I do not want publicity at the expense of other people."

"It's not at their expense, Olaya. They have stories worth telling. And your bread? It's epic. People all over the country will know about it." The whole concept behind Bread for Life was to lift up and empower low income and immigrant women in the community and help them develop hirable skills, as well as to build self-confidence. Olaya was teaching them to bake. They shared recipes, especially for indigenous breads, and each class offered the participants a chance to connect with one another. It had ended up being far more than a series of baking classes. It was akin to group therapy. A quilting bee or knitting circle, but with bread dough instead of fabric or yarn.

"*Pero*, will it exploit the women?" Olaya mused. "I cannot have that. I will not do that."

I didn't think so, but she needed to ease her own mind. "You should ask them what *they* think," I suggested. Olaya had designed the program to be three months long. The women met here at the bread shop once a week for three-hour sessions. We'd all come to love it. On class day, I woke up and started counting the minutes till it began. It wasn't just good for the women participating; it was good for Olaya and me—the ones running the sessions.

Olaya oiled the top of the round ball of dough she'd finished kneading and placed it in a proofing basket, covering it with an oiled cloth. "This needs three rises," she told me, then set it aside to let the yeast work its magic.

Olaya's office was more like a closet. It was barely big enough to fit the desk that held her computer, yet somehow she'd managed to squeeze in another chair facing the desk. That was usually my spot, turned in my seat with my knees facing sideways so they wouldn't bang against the front of the desk. But today I was in Olaya's chair, facing the computer monitor, the dashboard of the WordPress site I'd used to create the bread shop's blog, open on the screen. I clicked to open a new post—the first post—poised my fingers over the home row on the keyboard, and sat there, my mind empty of ideas.

I'd tried to write the inaugural post at home, but I'd drawn a blank. Thinking the scent of yeasty bread baking would inspire me, I'd walked Agatha, my fawn pug, then headed out to downtown Santa Sofia. The quaint, sometimes too touristy, California central coast beach town was home to me. It's where I grew up; where I first fell in love; where my heart had been broken clean in half; and where I'd come back to after my mother had died unexpectedly. Now I looked at Santa Sofia through a different lens. It was the place I called home; it's where I found love again; and it's the place I found *myself* again. I had Mrs. Penelope Branford, my neighbor across the street, an octogenarian of the most spritely order, and a fellow lover of Agatha. Mrs. Branford was like my grandmother, which made Olaya Solis something along the lines of an aunt. They were the family I'd chosen, and thankfully they fit in perfectly with the family I had: my father, Owen; my brother, Billy; and Emmaline, my best friend from my early school days forward and also my brother's fiancée.

I missed my mother beyond measure, but I knew she was an angel on my shoulder, ever-present, at least in my mind.

"Ivy."

I looked up to see Maggie Jewell, a high school girl who worked most afternoons, standing in the doorway waving at me.

I blinked. "Sorry. Guess I was daydreaming."

Maggie had her straight dark hair pulled back with a barrette. She was on the quiet side so it had taken a while to get to know her, but now that I did, she'd turned into a Chatty Cathy. She tilted her head to one side, pulling her lips right along with it. "Are you okay, Ivy? You looked like you were in a trance. Like, a million miles away."

I waved away her concern. "I'm fine! Just thinking."

"About . . . ?"

I pointed to the computer screen. "The blog is ready to go. I'm just not sure what to write about yet."

She took a step into the office—a single step—then scooted around to the chair squeezed between the desk and the wall. She was smaller than me by a few inches, so while my five-foot-eight inches felt smashed in the little space she was now occupying, the small space didn't seem to bother her any. "I can help you with that." She held her hand up and started ticking ideas off on her fingers. "You can write about Olaya's sugar skull cookies—"

Olaya made the traditional Day of the Dead cookies year round, decorating them before hiding them amidst the baked items in the bakery cases like Easter eggs for the kids to find.

"—do features on all the catering events she's done. You have pictures of everything, right?"

"I do—"

"So the pictures will tell half the story, and whatever you write will tell the rest." She went on before I could respond. "I mean, look. She did the Art Car show. She works with all those restaurants, like Baptista's Cantina and Grill, she catered the funeral for that friend of yours—"

"I'm not sure about featuring a funeral on the blog."

She nodded. "Yeah, I guess you're right about that. A funeral is kind of a downer."

It was, indeed, a downer.

"What about the classes she holds? She does those baking classes. That's how you met her, right?"

"It is." I'd come to Yeast of Eden practically every day once I'd returned to Santa Sofia. I'd been sad and lost, but Olaya's bread had helped heal me. Bit by bit, my grief over losing my mother had subsided and I decided I wanted to learn to bake bread, not just eat it.

"And the classes she's doing now? With all those women? The Bread for Life thing? That would make a great post."

And doing the reality TV gig would be huge, but I didn't want to start off with any of this. I needed an opening of some sort. Something to ground the blog and show what Yeast of Eden was all about. The bread shop had been around for years, so it wasn't a grand-opening kind of thing, but it was a grand entrance. It seemed silly to say something as simplistic as: This is our new blog! Check back to see mouthwatering pictures of bread, bread, and more bread!

Maggie tucked a strand of hair behind her ear. I stared. I'd never noticed how many piercings she had. With her hair out of the way, I could see her entire right ear. She had three earrings in her lobe, one toward the top, and several small hoops or studs in various other cartilage-heavy positions. My ear hurt just thinking about getting one of them.

I caught a glimpse of something on her collarbone. A smear of ink? No, it looked defined, even if I couldn't see what it was. "Maggie, you have a tattoo?"

By instinct, her hand went to the collar of her shirt. "Yeah. It's a dragonfly. My mom and I both got one. To, you know, show our solidarity with each other."

Solidarity. Would Olaya and Mrs. Branford get a tattoo with me? If there were ever three musketeers, that was us. But that led me to the *what* of the matter. If I were to get a tattoo, what would I choose? What would I want on my body for all of eternity?

An idea formed—not about a tattoo, but about the blog. "What about a short feature on the different people who work here? One on Olaya." I looked at Maggie. "One on you."

She puffed out her lips while she considered the idea. "Do you think people care about that? About us?"

"I think that's exactly what people care about. Olaya, the morning crew, you, me . . . we are what makes this place come alive. Remember when you spoke to the little boy in sign language? That shows who you are. Your heart. I think that's the kind of thing people want to read about."

Color flooded her cheeks. "Maybe . . ."

"It does. I melted when I saw you do that. And the skull cookies? Olaya doesn't have to spend time making those; decorating them; hiding them. But she does, and it's all for the kids. I need to ask her why she does it. Then I can write about not just *that* she does it, but *why* she does it."

Olaya's voice drifted to us from the front of the bread shop. Maggie bolted upright. "Whoops! Break's over. Gotta go," she said as she jumped up and ran out.

I went back to the computer, newly inspired. Instead of typing straight into the site, I opened up a Word document. It was going to take a few drafts and some editing to get it right, I suspected.

I was just getting my mojo, my fingers racing across the computer's keyboard, the words flowing, when Olaya opened the door and stuck her head in. "I called them."

My hands stopped their typing, hovering over the keyboard. "Called who?"

"Zula, Claire, Amelie, and Esmerelda."

I sat up straight. She'd called the four women in the Bread for Life program. "Oh! And?"

"And we will do this reality TV."

"They're in?"

Olaya nodded. "They are, as you say, in."

Chapter 2

Once Olaya made the decision to go ahead with the reality TV show, things moved with lightning speed. I imagined the filming would be weeks away. Boy, was I wrong. Olaya had been sitting on the reality TV proposal, so when she finally gave the green light, the production team was ready to get started.

Today was the day. I walked into Yeast of Eden's professional kitchen to find the Bread for Life women already at their stainless steel stations, chattering to one another. Only Esmé held back, quietly observing.

Zula was the most boisterous of the group. She was a thirty-something woman from Eritrea and had first come to the United States with her husband. He'd left her with a newborn daughter and a body covered in bruises. Her daughter, Ella, was twelve now, and despite the fact that they barely scraped by, Zula was inherently optimistic. She stood about five feet eleven inches, and with her high cheekbones, flawless glowing skin, and long braided hair, she could have competed with any supermodel in the world.

Claire was an American, was the youngest of the women, and from my knowledge of her, she didn't have two nickels to scrape together. She was a twenty-two-year-old woman who seemed to be on her own. She was the observer of the group—not a talker, so while I was curious about her, I couldn't get her to share much. She'd come into the bread shop a few times, always paying with a collection of coins she'd managed to gather. She was exactly the type of person Olaya and I hoped would benefit from the Bread for Life program, so I'd invited her. Truthfully, I hadn't held out much hope that she'd take me up on it. But then she'd asked, "How much does it cost?"

"It's free. We want to get women baking, and we want them to share recipes from their cultures."

She'd looked at me cockeyed. "I don't have any culture."

"Culture doesn't have to come from another country. It can be a family tradition. My mom always made these little thumbprint cookies called *kolaches*." The recipe had been passed down from my grandmother. I remembered the kolaches sold in Texas. I'd been so excited to discover the tradition my mother had passed on to me, but they were not the same thing at all. A dream dashed.

I didn't think Claire would come to the first

Bread for Life class, but she did. Now I hoped she'd get something out of it.

Amelie was in her early forties and had emigrated from Germany just a year before. "I had to get away," she'd told us. "I mean, what was I going to stay for? I have no more family. That is a strange thought. I am completely alone in the world. Coming here I thought I could get away from thinking about that. Actually, though, it does not help."

She had never revealed what had happened to her family, or why she was alone in the world. Whatever her story, it hadn't dampened her animation. The woman was always smiling and laughing.

"We will help each other," Olaya had said, squeezing Amelie's hand reassuringly.

Amelie had smiled, but this time it didn't quite reach her eyes. "*Danke*," she'd said, managing a faint smile.

Finally, there was Esmerelda. Esmé for short. She looked to be about my age—somewhere in her early to mid-thirties. She'd been in the US ten years ago, had gone back home to Zacatecas in Mexico, and now was back. She'd left her country behind, as had Amelie and Zula, and was starting over here. They'd left behind not only their families, whatever that meant to them, but their native languages, their cultures, the cities and states they'd grown up in, the food they'd spent their lives eating. Would any of them ever go back again, or would America become their permanent home? "I do not have a creative bone in my body," Esmé had said when she'd introduced herself, "but baking bread, that is not like holding a pencil or paintbrush. I can mix dough, so that is my creative outlet."

I looked at them, laughing and talking. They had started out as strangers, but now, after classes every week for a month, they were on the way to being friends. They were an eclectic group, each coming from a different country and each with a unique background. I thought they might get to the point where they felt like long-lost sisters, but it was too soon for that. They were still tentative about sharing their stories or about giving too much information about themselves, but it was clear they were becoming close.

Olaya came out from her office, greeting me with a smile. She clapped her hands, gathering everyone's attention. "*Mujeres*," she said, addressing the five of us. "The television crew is here."

She passed through the archway leading from the kitchen to the front of the bread shop, reappearing a minute later with several people in tow. One man hauled a heavy camera propped on his shoulder while several others lugged more cameras and lighting rigs. Another man came in dressed in a casual short-sleeved, button-down chambray shirt and jeans. He looked familiar, but I couldn't place him. Was he a local?

Before I could figure out where I'd seen him before, I was distracted by a woman I instantly recognized: Sandra Mays, local TV food celebrity turned national food personality. Wow. I couldn't believe it, but I felt a little starstruck. It wasn't like Mary Berry and Paul Hollywood were standing in front of me, but it felt almost as exciting. Well, maybe *almost* was a stretch, but it felt pretty darn thrilling.

Sandra Mays had long brown hair cut in layers, each section perfectly curled and flipped. The style softened the all-business demeanor spoken by her power suit. She surged forward, her right arm outstretched. She was a study in incongruities. She greeted each of us in turn with a firm handshake, a penetrating look with her ice-blue eyes, but with a warm and engaging, "It's so nice to meet you. I'm Sandra Mays."

Zula, Amelie, and Esmé hadn't been around Santa Sofia or California or the US long enough to know anything about Sandra Mays's celebrity. Claire may have recognized her, but if she did, she didn't let on. They weren't awestruck or spellbound or anything else remotely in that arena. I was alone in that respect. I couldn't help the grin that plastered itself on my face.

My gaze drifted from Sandra Mays to the chambray-shirt guy, then to the cameramen and tech guys who had all stopped just inside the kitchen. From the bland expressions of the people behind the scenes, I imagined they'd been through this exact scenario more times than they could count. Sandra Mays's star power didn't faze them. If anything, they seemed to be slightly nonplussed at the lack of response or reaction from the women Sandra had greeted. What did *that* mean? How would Sandra take it? Was she vain and in need of external validation, or did the women's lack of reaction make Sandra feel uncharacteristically normal?

By the tight line of Sandra's mouth by the time she finished her greetings, I went with option number one. She liked her celebrity, and more than that, she didn't like not being recognized.

And from the tight-lipped expression of the chambray-shirt man as his gaze passed over me, he didn't like the starstruck attention I'd directed at her instead of him.

I met the eyes of one of the cameramen. He lifted his eyebrows while simultaneously the sides of his mouth turned up in complete amusement. One of the tech guys, on the other hand, looked as if he was ready to burst out laughing. Clearly they'd seen Sandra's side of this scenario before, but not the ambivalence of Zula, Claire, Amelie, or Esmé. The tech guy, in particular, looked pretty pleased to see Sandra knocked down a notch or two. The cameraman shrugged at chambray-shirt man in a way that said, *It's no big deal, dude. Just let her have her moment.*

Sandra Mays glided past the last workstation until she stood face-to-face with me. She smiled, locked eyes with me, took my hand in a firm shake, and said, just as she had to the others, "It's so nice to meet you. I'm Sandra Mays."

If my grin had been big and sappy before, now I was sure it was over-the-top. She'd been a host on one of the local morning shows for as long as I could remember. My mother had loved watching her segments because they so often focused on food. I'd watched her on her own talk show when I was a teenager, which again, often had cooking segments. I'd grown up, but she looked like she hadn't aged a day. "I've been watching you since I was a kid," I gushed.

Her smile wavered, but she managed to hold it in place. "Well, isn't that nice," she said drolly as she dropped my hand.

I blinked. Had she spoken through gritted teeth?

"I didn't mean . . . I just meant . . . You've always been so . . . ." Finally I landed on, "Very nice to meet you, too."

"So you are a celebrity?" Zula asked, her eyes bright and wide.

The guys on the periphery of the kitchen chuckled, but Sandra bristled. "I am Sandra Mays," she said, hand on her chest, emphasis on the *I.*

Zula didn't pick up on Sandra's self-aggrandizing tone. "Do you know Sunny Anderson?" Zula asked. "Or the Tasty girl who does all those short videos? I love her. Or Giada? Do you know Giada? She's so skinny! How does she eat all that food and stay skinny like that, that is what I want to know." She ran her hands down her sides to show how *not* skinny like Giada she was.

Sandra brushed her hair back behind her shoulders, and turned her back on Zula. The chambray-shirt man answered for her. "She doesn't know them and they don't know her."

Sandra turned and glared at the guy. "How do you know with whom I am acquainted, and with whom I am not?"

I was impressed by the grammatical structure of her sentence, if not by her attitude.

The guy threw his hands up in defense. "So sorry. Please, set the record straight if you're on friendly terms with Sunny, the Tasty girl, or Giada."

Sandra seethed, and turned her back again, this time to speak to Olaya. "We'll need a private space in which to speak candidly with each woman—"

"Sandy," chambray-shirt man interrupted curtly. "I'm the showrunner."

She glared at him and clamped her mouth shut. The man stepped forward. "Mack Hebron," he said.

I did a mental head slap. Of course! Mack Hebron had been a *Top Chef* runner-up a few years back. I *knew* I'd recognized him. That gave him a *lot* more clout than Sandra Mays. No wonder he was the showrunner. The whole concept of *America's Best Bakeries* was probably his. Why in the world, then, was Sandra trying to muscle in and overstep her bounds?

I placed Mack in his mid-forties, but only because of the crow's feet around his eyes. He looked fit and was handsome in a square-jawed, blond-haired Brad Pitt kind of way. He stretched out his hand, first to me, then to each of the four Bread for Life women, and lastly to Olaya. "Nice to meet you all. Sandy will be setting up individual interviews with you all today."

Sandra Mays spun around, her face as red as a beet. "Do. Not. Call. Me. Sandy."

Chambray-shirt guy, who I now knew was named Mack, smirked. "Sure thing, *Sandra*," he said, drawing out the name dramatically.

Oh boy. There was no love lost between these two. This reality TV show experience could be quite entertaining for us as a result.

Sandra crossed her arms, standing back to listen as Mack took over. He spoke to the room, but mostly to Zula, Claire, Amelie, and Esmé. "We've gotten a little bit of background on each of you from Olaya and we're so glad you agreed to be part of the show. Your life stories are very important to the success of our pilot," he said. "We'll get film of the session today. The candids today, along with additional background footage, and *your* story, Olaya, will all be cut together during editing."

I imagined an episode of *Project Runway* or the Food Network's *Spring Baking Championship* where the designers or the bakers gave a blow-by-blow of what they'd sewn or prepared, including every mistake, horror, and success. That type of filming added drama and gave the viewer a real sense of the people being featured, warts and all. If that was what Mack, as the showrunner, was going for, this could end up being a huge hit.

Olaya led the crew, including Sandra and Mack, to a private space in the back of the kitchen. It was a conference room, of sorts, which she used when she met with brides planning their wedding menus, or restaurant owners or chefs needing to discuss how Yeast of Eden could enhance their food offerings. Once in a while, however, she hosted dinners there for friends and family, or for her loyal staff members. Bakery work was challenging, at best. It required early hours for the bakers, and consistency was key. Olaya showed her appreciation to the people who had stuck with her, who showed up on time, who went above and beyond what she expected, who clearly loved the bread shop as much as she did. That meant a special meal, prepared by her, every other month or so. The people who worked for Olaya knew that they were loved and appreciated.

The camera and tech guys set up the space for filming with their lights and camera set on bulky tripods before bringing in the women, one by one, to do a test with Sandra and Mack. Zula bounced in, and then fifteen minutes later, she bounced back out. "I have never talked to a camera before. It is a very interesting experience. I must admit, I like it!"

Zula was a natural, and I imagined the camera loved her.

Claire almost shuffled as she started toward the conference room. The prospect of the on-camera interview had invigorated Zula, but it had enhanced every shy bone in Claire's body. She'd agreed to be part of the program, but for a second I thought I'd have to link my arm through hers and guide her in. She managed, though, with just a little coaxing by Sandra. "You're a natural beauty," the woman said, coming across as far more gracious than she had a few minutes ago with her co-host. "The camera will love you."

I wasn't so sure that had happened because Claire came back out of the room a mere six minutes after going in. I suspected her shyness got the better of her. It might take a lot of work to get her to open up on camera.

Amelie came and went without fanfare. She had an easy smile and lighthearted demeanor about her. I could picture her shining for the camera, her bright complexion glowing under the lights, her voice excited and her laughter contagious.

And then there was Esmé. She had the fingernail of her thumb pressed between her teeth when she went into the room, her nerves getting the better of her. By the time she came out again, her complexion had turned pallid and ghostlike. She had stage fright and I wondered if she'd ever spoken publicly in her life. I gave her hand a little squeeze and she gave me a faint smile in return as she went to join the others.

Finally, I thought, we were ready to begin the class.

"Ivy?"

I turned at Sandra's voice calling me from the doorway of the makeshift interview room. She beckoned me with a crook of her finger.

"Your turn," she said after I crossed to her.

My brain stuttered and I pressed the flat of my palm to my chest. "My turn?"

"Of course. We need test footage on everyone, and you're an integral part of the bread shop."

I started to back away, suddenly understanding Claire and Esmé's anxiety. "I just help out, kind of like an apprentice. Olaya and the other women are the story."

"They are, I agree," Mack said, stepping slightly in front of Sandra. "But from what I hear, you have an interesting story, too. You're part of the appeal of Yeast of Eden, and we want the whole story."

"But there's nothing interesting about me," I tried again.

Sandra shook her head, disagreeing with me—and maybe more importantly, agreeing with Mack. "Not true. From what we hear, you moved away from Santa Sofia after high school, had a successful photography business, then came back to be a support to your family after your mother tragically died."

My life wasn't a soundbite, but that's exactly what Sandra made it seem like. I bristled.

"Sandy's right," Mack said.

Sandra stiffened, opening her mouth to chastise him about her name, I felt sure, but then she closed it again. "People watch the shows to see us and to see the stories of real people just like them. Your story is important," she told me. "It's poignant. It's *real*."

I frowned. The network had done their homework. My nerves heightened. I wanted this show to happen for Olaya and the bread shop, and to showcase Claire, Zula, Esmé, and Amelie, but broadcasting my own story was unsettling. Before I could formulate an actual coherent thought about my feelings, though, Sandra went on. "Rumor also has it that you've been instrumental in solving some of Santa Sofia's recent crimes."

Well, *that* was true. A few situations had hit too close to home and I'd had no choice but to dig in and help. In the process, I'd discovered I had a knack for crime solving.

"Please, Ms. Culpepper. Just a few minutes." Sandra edged in front of Mack and smiled in a way that told me she was very used to getting what she wanted and didn't take no for an answer. Local-turned-national celebrity went a long way. She reached her hand out, lightly touching my arm to get me moving into the makeshift interview room.

Mack shut the door behind him after he came in the room and directed me to a stool. "I'll ask you a few questions, and you just respond to them. It's that easy."

Easy for him. He was used to being in front of a camera. I, on the other hand, like the cameraman getting ready to film me, preferred to be behind the eyepiece, which for me, meant my Canon. I sat on the stool, held my chin up, wished I'd worn a jean jacket on top of my Yeast of Eden T-shirt, and waited.

"*We'll* ask her a few questions," Sandra corrected. Mack didn't bother responding. Yikes. I didn't know how these two were going to pull off a successful television show when they clearly didn't like each other and couldn't get through five minutes without one of them contradicting the other.

Mack stepped back and leaned against the wall, sweeping his arm wide for Sandra to take the lead. She smirked at him, but when she faced me again, she was all professional. She launched right into her questions. "I understand you met

Olaya Solis during a bread-making class here at Yeast of Eden. Would you tell me about that?"

I drew in a breath to calm my nerves, telling myself that they could edit out my mistakes. "Well, as you know, my mother died—"

"Cut," Mack said. "Try not to say things like *as you know.* Pretend we're hearing it all for the first time, because the audience will be."

So what I needed to do was pretend like they hadn't done a thorough background check on me, probably looking under all manner of rocks in the process. I nodded and Mack rolled his index finger in the air. We started again. Sandra repeated her line. "I understand you met Olaya Solis during a bread-making class here at Yeast of Eden. Would you tell me about that?"

I inhaled to give myself a second to calm down. "After high school, I moved to Austin, Texas, to attend college."

"A Longhorn, eh?" Sandra extended her index finger and pinkie, pressing her thumb to her middle and ring fingers at the inside of her palm, then swept her makeshift horns down like her pinkie was going to hook onto something. It was the quintessential UT Austin hand symbol. "Hook 'em, Horns!" she said with a big smile.

I mirrored her action and repeated the line, a trifle less enthusiastically than she had because the inhalation had done nothing to calm my nerves. "Hook 'em, Horns."

"And there was a broken heart involved in the decision to leave California, I understand?" Sandra said.

As I'd thought—all manner of rocks. I wasn't about to dig into my love life on air, though. "There was," was all I said, but Sandra had more information to throw at me.

"And the broken heart, was it yours, or did it belong to the very eligible Miguel Baptista?"

Wow. She'd dug deep. "Um, both of us, I guess."

"But you two have reconciled, is that right?"

I managed a small smile, despite the intrusion into my personal life. "We have, very happily."

"It is truly wonderful when things work out the way they should," Sandra said.

Had they worked out the way they should? My mother's death had brought me back to Santa Sofia. If not for that, Miguel and I wouldn't be back together. There would not have been a second chance for us. I loved Miguel, but if I could have my mother back, I'd choose that.

Sandra seemed to read my mind. "A tragedy brought you back to your hometown, is that right?"

She knew it was. "Um, yes. I'd recently gotten divorced, and then my mother, um, died." I didn't want to go into the details of her death, so I left it at that. "It was time to come back to Santa Sofia and be with my family." I felt a swell of emotion rise inside me. When I stood outside the pearly gates, if St. Peter asked me what my biggest regret in life was, it would be that I hadn't come home in time to see my mother before she was gone.

"When did you meet Olaya Solis?" Sandra quickly asked, redirecting the conversation. I could tell she knew she was going to lose me if she didn't get the interview back on track.

"I did move back . . . after . . . but I felt really lost with my mother gone. My brother, my father . . . we were all struggling. I spent a lot of time on the beach and just walking around town taking pictures. Trying to get my mojo back, you know? And I stopped into Yeast of Eden one day to get a croissant. Then the next day I came again. Pretty soon I was coming every day. I'd tried every single thing Olaya baked and couldn't get enough. Her bread made me feel . . . better, somehow."

Literally. I remembered how Olaya had told me she came from a long line of *brujas*. Witches. Their family legend told the story of a woman who had been wronged by a man. She was a *curandera*—or a healer—and had gone on to bless the future women in her family line. She believed in the power of female relationships, so she blessed the family to ensure that mothers and daughters, grandmothers, aunts, nieces, godmothers . . . *they* would be the relationships that lasted beyond every other. She had also blessed the women in the family with the ability to infuse what they baked with a bit of magic. If someone ailed, whether from heartache, physical pain, or something else, bread from the Solis women could help make things right.

"Olaya sees bread baking as an art," I said, remembering what she'd told the women in the very first class I'd taken. "She comes in early every day. Four thirty. The rest of Santa Sofia is asleep, but Olaya is here baking." Granted, she had a small crew of people to help her, but she was the one who never faltered. "She says that bread must look right. Taste right. And must be completely natural. She uses a long-rise method. That gives you the payoff. Baking bread the traditional way takes time. That's something a lot of people don't have, but it's what she believes in. It takes patience. Baking bread for Olaya Solis is like meditation. For the people who eat her bread, it's healing."

Sandra nodded, smiling. She had liked that response. "What made you take the class with her that first time?"

Again, I remembered back to the moment I'd first spoken to Olaya. I'd been standing outside the bread shop, wanting to go inside but was scared at the same time. Baking was not in my repertoire. Olaya had opened the door and stood there in a colorful caftan and red clogs. She'd looked at me with her gold-flecked green eyes and told me that she'd been waiting for me and that coming inside would change my life. I didn't know her, but she seemed to understand just what I needed to begin healing. I'd felt an instant connection with her, and as I'd walked into Yeast of Eden's kitchen, the heart and soul of the bread shop, feeling the scent of fresh-baked bread wrap around me like a warm blanket, I knew that she was right. This was where I was meant to be.

How could I explain all of this to Sandra Mays and Mack Hebron?

"Ivy?" Sandra looked at me expectantly.

I scanned the room. Mack leaned against the wall, nodding with encouragement. The cameraman, whose name I'd learned was Ben Nader—a fifty-something man who was tanned and fit and looked like he spent every spare moment in the sun—stood quietly with his equipment. He looked a million miles away, as if he could do his job without giving it a second thought. The rest of the crew melted into the background.

"Ivy?" Sandra said again. If it wouldn't have been rude, I imagined she would have snapped her fingers in front of my face to draw me out of my memory.

I blinked, reminded myself of the question, and said, "This place is magical. There's no other way to describe it. Olaya has a way of knowing what people need. She's taught me so much, not only about bread, but about myself, what I want, and what makes me happy. That's what the Bread for Life program is all about. Every person and every culture has a story, and food is almost always part of it. Bread is part of it. She had this idea to bring us together through our stories. Through our cultures. Through our bread."

Sandra sliced the air with her hand and looked at Ben. "Cut." To me, she said, "That was perfect." She ignored Mack, looking at Ben instead. "Wasn't that perfect?"

Ben had taken out his cell phone and looked like he was texting someone, only half paying attention to the on-air host, but he nodded. "Sure, Sandy-*ra*."

Sandra's lips parted like she was going to

chastise him, but then she changed her mind, closed them again, and let it go.

Mack jumped in. "Here's the plan. We're going to jump into the bread-making today and tomorrow. We'll do the intro, get any additional footage we may need, and we'll wrap on day three, unless we decide we need more. Questions?"

I just stood there while Sandra gave him a curt nod before walking out in front of me, not bothering to hold the door open for us.

Ben put his phone away, removed the camera from the tripod, and propped it on his shoulder. He had a ball cap with the news station's call letters embroidered on the front pulled low over his forehead. I held the door while he passed by me with a little nod of thanks. Mack brought up the rear. "She's a piece of work," he said as his hand gripped the door, relieving me of it. "Don't let her get to you. You're a natural. You did great."

I didn't think she was the only piece of work, but I didn't bother saying so. "Thanks, and I won't," I said, but he'd already passed me by.

Chapter 3

If I was a natural in front of the camera, I didn't know what that made Zula. That woman was born to be a reality TV show host. As she led us through the history of *hembesha*, a traditional Eritrean food, she had an animated conversation with the camera Ben Nader held. Her personality blossomed with each word she spoke.

Sandra walked up and looked at the ingredients on the counter in front of Zula. "Tell me more about this . . . hembesha."

Zula adopted a serious air. "It is an East African bread. Soft. Fragrant. Very earthy. I know you will like it very well—"

Sandra bent at the waist to look at the collection of ingredients at Zula's station, examining each container, picking one up to look at it before putting it down again and replacing it with another. "I'm sure we will."

Zula's eyes were wide and uncertain as Sandra

abruptly walked away from her and came over to where I stood. "Ivy, you're what Olaya has called an apprentice baker at Yeast of Eden. You're here helping out today?"

I smiled at her, trying to tuck away a few wayward strands of curls that had slipped from my topknot. I was going to be on national cable television representing Santa Sofia and Yeast of Eden. Of course my hair hadn't cooperated. It felt strange rehashing the same story we'd talked about just a short time ago during my interview, but I launched into it nonetheless. "That's right. I took a bread making class from her and—"

"Right. Interesting. And today you're all making . . . what's it called again?"

"Hembesha," I said, my smile becoming strained. Sandra Mays was clearly going through the motions. She didn't seem to have much real interest in what we were making or the group of women here. "It's an Eritrean bread."

"Yes, of course. Hembesha. What can you tell us about it?"

Aside from what Zula had already shared? Not much. "Zula can tell you more about it than I can." I looked at her instead of at Sandra. "You ready?"

"I am ready," Zula said, meeting my gaze with more composure than I was feeling. She turned to the other women. "You have everything you need, including ground coriander, cardamom, and fenugreek."

Mack came up next to Zula. Ben turned his body and directed his camera at the two of them. "Tell me about this . . . fenugreek," he said amiably. His demeanor was night-and-day different than Sandra's and he'd asked the obvious question given that most of us probably had never heard of fenugreek. I knew I hadn't. As Zula unscrewed the cap of one of the jars at her station, I did the same. As she held the jar out for Mack to smell, I put the jar of ground seeds to my nose and took a whiff. I tried to put my finger on what it reminded me of when Mack exclaimed, "It's like curry!"

Ah, exactly!

Sandra elbowed her way back into the frame, crowding Zula on her other side. "These are spices specific to Africa, I assume?"

Zula shook her head. "No, not to Africa. Asia, I think. The fenugreek seeds were discovered in Iraq, too."

"Fascinating," Sandra said, although her fascination didn't feel authentic. Looking back to Ben and his camera, she continued. "Learning about different cultures is a big part of the Bread for Life program here at Yeast of Eden. Where else would you learn about—" She looked at Zula. "What's it called again?"

Mack answered instead. "Fenugreek."

Claire pressed her lips together, stifling a laugh. She and Amelie listened intently, but Esmé stretched one hand across her forehead and rubbed her temples with the thumb and middle finger like she was fighting a headache. I watched her as she slipped her cell phone from her back pocket and quickly texted someone. She put her phone away again and went back to massaging her temples. Her expression was pained, but she closed her eyes and took a deep breath. A moment later, when she looked at Sandra again, she looked calm and collected.

Odd, I thought. What was wrong with her?

Zula began mixing the ingredients together, talking through each step as she added all-purpose flour, wheat flour, dry yeast, the mixture of spices, crushed fresh garlic, one egg, and warm water to the bowl. She dug her hands in, combining it all together.

Each of the women did the same, myself included. In seconds, my hands were covered in the sticky mess of dough, but as I incorporated more flour, it became less sticky.

"Keep kneading," Zula said. "You must mix in every last bit of the flour. After a short while, it will become soft and smooth."

For a minute I doubted her, but she was right. It took some time, but the dough formed a smooth ball. After she instructed us to cover it and we each set the dough aside so it could rise, she called "Cut!"

Mack laughed, but Sandra scowled at Zula usurping her reality TV authority. Or maybe she was irritated at Mack for indulging Zula. If Sandra had called *Cut!* I imagined Mack would have been testy about it. Those two had some issues to work out if they were going to make *America's Best Bakeries* a success. TV viewers wanted to see chemistry between the hosts, not tension.

We all followed Zula's lead and covered our bowls. "Oh! Uncut!" She looked at Ben and rolled her finger. He counted down with his fingers and pointed at her. Mack bit his lip, holding in his burgeoning guffaw. Sandra, however, didn't have any mirth in her. Her scowl was back, front and center. Or, rather, it had never left.

"We must wait forty-five minutes for the dough to rise," Zula said. "Maybe we could let it rise longer, but we will use the magic of television to show the best finished hembesha." She crouched in front of her station, retrieving something from the lower shelf.

When she stood, I laughed. She held a tray with a fully baked, golden tear-apart round of hembesha. Impressive. I gave her a thumbs-up and mouthed, "Good planning." She was determined to make sure her segment for this new show was as good as it could be.

Mack nodded with approval as he tore off a piece of the bread. The others gathered around and did the same. All except Sandra, who remained on the periphery. Ben swiveled the camera to face her. "And that, friends, is hembesha."

She signaled for Ben to cut. "The bread has to rise for forty-five minutes?" she asked. Zula confirmed with a nod and Sandra continued. "So we'll pick up then."

"Nicely done," Mack said. Zula beamed, her smile illuminating her face. Mack pulled her aside and they chatted. I wondered about what, but turned my attention to the camera, sound, and light people as they put their equipment in the makeshift conference room. When Ben came back into the kitchen, he held up a pack of cigarettes. "Where can I smoke?"

It was a good question. Santa Sofia was a smoke-free town in public spaces. "The back parking lot is the only place around here," I said. I showed him the door and followed him outside. "There's a bench over there." I pointed out one of the flowerbeds.

He angled his head to look, raising his eyebrows at me. I led him closer. The spring blooms in the flowerbed had exploded with color. The hydrangeas, lavender, coral bells, columbine, bellflowers, and daisies flourished to the point that the little black wrought-iron bench was well hidden.

Ben made a face. "I think—"

He broke off and wandered past the bench, looking up at the building. I followed, curious about what he'd been about to say. And also to make sure he didn't make his way all the way to the front of the bread shop to light up. No smoking in public spaces was a strict ordinance that the city took very seriously.

I needn't have worried. He stopped beside a lemon tree. Behind it, vines climbed the brick walls. I stood beside him, watching him curiously as he adjusted his ball cap and peered up to the roofline, then straight ahead at the vines. "It used to be here."

"What used to be here?" a man's voice said, coming up beside me. It was a voice I recognized well.

I spun to face him, knowing that a smile had lit up my face. "Hey, you," I said.

Miguel Baptista stood six feet, which meant he lowered his head and I arched my neck for our lips to meet. "Hey," he said, smiling back at me.

I did a quick introduction. "Miguel Batista, Ben Nader. Ben, Miguel." To Miguel I said, "Ben is the local cameraman for *America's Best Bakeries* segment. They started taping today. He works with Sandra Mays and Mack Hebron." To Ben I said, "Miguel is the owner of Baptista's Cantina and Grill." I left out that part about Miguel being my boyfriend. As a thirty-six-year-old woman, it sounded silly to phrase it that way. We'd been boyfriend/girlfriend back in high school. Now we were on a path toward a life together, but how did you work that into casual conversation?

Miguel and Ben shook hands, then both turned to stare at the vines climbing the wall. Ben had lit his cigarette and taken a few drags, but now he tossed it on the ground and stamped it out with a twist of his foot. "Me and my friends used to go up to the roof here."

I followed his gaze. "Like *climb* up?"

He adjusted his hat. "Yeah. God, it's been a long time, but I'm sure this is the spot. This place wasn't a bakery back then. Or . . . at least I don't think it was." He stepped into the flowerbed next to the lemon tree and reached his hands out, pulling some of the vines apart. "There used to be a ladder here." After a second, he moved a few steps and tried again.

"You think it's still there?" I asked. Ben looked to me to be in his fifties, which meant high school had been more than thirty years ago. Enough time for an old ladder to the rooftop of the bread shop building to be long gone.

He made no acknowledgment that I'd spoken. Instead, he walked farther down the parking lot, looked up at the side of the building, then stopped and split the vines apart again. "Bingo," he said, looking back at us, a goofy grin on his face. "I knew it was here."

Miguel and I both stared. "Wait," he said. "There's actually a ladder there?"

Ben yanked some of the vines away, clearing them away from the ladder, then stood back to show us. "Hidden right here."

The guy was right. A metal ladder, which looked like a rusty fire escape contraption from an old San Francisco brownstone or painted lady, had become a makeshift trellis for the vines. I peered up, shading my eyes from the glare of the late afternoon sun. "You used to climb this?"

"Santa Sofia was a lot smaller back then. Not many places to get away from life." He grinned, remembering. "My friends and I, we used to climb up here, stare at the ocean, and philosophize as only teenagers can. We were going to save the world, you know?"

I did know. Miguel and I had both been young idealistic teenagers once upon a time. Instead of wanting to save the world, though, we'd been ready to conquer it . . . together. That is, at least, until things fell apart for us.

Ben's voice turned a little melancholy as he philosophized. "There aren't many places you can truly be alone, you know? If you find the right moment, you might get a little piece of the beach to yourself, but not usually. If you live alone—but that's where you live, not necessarily where you can just think. Not enough people just think."

"That's why people meditate," I said. "You can get apps that take you through guided meditation, so you can think . . . or turn off your thinking, as the case may be."

Ben rolled his eyes, but not dismissively. It was more a *that's not for me* motion. "I'm not into meditation, but . . . Christ. If only I'd remembered this place—if I'd had time and a place to think—a lot of things might have turned out differently." He hiked up one leg, testing his weight on the bottom rung of the ladder. He hauled himself up onto the next rung, taking it slow.

"Do you think it's safe?" I asked, stretching my hand out as if I could catch him if the rungs gave way and he tumbled backward.

He hung on to the vertical rails, moving his body to shake the ladder. It squeaked and rattled, but it stayed put. I thought he was going to keep climbing, but instead he dropped down, dug his packet of cigarettes from his pocket, knocked one free, and lit it. He looked longingly toward the roof.

"Ben!" Sandra Mays's shrill voice sounded loudly from behind us. I turned sharply, thinking she'd been lurking, but she wasn't there.

Ben frowned, his nostalgic moment interrupted.

"Ben, where are you?" Sandra hollered again.

He sighed and took a deep drag of his cigarette. "Over here," he called.

Her voice came at us loudly again. "I need to talk to you. Now."

This time the roll he gave with his eyes clearly conveyed frustration. He didn't look like he appreciated being summoned by Sandra. "The diva beckons," he muttered, his mouth twisted into a grimace. To her he didn't respond.

"Ben!" she said shrilly. More insistent. "Goddammit, come here."

He sighed, took another mighty drag off his cigarette, and stepped out of the flowerbed. "On my way," he snapped, then followed with an annoyed, "Jesus."

He walked toward the corner. Slowly. And taking in as much of the nicotine as he possibly could before he dropped his cigarette, grinding it out like he had the first one. After a backward wave to Miguel and me, and a somewhat longing glance in the direction of the ladder he'd rediscovered, he turned the corner and disappeared from sight.

Chapter 4

Olaya scheduled a special Bread for Life class the next day so the television crew could come back and finish their filming. She had gotten to Yeast of Eden at four thirty in the morning, as usual, then had spent the entire day baking and working in the front of the shop. By the time I showed up at three thirty in the afternoon, a half hour before everyone else was due to arrive, she looked dead tired. Or maybe it was more than that. Black circles ringed her eyes and her olive skin was unusually pale.

The bread shop closed at four and, as usual, a line queued along the bakery cases. Maggie had been working for Olaya long enough to know how to work the counter. She was one of those students who had graduation credits piled up, which gave her three off-periods. She was the perfect employee and made the afternoon shifts run like clockwork. She worked through the customers one by one, quickly and efficiently.

Olaya made her way to one of the bistro tables. She sat, folded her arms, and rested her forehead on them.

I sat down opposite her. "Are you okay?"

She lifted her head just enough to peer up at me with her glassy eyes. "I never get sick . . ."

"But you are now," I finished for her.

She nodded, lowering her head again. Even her normally vibrant silver curls looked lackluster, as if whatever virus she had had seeped into the hair follicles.

"I can run the class," I said. "You should go home and rest."

"They are filming this afternoon. I have to be here."

"Not if you're sick." I didn't want her to miss it, but she didn't look like she'd be able to stand, let alone help with the class.

The doors between the front of the bread shop and the kitchen swung open and Sandra Mays and Mack Hebron strolled in followed by Ben Nader and his camera. Ben wore the same cap he'd worn the day before, loose jeans, and a button-down. He dressed like a much younger man than he was. I kind of liked that about him. He lifted his chin in a subtle greeting as he passed us by, heading through the swinging doors and into the kitchen. The other tech guys were nowhere to be seen. Sandra was dressed down in a navy blouse and jeans, but her hair was styled exactly as it was every time she was on television. It was, I surmised, part of her brand. She would have fit in well in Texas, with the back-combing that gave her hair height on the crown and the curl that lightly flipped her hair up at her shoulders. Mack, on the other hand, looked completely natural, as if he didn't give a single thought to what he wore or how his hair looked. I knew that wasn't the case and his effortless look, especially the careless spikes of his hair, were all by design. He probably spent a fair amount of time in front of the mirror with his hair gel, but he pulled off the carefree look very well.

He stood back, arms folded over his chest as Sandra waved jazz hands in the air, clearly ready to hold court. "Hello, hello, my darlings!"

The people in line turned. A collective gasp rose up, before the eyes of a twenty-something woman buying a dozen croissants and two baguettes opened wide and she exclaimed, "You're Sandra Mays!"

Sandra smiled indulgently. "Guilty as charged."

The young woman dropped her bread on the counter, whipped her cell phone out of the back pocket of her jeans, and hurried over to the reality TV star. "Can I get a selfie with you?"

Sandra's smile widened. It was clear that she lived for moments like this. "Abso-*lute*-ly."

They stood side by side. Sandra's groupie held her phone in her outstretched hand. I held in a laugh. They were both well practiced at the art of the selfie. They each held their eyes open—no blinking! Sandra curved her lips into a sleek, practiced smile, while her biggest fan positioned her lips in what I was sure she thought was an alluring pucker. She pressed her thumb against the button on her screen, snapping several pictures before letting her face morph back into its normal expression. "Thanks," she said, but she was looking at her phone rather than Sandra. Already posting her story on Instagram, no doubt.

Which seemed fine with Sandra. She glided to the people who'd stayed in line but who were taking pictures with their phones or holding out pens and Yeast of Eden bread lists for her to sign autographs. She was in full star mode, even if her star still mostly shone over Santa Sofia and the surrounding areas. Mack was the real star, but nobody had noticed him yet. I snuck a look at him, half expecting him to be irritated at not being recognized, but his amused expression seemed to communicate the opposite. The guy didn't look bothered at all by Sandra hogging the spotlight, which was interesting given their dynamic the last time they'd been together. Maybe they'd buried the hatchet, so to speak.

The clock struck four—without any fanfare— and I flipped the sign hanging in the door from OPEN to CLOSED. Maggie finished up with the last of the customers, ushering them out, and then turned the lock on the door. It was unusual to have any bread left at the end of the day, but when there was, Olaya donated it to a food closet in town. Today, there were two baguettes, an olive loaf, and a handful of plain croissants, all of which I'd pack up and drop off after filming.

With the fans gone, Sandra turned to Olaya and me. "Ready to start taping?"

"We are," Olaya said as she stifled a cough.

Sandra spun around, her mouth agape. She took a step backward. "Are you . . . sick?"

The bags around Olaya's eyes looked darker than they had a minute ago. She started to shake her head, but I stopped her by saying, "Yes. You are." To Sandra, I said, "She is. Sick. Very."

Olaya listed to one side, unsteady on her feet. Sandra put more distance between them. Her eyes were wide with horror. Actual horror. "Do. Not. Come. Near. Me. I do not want sick germs. Do you hear me? I. Can. Not. Get. Sick."

Mack shook his head and shot Sandra a disgusted look. He hurried right up to Olaya and held her by the elbow. "Whoa there. Let's get you to a chair." He looked at me, his raised eyebrows asking where he should take her.

I moved quickly behind the counter and held open the swinging door, stepping aside for him to pass through. Sandra stayed far, far behind, but Mack was right there, guiding Olaya, following me to her office. He deposited her in her chair. "I'll get her some water," he said. I waited until he was out of earshot before I spoke. "You are sick, Olaya. You need to go home."

"But the taping. The show." Her voice was low and she closed her eyes as she spoke.

"I can handle it tonight, but this place doesn't run without you. You need rest."

Olaya managed to stand up. She opened her mouth to speak. To disagree with me, I thought, but she stopped. Her eyes fluttered, she wobbled on her feet, and she grabbed for me. "Okay. *Por favor.* Take me home."

Chapter 5

Not wanting Olaya to be alone, I called her sisters, first Consuelo, then Martina. Unfortunately, they were not women who had their phones glued to their hands at the ready for any call that came in. Neither answered.

I thought about asking Maggie to go home with Olaya, but she'd worked a full shift. I didn't have the heart to pull her away from whatever she had planned that night. My father? He'd help me out in a heartbeat, even if he didn't know Olaya very well. I started to dial him, but changed my mind at the last second, instead dialing Penelope Branford, my intrepid octogenarian neighbor from across the street. The woman was as spunky as someone half her age and I was pretty sure she would do just about anything for me. The feeling was mutual. Mrs. Branford and Olaya Solis were not women who'd been born into my family, but they were people I chose to *be* part of my family.

"I'll get a Lyft," she said when I told her what I needed.

I laughed. The woman was elderly, but she was far from old. She was as in-tune with the world as they came. I wanted to be just like her when I hit my eighties. I gave her Olaya's address, knowing she was typing it into the ride-share app as I spoke. She'd be across town in ten minutes flat.

I'd been right on the money. I'd barely gotten Olaya out of my car when a hunter-green sedan rolled up behind me. I expected the back-seat door to open so I did a double take when the front passenger door creaked open instead. Penelope Branford appeared. She swung her legs out, propped her cane in between them, and used it to propel herself out and up.

The Lyft driver, meanwhile, had scurried around to help her, taking her gently by the elbow and guiding her onto the sidewalk. "Mrs. Branford, it was a real pleasure," the man said. He clasped his fingers to the bill of his hat, tipping it so gallantly that I could imagine it being a top hat instead of an Oakland A's cap.

"Spencer, my boy, the pleasure was all mine. You take care of yourself, and if you want to talk more about your plans, you just let me know. You have my number now. Don't be shy about calling."

"I won't, Mrs. Branford," the guy said. "I definitely won't."

"You know that guy?" I asked her as she came up to Olaya and me.

"You have to ask?"

Touché. The decades Mrs. Branford spent in the classroom teaching English at Santa Sofia High School meant she, quite literally, knew everyone. Spencer the Lyft driver sped off. By my side, Olaya was fading fast. I helped her inside her little house, surreptitiously looking around as she directed me to her bedroom. The house was her in every way. Colorful teal, white, and orange pillows dotted the pale yellow couch and off-white chairs. A woven Mexican cloth lay across the coffee table. From the corner of my eye, I caught a glimpse of the kitchen. It wasn't fancy, but even from my vantage point, I could see that it had every tool Olaya could possibly need to bake the bread she was famous for. Open shelves were lined with glass jars filled with what looked like dried herbs.

Mrs. Branford followed us down the hallway, her cane lightly striking the floor as she walked. It was more of an afterthought than a necessity. At least that was true most of the time. Once or twice, I'd felt like she had really needed it, but usually, it was more of a prop. She put it to good use when she felt it would benefit her—not in a diabolical or wicked manner, though. Mrs. Branford was simply pragmatic.

"I will be fine," Olaya said. She started to turn her head to look over her shoulder, but wobbled on her feet again.

"Well, of course you will," Mrs. Branford replied.

"But no one should be alone when they feel miserable."

Now Olaya did manage to turn around. "You are staying here with me?"

Penelope Branford and Olaya Solis had a history, and it wasn't a pleasant one. They'd figured out how to overcome it, but I wouldn't say they were exactly friends. More like frenemies. Kind of like the dowager countess and Isobel Crawley on *Downton Abbey*. They enjoyed each other's company in a complicated and passively adversarial way, but deep down, they really adored one another.

We got Olaya settled in bed, I quickly filled Mrs. Branford in on what was happening at the bread shop, and I left her to her crossword puzzles and her e-reader. "Don't worry about us," she called to me as I opened the front door. "I'll make sure the stubborn woman gets her rest."

I waved back at her. I had no doubt. Mrs. Branford might even use her cane, if necessary.

Chapter 6

I walked back into the bread shop, half expecting the taping to have started. It hadn't. Instead, the crew had spent the time holding more one-on-one interviews with the Bread for Life women. Additional crew members for the show leaned back against the baking stations or perched on stools thumbing through Instagram posts or sending texts. I raised my eyebrows, asking a silent *What's going on?* No one noticed, so no one responded.

"At long last," Sandra said when she spotted me. "Can we finally begin now?"

Now that I was back at the bread shop, Sandra walked around the kitchen, dusting her fingertips on the stainless counters of the stations she passed. "Who's leading the class today?" she asked, her back to us.

Amelie raised her arm. "I am."

"Very good."

From behind her, Mack gave a heavy sigh and shook his head. I could hear him saying in his head that he was the showrunner, not Sandra, but he didn't stop her this time.

Sandra, for her part, completely ignored Mack. She looked around, her gaze landing on Ben. "Are we ready?"

The cameraman looked up from under the brim of his ball cap and gave a thumbs-up.

"Are you taping the entire class?" I asked him.

"Yep." That was all he said. Yep. He was a man of few words.

Sandra filled in the details. "We'll edit it later. The more tape we get now, the better. We'll cut in pieces of everyone's story."

"We will," Mack said, the words dripping with sarcasm. The message was clear. Sandra wouldn't be doing any editing, but Mack would.

"What about Olaya?"

"She can't be here if she's sick," Sandra said. She was all heart.

Mack jumped in, supplying the empathy. "Is she okay?"

"She's resting," I said.

Sandra fluttered one hand in the air. "We've got lots of tape on her. We'll cut it together. It'll be great. Don't worry."

The words she said sounded right, but I did worry. What if Olaya didn't come across strongly enough as the person behind Yeast of Eden? It would be like featuring La Brea Bakery without Nancy Silverton. Without Olaya, there was no bread shop. She was the beating heart of the place and that needed to be represented in the final cut of the show.

Mack excused himself, saying that he'd be right back. Sandra's head swiveled as she watched him disappear into the front of the bread shop. She tapped the mic clipped to her blouse. "Testing."

"All good," one of the crew said.

I couldn't shake the feeling that there was something a little shifty about Sandra Mays. Maybe Mack Hebron's disdain for her had unwittingly rubbed off on me, but I didn't think I could trust her. I had the feeling she would say whatever she had to say to get the story she wanted—to hell with the consequences. I'd heard rumors that she'd tried to transition into bigger markets over the years, but she was still in our sleepy little coastal town. Until now. What had she done to get this gig?

She took a moment to primp, then turned to face the camera Ben had aimed at her. He held his hand up as he counted down from five, verbally at first, then silently on the last two numbers. He pointed at Sandra and she began.

"We are here today at a Santa Sofia gem— Yeast of Eden. The bread shop's owner, Olaya Solis, has been in business for—well, for as long as I can remember. This town, as some of you may know, is where I got my start." She chuckled. "Olaya Solis is an institution here in Santa Sofia, as much as I am." Another self-deprecating chuckle.

I looked around for Mack, but he hadn't come back yet. Where had he gone and why was Sandra filming without him?

She paused long enough that I figured this is where they'd cut in some footage from an interview with Olaya. Sandra started again. "Olaya is a magician with bread. Everyone in Santa Sofia knows firsthand that anything baked at Yeast of Eden will change their lives for the better. Olaya is quite the community activist, as well. As an immigrant with a heartwarming success story, she hasn't rested on her laurels. Instead, she's worked to pay it forward, as they say, by developing a program called Bread for Life. It's kind of like the old adage, give a man a fish, he eats for a day; teach a man to fish, he eats for a lifetime. That is exactly what Olaya intends to do with the Bread for Life program. These women come together for fellowship and baking, sharing the breads of their different cultures with one another, and then, hopefully, taking what they've learned and spreading that love through their continued baking. We are thrilled to be featuring Yeast of Eden as our first bakery featured in *America's Best Bakeries.*"

So this was the intro Mack had referred to yesterday. I had to admit, it was good. I started to say so—to no one in particular—but stopped when Mack came back in from the front of the shop. He took one look around and stopped short. "What the hell?"

Sandra gave him a withering look. "Where did you go, Mack? We had to start without you."

He surged forward, his amiable demeanor gone, his lips suddenly thin and tight. "Who do you think you are, Sandy? This is not a one-woman show. I am the goddamned showrunner and we are co-hosts. Co. Hosts. That means I am involved in everything connected with this show." He quickly scanned the room and threw up his hand apologetically. "Sorry for the inconvenience, folks—"

Sandra surged toward Mack, red creeping up her neck and onto her cheeks. "Let me tell *you. I* am going to be the star of this show. After that stunt you pulled in New York, you're lucky I even agreed to be seen with you—"

The veins in his neck flexed, but his voice miraculously remained controlled. "The stunt I pulled? That was all on you, Sandy."

Her eyes bulged, her face turned fire-engine red, and for a second I thought she might spontaneously combust. "Don't call me that!" she screeched.

I shot a frenzied look at Zula, Claire, Amelie, and Esmé, wanting to get them out of the kitchen, but they were completely focused on the unfolding drama in front of them, drawn to it like moths to a flame. The other crew members watched Mack and Sandra, too, for that matter, but where the four women were enthralled (and looked slightly terrified) the crew watched as if the scene unfolding before them was no more entertaining than an amateur golf tournament on a cloudy day being watched by people who couldn't care less about putting a tiny ball into a tiny hole.

Mack folded his arms across his chest, looking altogether unconcerned about the state Sandra was in. "It's your name," he said before leaning in close to her and whispering something in her

ear. She recoiled, then let loose her arm and
shoved his shoulder. The blow hardly fazed him.
His upper body jerked back slightly, but his feet
never moved. He was rooted to the ground.

Sandra's hands were fisted next to her sides. A
vein in her forehead bulged. God, I hoped she
wouldn't have an aneurism. Somehow she managed to control her voice. "You are a horrible
human being, Mack." She turned her back on
him and muttered something under her breath
that sounded like, "Karma, Mack. You can't fight
karma."

I had no idea what he'd actually whispered to
her, but I got the distinct feeling that their relationship had gone beyond the professional at
some point. I didn't want to be on Sandra Mays's
bad side.

I looked at the baking racks, hoping something
was still left that could calm her down, but it was
the end of the day, the racks were empty, and
there was nothing magical about the crumbs that
remained. She sucked in a breath. Then another.
None of us could tear our eyes away from her.
The vertical vein in her forehead sunk back into
place. Her color returned to normal. If not for
her fisted hands, I would have thought the crisis
had been averted, but I could sense the hard
simmer just under her skin. She was one degree
away from a boil.

She looked at Ben. A silent communication
transpired between them and he raised the camera to his shoulder, giving one succinct nod.
"Ready to go again."

Sandra didn't look at Mack. Didn't make eye

contact. Although Mack, with an expression I couldn't quite read—Was it contempt? Or disinterest?—did look at Sandra. He wasn't fazed by her, which gave him a leg up in their battle. She, on the other hand, was struggling to maintain control. Mack had completely unsettled her. Com-plete-ly. Everyone scurried to their positions. Zula, Claire, Amelie, and Esmé shot puzzled glances at each other, then at me. I forced a smile. Was this the way things were in the volatile world of reality TV?

I tied on my apron and took my place next to Esmé. Sandra turned to face us all, her smile as strained as mine was. "Are we ready?"

Mack looked at Ben and rolled his index finger in the air. It was the okay for Ben to count down. He held up his hand and counted down on his fingers, saying, "Five. Four," then he mouthed, "Three. Two. One," and pointed at Mack.

Mack Hebron was a pro. I knew he'd studied in France and had had a restaurant in North Carolina, where he had been close to being a Top Chef—his foray into reality television. He'd transitioned to pastries at some point and had worked as one of the head pastry chefs at a dessert bar restaurant in Manhattan before being tapped by the cable network as the next big thing. And he was. His expertise and success with his first baking show on a cable food network had been the impetus for multiple other shows, including this one: *America's Best Bakeries*. How Sandra Mays got involved was a mystery, but she seemed to think she was the star, not Mack.

Mack started the same intro Sandra had just

given, pausing when it was time for Sandra to say her lines. They'd clearly rehearsed it. The fact that she'd gone through it alone meant that she'd intentionally pushed his buttons.

Once the intro was done, I gestured for Amelie to step up to the demonstration station. It was just like the other stations with the exception of the huge overhead mirror angled to allow the other people in the kitchen to see what was happening. Olaya used that spot to lead her classes. Her students could see the ingredients, how she mixed things together, and her method for kneading.

Amelie raised her arms, waving her hands. She was summoning up her on-camera personality. "Attention!" Her voice bellowed and everyone's attention came to her. "Today," she said, "we are going to make *Brezel.*"

We looked at her blankly.

"It is German for . . . can you not guess?"

I said the word over and over in my head, mouthing it, then saying it under my breath. "Brezel. Brezel. Brezel—Oh! Pretzel!"

Amelie's face lit up and she clapped. "Exactly! Pretzel! I thought and thought about what German bread to teach to you. Pumpernickel came to my mind. I do love the pumpernickel. I also thought of *Fünfkornbrot*—five-seed bread. But after Zula's hembesha, I thought, no, no, I must do the Brezel. The pretzel." She grinned, feigning shyness. "It is very good."

"Who doesn't like a good pretzel?" Sandra asked, inserting herself into the frame.

Amelie clapped again. Her enthusiasm was contagious. I couldn't help but smile along with

her. "Right. Yes! Everyone loves pretzels." She
set to work, taking us through the process of
mixing the dough. "The Brezel is really like a
bread. Traditionally, they are dipped in a lye
bath. It is science. The lye reacts to the dough to
give the crust the dark brown and crunchy outer
layer."

"Lye?" Sandra's eyes went wide. "Isn't lye dangerous?"

"Yes, yes. You must protect the eyes especially.
But we will not use lye. Instead, we will make a
baking soda solution that mimics the chemical
reaction we want to happen."

Okay. Interesting. Pretzels were not something Olaya had ever made at Yeast of Eden, at
least to my knowledge. She was going to be so
disappointed to miss learning about something
new.

We followed Amelie step by step as we dis-
solved the yeast in warm water, then mixed it
with the flour and sugar. We kneaded butter
into the dough, adding drips of water to get to
the right consistency. "We let the dough rest,
meanwhile we clean up."

That's just what we did, putting the ingredients away and washing the dough hooks from
our mixers. Amelie brought us all together
again and we moved on to the next steps. "We
knead the dough, then cut it into twelve pieces.
Make sure they are the same size," she said. We
watched her, then copied the action, as she
rolled the first piece into a twenty-inch thin
length, tapering the ends. "Now we form the
Brezel," she said. We all watched the mirror

above her and did as she demonstrated. First she formed the length of dough into the letter U. Next she crossed the ends over one another, twisting them in the process. Finally, she brought the ends down and placed them at the bottom of the U, just at the curve.

I looked at hers, then looked at mine. Hers looked like a pretzel. Mine looked thin and unappetizing. I frowned. It was harder than it seemed.

One by one, we rolled and folded our dough into the traditional pretzel shape, laying them on a piece of parchment.

"They must go into the refrigerator now," she said. "One hour."

Ben filmed us taking our baking trays to the walk-in refrigerator and sliding them onto a rack inside. "Why do you need to refrigerate them?" Sandra asked.

"If you baked, you'd know the answer to that." Mack's voice had been quiet, the muttering not meant for anyone to hear. I pretended like I hadn't.

"More science," Amelie said. "The Brezel forms a hard layer, like a skin, you know? Then when we dip the Brezel into the baking soda solution, the skin absorbs that liquid in a unique way. It is what makes the traditional shiny brown crust of the Brezel."

Made sense. Science in action. The hour passed quickly as we all fielded questions from Mack and Sandra, finished cleaning our mixing bowls and stations, and prepared the baking soda solution on the stove. When the water-and-soda mixture was boiling, we retrieved our pretzels and used slotted spoons to carefully drop the pretzels into the bubbling water. "Turn them over after ten seconds," Amelie said. We had only six burners on a commercial stove, so took turns dipping and placing our pretzels back on our parchment-lined baking sheets.

"Now, we score and salt," Amelie said. She went back to her station with her tray. We followed suit, each of us taking up our sharp knife and drawing the blade across the dough. She sprinkled her pretzels with coarse salt, and we did the same. "Now we bake at four hundred degrees for just about fifteen minutes. Twenty minutes for a darker crust. Very, very easy!"

After we took them out of the ovens to cool, Sandra sighed as if she was expelling the weight of the world. "Let's take a break, shall we?"

The crew looked longingly at the cooling pretzels. "They must cool a little bit," Amelie said. "We will burn our mouths otherwise. In Germany, we have them with butter, but you can do like the Americans do and have them with mustard. It is your choice."

"Cut," Mack said. "We'll take a break. Pretzels afterward."

That was all the permission any of the crew needed. They scattered to the front of the bread shop and out to the street, while Mack headed out to the back parking lot.

The four Bread for Life women fell in together and disappeared through the swinging doors into the bread shop. A second later, the bell on the front door tinkled and their chatty voices faded away.

Ben lowered his camera. He grabbed a piece of bread that had been left on one of the bakery racks in the kitchen, uncapped a water bottle to take a long swig, and disappeared to put his camera down in the back room. He reappeared, bread in hand, and walked out the back door of the kitchen to the parking lot without a word to anyone. Smoke break, I thought.

Sandra watched him intently. She gave a little shake of her head as she watched him go

"Is he okay?" I asked.

She took out her cell phone and checked the screen. "I don't know. Something's up, but he doesn't share like he used to."

Which implied that he had shared once upon a time—and that they'd been close enough to have that type of friendship. All I could think was that everyone was acting so strangely. Reality TV seemed to bring out the weird in people. Before I could ask Sandra about her history with Ben the cameraman, she dialed a number and promptly vanished into the front of the bread shop. Once again the bell on the door tinkled, and she was gone.

My break was going to be spent cleaning up the front of the bread shop. I found a brown paper bag in which to put the remains of the day so I could deliver them to the food closet on my way home, grabbed a cloth, went out to the front, and started wiping down the counters. I moved on to the little bistro tables, running the cloth over them, then the seats of the chairs. People strolled by the shop, glancing in through the windows. One couple stopped and peered in. The woman said something to the man, who nodded. They walked on, but I knew they'd be back another day to buy bread.

From the corner of my eye, I caught a glimpse of Ben turning the corner from a side street onto Cambria, cell phone to his ear. He'd walked from the back parking lot to the beach side of the bread shop, immersed in whatever conversation he was having. It did not look like a pleasant one. His eyes were still shaded by his cap, but red crept up his neck and onto his cheeks. He gestured wildly with one hand. He wasn't yelling, but he was definitely agitated.

I was inside with windows between us, but I still turned away to give him privacy. Strands of my hair had come loose, so I undid my topknot, bent over, letting my hair fall over my head, then gathered it up, twisted it up again, and secured it with the band.

The sudden sound of screeching tires, followed by a loud *thunk* and screams sent a chill through my body. I spun around to face the window again.

A car sped away into the distance, nothing but a blur of color and taillights. And there, in the middle of the street, lay Ben Nader.

Chapter 7

Chaos. There was no other way to describe the time immediately following the accident. Sirens screamed in the distance, growing closer by the second. Blue and red ambulance lights flashed. The police closed the road on both sides, cordoning off the area. Passersby stopped to stare, cell phones out and at the ready.

The Bread for Life women had come back and stood in shock, staring first at the body in the road, then at each other. Even from where I stood, just outside the bread shop, I could see Claire swipe tears away from under her eyes.

I watched helplessly as, a block away, Sandra Mays strutted down the street on her way back from wherever she'd been. As she grew closer, she stopped, gawking at the crowd that had gathered and at the blocked-off street. She scanned the area and spotted me standing under Yeast of Eden's awning. She hurried toward me. "What's

going on—" she started, but her head swiveled
to look at the street and the words fell away. "Is
that—" She lurched forward. "Oh my God! Is
that Ben?"

I looked back at the cameraman's body, lying
in an awkward, unnatural position, legs splayed,
head cocked, blood pooling, and could imagine
the anguish Sandra was experiencing. I hadn't
sensed a lot of love or affection between the TV
personality and the cameraman, but it was clear
they had some sort of history. Chances are
they'd worked together for a long time. Of
course she'd be distraught. She made her way
through the crowd toward Ben. The paramedics
were working carefully now, moving Ben onto a
backboard and into the ambulance. I wondered
if I should go with Sandra—to stop her . . . or to
help her . . .

"Jesus, Ivy, what happened?"

I jumped at the voice behind me, turning to
see Emmaline Davis, Santa Sofia's sheriff, my best
friend since forever, and my soon-to-be sister-in-
law. She took one look at my face and took my
hand in hers, giving it a squeeze. "Hey, Ivy. Are
you all right?"

"I-I don't know, Em. Is he dead? It looks like
he's dead."

She shook her head. "I just talked to the paramedics. It's dicey, but they think he'll make it.
He's got a battle ahead of him, though."

We stood side by side. She dropped my hand
and we both folded our arms over our chests.
Ben Nader. He'd just been inside with us all, ag-
gravating Sandra with his non-conversation. Just

yesterday, he'd told Miguel and me about his philosophical escape as a kid. How could he be laid out on the road fighting for his life?

Em held a small notepad. She went into detective mode. "Did you see it happen?"

I shook my head. "I saw him standing by the curb talking on the phone. I looked away and then . . . and then . . ." The sound of screeching tires roared in my ears.

"Any idea who he was talking to?"

"No, but—"

"But what?"

I hesitated. Was I entirely sure that he'd been upset? I thought back. Yes, I was sure. I described what I'd seen. "It didn't look like a happy conversation."

"We have his phone. We'll check the call history."

Something about that statement made me snap my head up. Had he been so upset that he'd stepped out in front of the car that had hit him? Or had the phone call distracted him and he hadn't seen the car? "What are you thinking?"

"It's not what I'm thinking. It's what I saw."

I turned to her. "What do you mean?"

"We found a bystander with video."

Now I stared. "Of the hit-and-run?"

Em adjusted her navy Santa Sofia Sheriff's Department cap over her braided hair before she answered. "There's a woman. She was taking a video of the ocean view. She didn't catch the whole thing, but she got part of it."

My heart was pounding out of my chest. Had

she caught the part that would identify the driver?
"So you got a license plate?"

"Unfortunately, no. She only got the side of
the car."

"Make and model?"

"Working on it."

"Can you see the driver?"

Again, she shook her head. "The car was heading west. Empty passenger seat and no view of
the driver from what I can tell. I'm going to have
our tech guy see what he can see. Maybe we'll
get lucky. Mr. Nader was crossing the street and
didn't see it coming. Like you said, he looks to
have been talking on his phone. Either the driver
also didn't see him, or . . ."

She stopped talking, but I didn't need her to
finish the sentence. I'd known Emmaline Davis
since we were kids playing on the beach together. Even on my worst day, I could finish her
thoughts. "Or the driver meant to hit him."

Em snapped her notebook closed. "Exactly.
And based on what I've seen, I'm going with op-
tion two. The car didn't swerve. Didn't slow.
Didn't stop. The guy is lucky to be alive."

She left to talk to her deputies and left me to
my thoughts. After Sandra had called for a
break, Ben had walked out. What had been on
his mind and who had he been on the phone
with? Em would get to the bottom of it, I was
sure. My biggest question was—and I knew it was
hers, too—had Ben Nader been hit by mistake,
or had it been intentional?

* * *

After Ben Nader was taken away by the paramedics, the people scattered and the street went back to normal. Not that anyone could feel normal after seeing a man mowed down. I know I didn't. In fact, I felt like I was carrying weights on my shoulders. The man had been standing in the bread shop just hours ago. How had this happened? *Why* had this happened?

It didn't surprise me that both Mack Hebron and Sandra Mays had disappeared. They'd probably gone to the hospital to be with Ben and his family. Zula, Claire, Amelie, and Esmé had come back into the bread shop looking spooked and helpless. "You're back!" I said, sounding far more enthusiastic than I felt inside. What I really wanted was to send them home, but we had Amelie's Brezels to bake.

"I have been outside watching the commotion." Zula stared, doe-eyed and dazed. "It is unbelievable."

Claire's eyes pooled. She hadn't known Ben any better than I had, but we did know him a little bit, and seeing him suddenly fighting for his life was enough to send anyone into an emotional tizzy. She swept away her tears. "It doesn't seem real."

Esmé and Amelie nodded their agreement. Esmé rubbed her temples as she had earlier. "I went to the pharmacy down the street and when I came back, he was . . ."

"We have to hope he'll be okay," I said, squeezing her arm, hoping she'd gotten some headache medicine.

Amelie nodded along emphatically. "I was

going to the beach for a few minutes. I heard the screams and I saw the car race away. I-I had no idea it was . . . it had . . . that the car hit that man."

"And then left," Claire exclaimed. "It hit him, then just drove away. Isn't that illegal?"

One hundred percent illegal. "Yes, but without a license plate, the police don't have much to go on."

We sat in silence for a minute, then retreated to the conference room where Ben and Sandra and Mack had held the interviews with each of us. We stared at each other from around the table. "I cannot believe this," Amelie said, her German accent heavier now than it was normally.

Esmé and Claire both shook their heads. "Everybody told me to be careful," Claire said. "Watch out for crazy people in America. They were right."

"Not everybody is crazy," Esmé said, but she didn't sound very convincing.

Zula stretched her long legs out under the table and folded her arms. "But whoever did this is crazy. That car, it did not stop. It was like a bowling ball going for those—what do you call them?"

Claire and I answered at the same time. "Pins."

Zula gave a succinct nod. "That car was like a bowling ball and Ben Nader was a pin."

Esmé's mouth gaped open. "That makes it sound like it was on purpose."

Zula nodded. "That is what I am thinking exactly. That man, he did not have a chance. I will be surprised if he survives."

"What do you mean?" Claire asked, horror coloring her voice.

Zula dropped her arms and sat up straight. "I am saying that the car meant to hit our cameraman, Ben. It went right for him, did not swerve, did not try to stop." She took a breath. Looked at each of us in turn. "It went right for him."

Chapter 8

The food shelter had long since closed, so I'd given the few remains of the day to the crew members who'd finally returned for their equipment. I needed to distract myself, so I pulled out all the cleaning supplies and gave each baking station a thorough scrub. I moved on to the refrigerator, then to the baking racks. Finally, I went into Olaya's office and worked on the bread shop's website. By the time I finished, it was nearly nine o'clock and pitch-black outside. Where had the time gone?

I knew Olaya would want an update on how the day went after she left. I also wanted to drive Mrs. Branford home. I stopped by my house to pick up Agatha, then turned around and headed back to Olaya's for the second time that day. As I drove, Zula's words circled in my head. *It went right for him, did not swerve, did not try to stop.*

The video Emmaline had found seemed to show the same thing. Which meant that if Ben died, it would be murder.

Cloud cover blanketed the night sky, tamping out any starlight. A shiver ran through me. It was too dark. I could hear the crashing of waves as I wound through town, but to my left, the Pacific Ocean was nothing but a dark expanse in the distance. The dark roads were unusually quiet. The townspeople were safe and sound in their homes.

From out of nowhere, blinding headlights appeared behind me. I peered through the glare in my rearview mirror to see a looming dark SUV. I pressed my foot on the gas. My crossover kicked into gear and jerked forward, putting distance between me and the menacing car. It didn't work. The driver sped up right along with me, getting closer and closer. I considered my options. If I slammed on the brakes, the SUV would plow right into me. I could stay at my current speed and hope the other driver would decide to go around me. Or I could speed up again, outpacing him. I'd never felt vulnerable in my car, but I suddenly did. I imagined the front grill of the SUV as a growling mouth, the headlights as fiery eyes.

I shook my head, pushing those images away. It was just an obnoxious driver. I kept at my speed, wishing there were more cars on the road. A sedan came toward us on the opposite side of the street, passing us by. The SUV stayed close, but wasn't on my tail.

The guy needed to learn some road boundaries.

A red light glowed in the distance. I tapped my brake pedal a few times, slowing incrementally. The car behind me fell back. I exhaled a sigh of relief as I pulled to a stop at the traffic signal, my eyes glued to the review mirror. The black SUV idled behind me. It was close, but not too close.

I tapped my fingers against the steering wheel, impatient for the light to change. A car came up beside me, stopping at the light. I looked over, but the driver looked straight ahead, not even giving a cursory glance in my direction.

It was a four-way intersection. Several cars drove through the green light, passing in front of me, but my focus was on the car behind me. "Come on," I muttered, willing the light to change.

Behind me, Agatha shifted, then settled down again, snoring loudly.

The light turned green. I slammed my foot on the gas pedal and two-fisted the steering wheel. My car responded by jerking forward. My goal was to put distance between the two cars. In two seconds, though, he was right behind me again, closer than he'd been before.

"What's wrong with you?" I flipped on my blinker and moved over. "Just pass me already," I said, using my left hand to wave him ahead of me. The hit-and-run earlier had me spooked. I didn't want any type of encounter with a car. Period.

Finally, the car moved to the left lane next to

me. Now it seemed to be taking its sweet time, though, coming up alongside me slowly. Something wasn't right. It kept a steady pace with me, moving up just enough that I couldn't see inside any of the windows. All this time, I'd been thinking it was just an obnoxious driver, but now I wasn't so sure.

I slowed, holding my breath to see what the other car would do. I'd been afraid that it would slow, too. I didn't know what I'd do if it did—but instead, it finally sped up. The space between us grew and finally its taillights disappeared into the distance.

"Thank God," I said, breathing out my relief. I pressed my foot on the gas pedal until I was up to speed, once again. One or two cars came and went, leaving me mostly alone on the road. "What was that about, Agatha?" I asked, glancing over my shoulder at my pug. She rode in the back seat, stretched out on her blanket with her front paws crossed over one another, totally oblivious to the encounter I'd just had.

This time when she heard her name, she opened her eyes and lifted her head slightly.

"That was disconcerting, wasn't it?" I said to her, my heartbeat slowly returning to normal. I looked in the rearview mirror in time to see Agatha give me a slow blink.

My thoughts returned to the day's events. I looked at Agatha's reflection again. "Someone had a big gripe with Ben Nader to run him over," I said to her. "If that's what happened."

Agatha's bulbous eyes were at half-mast.

I continued, as if she'd responded by asking who could have had such a gripe.

"Good question. I didn't know the man. He has at least one enemy." I immediately thought of Sandra, who seemed to collect enemies like other people collected Starbucks stars.

Agatha gave a guttural growl of a sound, blinked again, then lowered her head on top of her legs.

"You're right," I said. "I'll talk to Em about it. Maybe do a little digging myself . . . just to, you know, ease my mind."

This time Agatha peered at me, not bothering to raise her head. "I'll keep it to myself," I told her, as if she'd issued a warning, telling me to be careful. Excluding Olaya and Mrs. Branford. And Miguel, of course. They were my A team.

Blinding light, reflected in my side and rear-view mirrors, intruded into the darkness. Another car zoomed up behind me, riding my tail so closely that I thought it might plow right into me. My heartbeat ratcheted up again. Muscle memory. What the hell was going on? Who was in that car?

I sped up to put space between us. The car fell back for a few seconds. I started to exhale with relief when it sped up again, riding my bumper like the boxcar on a train.

"Hang on, Agatha," I said as I jammed my foot on the gas pedal. The engine revved, caught, and my car shot forward with a jolt. The headlights behind me faded with the distance I put between our two cars. From the back seat, Agatha grumbled.

"Idiot driver," I muttered under my breath. The words barely escaped my lips when an impact came from behind. Something hit my bumper, lurching my car forward. My body jerked, my head whipping back again. I kept my hands gripping the steering wheel. I searched the rearview mirror, frantically looking for the car that had careened into me. The street behind me was dark. Empty. I peered at my side mirror and drew in a sharp breath. A car had moved to my blind spot, its headlights off. I could just make out the front bumper. It was the black SUV.

Under normal circumstances, the people involved in a fender bender would pull over, exchange insurance information, and call the authorities, if needed. That was not happening now. There was no way I was stopping on this dark starless night on a deserted street with a car that had been tormenting me.

The black blob moved out of sight. I tried to calm down, but it didn't work. My hands shook. My breath was ragged. I needed to pull over and calm down, but that wasn't happening until I could lose the car and find a safe, well-lit place.

I merged right so I could take the next turn, but suddenly I was blinded by lights in my rearview again. The menacing SUV was directly behind me. My heart thrummed in my chest. I sped forward, swerving to get out of the way, but the car behind me was like a heat-seeking missile locked on me. I had to lose it. Were my driving skills good enough? God, I hoped so. I was close to Olaya's but I couldn't drive straight there. I needed a place to hide.

Crazy thoughts circled through my mind. Who- ever was behind me seemed to have some sort of personal grudge. It did not feel random. But who would be targeting me . . . and why? Could it be related to Ben Nader's hit-and-run? I quickly dismissed that idea. It didn't make any sense. I didn't know the man—had no connec- tion to him beyond our brief reality TV interac- tion.

My opportunity to outmaneuver whoever was behind me came the next second. I veered into the left lane, not slowing down. I didn't want to give the person any clue that I was about to try to make a wide and erratic right-hand turn. With one eye on the rearview mirror, and the other straight ahead, I raced forward. I was itch- ing to get ready for the turn, but I made myself take a breath.

Wait.

Wait.

Wait.

Finally, at the last second, I jerked the wheel right. My tires skidded. "Hold on!" I told Agatha, as if she could understand and actually grip something to keep her from flying. I cursed under my breath for never getting one of those doggy seat belts for her. She rolled off her blan- ket, but righted herself before she plunged to the floor of the car. I checked the rearview mirror.

My heart was in my throat, but there was no sign of the car that had been behind me. I didn't take any chances, though. I took the next right, followed by a quick left, then another right. I came up to row of apartments and made a split second decision. I cranked the steering wheel and turned in. I slowed enough to follow the curves of the parking lot around and away from the street I'd been on. I pulled into a vacant spot, cut the engine and the lights, threw my arm back to give Agatha a reassuring pat, and tried to steady my jackhammering heartbeat.

I waited.

And waited.

All was quiet. No one had followed me into the apartment complex's parking lot. No car appeared cutting a swath of light in the darkness.

Finally, I breathed again, dropping my forehead to the steering wheel. My whole body trembled, the adrenaline that had been surging through me seeping right back out again. Had I really lost the car? Had it really been after me, or was it just some crazy person who'd had one too many and decided to play a dangerous game of chicken?

This time, it took fifteen minutes for my breathing to return to some semblance of normal, and for my heart to slow to an almost regular beating pattern. I checked the time: 9:40. There should be cars on the road, but even if there were, what would that matter? If that car wanted to torment me—which it had done expertly—other cars on the road wouldn't stop it. I

made a decision. I'd take the back roads to
Olaya's. I did not want to get onto the main road
again for fear of facing the dark SUV again.

By the time Agatha and I walked into Olaya's
house, I thought I had myself together, but
Mrs. Branford took one look at me, jumped up
from where she'd been cocooned on the couch,
and raced over to me. "Ivy, what in world happened? You look like you've seen the ghost of
Lady Macbeth."

Only Penelope Branford would name a specific ghost in this situation.

"Someone hit my car," I said, my voice shaking.

She guided me to the couch, where we sat
side by side. "While you were in it?" she asked.

I nodded. "While I was driving."

"You were in an accident? Just now?" She
looked me over. "Are you okay, my dear?"

My head moved in a half nod, half shake as I
tried to puzzle out what had actually happened.
It had been intentional, right? I'd seen the same
car twice—once when it had blinded me with its
lights, and again when it plowed into my bumper.
"Someone rammed into the back of my car."

Mrs. Branford's mouth collapsed into a wrin-
kled frown. "Just now?"

She was checking for understanding. This time
I made my head simply nod. "I was heading here.
A car came up behind me, flashed its brights,
then rammed me."

Mrs. Branford perched on the edge of the

sofa, her cane propped on the floor between her legs. "On purpose."

The more I pondered that question, the more convinced I was that it had not been a random act of violence. "On purpose," I confirmed.

"But why?"

I proceeded to tell her about the hit-and-run that had nearly taken Ben Nader's life earlier that afternoon.

Her snowy curls framed her face as she swiveled her head to look at me. "Will he be all right?"

I lifted my eyebrows in response. "I don't know."

"And you think it's related to the car that hit you?"

I shook my head. "I can't think of a reason why. I don't know the guy."

She put her gnarled hand on my knee. "Have you angered someone, Ivy? Taken a photograph you didn't get permission for?"

I'd spent the rest of the slow, torturous drive to Olaya's thinking about what kind of grudge anyone could have against me. A year ago, Laura, Miguel's sister, might have crossed my mind, but we'd buried the hatchet, so to speak. Our history was in the past, and our future was all positive. I hadn't made any other enemies— that I knew of, anyway.

"No and no. It had to be an accident," I said, but saying the words aloud didn't make it true.

Mrs. Branford's mouth twisted into a puzzled frown. "You should talk to Sheriff Davis," she said.

I'd considered it, and I probably would—eventually—but I didn't want to commit to that quite yet, so I replied with a vague, "Maybe."

Mrs. Branford wasn't giving up that easily, though. "Not maybe. Definitely. You may not think you have an enemy, and you may not know who it is, but it seems you do, indeed, have one." She wagged her finger at me. "You are to take no chances, do you hear me, Ivy?"

I couldn't help but grin, despite myself. "I understand, Mrs. Branford."

She heaved a put-upon sigh. "One of these days, you will call me Penelope—"

"Never—"

"Or Penny—"

"Uh-uh, I can't do it."

"Or at least Mrs. B."

I stared at her, my mouth agape. "Mrs. B?"

She fluffed her snowy hair. "That is not my preferred choice, but it will do if you so choose."

"I don't so choose," I said.

"Someday you will," she said.

I shifted subjects. "How is Olaya?"

She cocked a gray eyebrow at me. "Answer this for me. Why can you call Olaya by her first name, but not me?"

"Because I met her as Olaya, but I met you as Mrs. Branford. I'm a creature of habit," I said. I'd tried to call her Penelope and Penny, but calling Mrs. Branford anything other than Mrs. Branford was like trying to drop the Aunt or Uncle after a lifetime of that formality. It didn't feel natural or right. "It would be like your students suddenly calling you by your first name. That would be weird, right?"

She narrowed her eyes, considering my explanation. "It is . . . unfamiliar."

"Aha! So you've experienced that."

"I have. Every once in a while, I see a former student. They're all adults now, of course, and sometimes they try out my first name. It is always unfamiliar, but not necessarily bad."

"You two need to go home now."

Mrs. Branford and I turned at the sound of Olaya's voice. She stood in the hallway, her wavy iron-gray hair sticking up on end, her cheeks flushed, and her skin pale. I jumped up and hurried over to her, placing the back of my hand against her forehead.

She shook her head. "I have no fever."

I eyed her. She felt a little warm to me. "I don't know about that."

"I know," she said, as if she had just this second accepted the fact that she was sick. "*Pero*, you can go home. Both of you. I can manage by myself."

"Of course you can," Mrs. Branford said, "but friends help one another."

Olaya's mouth lifted in the slightest hint of a smile. "Are we friends now, Penelope?"

"I think we are, yes," Mrs. Branford said. "I mean, I've seen the best and the worst, and despite our past, I've moved on. I accept your friendship if you accept mine."

I looked from one to the other—my favorite women in the entire world. They had a complicated history, but Mrs. Branford was saying aloud what I knew they both felt. Of course, I thought they'd already crossed this bridge, but what did I know. A man was involved in their shared past, and that always complicated things. Still, they were definitely, 100 percent, friends.

Olaya sighed. "*Pues*. Fine. If you insist, I accept your friendship."

"Then sit down," Mrs. Branford said.

Olaya didn't budge. "Why?"

"We have something to tell you."

Olaya looked at me, a slightly bemused expression on her face. "What do you have to tell me?"

Mrs. Branford drew in a breath, let it go, then said, "There's been an accident."

Olaya stared. "What are you talking about?"

I shot Mrs. Branford a reproachful look. Friends or not, Olaya was sick. She didn't need to know right now. "It's not important," I said, instantly regretting the words and wishing I could take them back, because of course it was monumentally important to Ben Nader and to his friends and family.

Mrs. Branford, for her part, lifted her eyebrow again in a way that said *She needs to know.*

I sighed and nodded. "Ben Nader was hit by a car outside the bread shop today."

Olaya placed her hand against the wall to steady herself. "What?"

"He was crossing the street, on the phone. He didn't see it coming. He's in the hospital."

"He will recover?"

I didn't have the answer to that, but my phone

dinged with an incoming text, as if on cue. It was
a text from Emmaline. Ben Nader in ICU. Swelling of the brain. Doctors putting him into a
medically induced coma.

I read it aloud. Olaya's knees seemed to buckle
under her. I helped her to the couch where she
sat, back erect, next to Mrs. Branford. I sat on the
chair opposite them and filled her in with whatever other details I knew.

"It was not an accident?" she asked.

"The sheriff doesn't think so," I said.

She was silent for a minute, then propped her
elbow on the arm of the couch and cupped her
hand against her forehead. "I am sick."

Mrs. Branford smirked. "An astute observation."

Olaya ignored her and raised her eyes to me.
"I cannot go to work tomorrow. Will you help,
Ivy?"

"Of course," I said immediately. "Just tell me
what you need."

What Olaya needed was for me to take her
place beginning at four thirty in the morning. I
would do anything for her. The woman had
helped me grow in ways I hadn't known I
could—or that I'd needed. But when my alarm
went off at four o'clock the next morning, my
eyelids felt like lead and I would have given anything to sleep another two or three hours.

But a promise was a promise, and Olaya was
the most independent woman I knew—right

alongside Penelope Branford. She didn't ask for much, and I felt that I owed her a lot. The bread shop was a Santa Sofia staple. It was closed on Sundays and Mondays—and on major holidays, of course—but other than that, Olaya never closed it for any reason. I wasn't going to let her down.

Agatha was curled in a ball at my feet. I sat up in bed, rubbed the sleep from my eyes, and poked her with my toe. She gave a grumbly snort, raised her head just slightly, then lowered it again, closing her eyes and sinking back to sleep. "I don't blame you," I said, leaving her be while I got myself ready for the day. Just before I headed out, I tried to rouse her again, to no avail. She did not want to wake up. I scooped her up into my arms and carried her hefty body outside, putting her down in her favorite flowerbed. She groaned again, but circled around and took care of her business. Back inside, she jumped up onto the couch and settled into sleep again. "I'll be back," I said, giving her a head a little rub.

A short while later, I had let myself into Yeast of Eden's kitchen, the list Olaya had dictated to me the night before on the stainless steel counter in front of me. Lucky for me, Olaya's bread-baking philosophy was all about the long rise. That meant that much of the bread for the day's offerings was already made and in the walk-in refrigerator, just waiting to be baked. The croissant dough had been filled with butter, folded, rolled out, folded, rolled out again until it was ready to be cut, shaped, and baked. I'd worry about making new dough for tomorrow later. Dinner rolls, baguettes, French loaves. The list went on and on. I set to it, working my way down the list. With each passing minute, I was more and more in awe of Olaya. How she did this day in and day out was astounding.

At five fifteen, the kitchen door leading to the outside parking lot opened. In walked a young man who looked to be in his twenties. His eyes were light in contrast to his black skin, and he wore an amiable smile that etched a tiny dot of a dimple into one cheek. His white chef's shirt with three-quarter sleeves and buttons running up the right side strained against his rounded belly. His hair was shorn close to the scalp.

"You must be Ivy," he said, walking right to me. My hands were elbow-deep, kneading a massive mound of dough. He bent his arm and bumped my elbow. His smile never waned. He was the kind of person, I realized, who was inherently happy and whose lips always curved upward. "And you must be Felix," I said. "I can't believe we've never met."

Olaya had hired Felix Macron a few months prior to help her with the morning baking routine. She'd come to rely on him. Experiencing the work for the first time, I could see why she needed the help and I couldn't believe she'd waited this long to bring someone else in. Based on the amount of bread she made throughout nearly every single day, I think she needed an entire team.

In that moment, I decided that I was going to

increase the hours I worked at the bread shop. There was no way Olaya could keep up the pace she was going. She needed others to take some of the workload off her shoulders.

"My hours here have been pretty limited," he said, "but that's changing. I want to learn every last bit of what Olaya has to teach me."

The dough I'd been working had transformed from a sticky mass to a soft ball. I set it aside and turned to Felix, giving him my full attention. "Olaya mentioned that. You're always gone before I come in. So you'll be staying longer now?"

"Five to noon," he confirmed. "I don't know how she's managed all this time without more help," he said, saying aloud what I'd just been thinking.

Felix moved to the sink and gave his hands a good scrubbing. "So, where are we?"

I breathed a sigh of relief that he was here and consulted my list. "Croissants are baking. Baguettes are formed. We need the wheat and rye breads next." I followed his gaze to the empty bakery racks. "Or, you know, basically everything."

"We'll get it done." He moved around the kitchen as if he owned it. He knew where everything was and got right to work, starting with the massive floor mixer, fitted with a giant dough hook. Before long, he had the ingredients added and formed a dough.

"You're quick," I said. Thank God, because I was not. The skill and speed needed to bake the vast quantities of bread that Olaya made on a daily basis far exceeded my abilities. Felix was a lifesaver.

"I grew up eating Yeast of Eden's bread. It's what made me want to run my own bakery. She's been mentoring me since middle school."

"You're going to run your own shop one day?"

"You better believe it. But not here," he added quickly. "I'd never compete with Olaya. I'll go up the coast, or maybe down to L.A. Of course you have La Brea down there, and plenty of other artisan shops. I don't know. I'll figure it out when the time is right. I have too much to learn still. If it wasn't for Olaya, I don't know what I'd be doing. Not this, that's for sure."

"She has a habit of saving people," I said.

He looked at me, his smile growing bigger. "You too?"

I realized that just like I knew next to nothing about him, he probably knew nothing about me. Olaya kept other people's stories to herself. It was one of the many things I loved about her. "Me too."

We worked in companionable silence for the next three hours, making our way through Olaya's list of daily baking. By eight o'clock, the morning crew had clocked in, the coffee was made, and the bakery cases were filled with enough breads, croissants, rolls, and everything in between to open the doors. The regulars shuffled in, standing in line to get their cup of joe and their morning carbs.

After the rush died down, I left the front and

rejoined Felix. Another of Olaya's late-morning crew showed up. After another few hours, with Felix's help, we'd finished the baking and had cleaned the kitchen. I tossed my apron into the laundry bin Olaya kept just outside her office, debating whether or not I should log on to the computer and spend some time working on the bread shop blog, go home to take a nap, or stop by Baptista's Cantina and Grill to visit Miguel.

It wasn't a hard decision. I was off to Baptista's. "I'll see you in the morning," I told Felix, planning to be back. If Olaya was still sick, I'd fill in again. If she was better, I'd help out so hopefully she wouldn't relapse.

He gave me a playful salute and said, "Okay. See you *mañana*, as Olaya says."

"See you *mañana*."

I was halfway to Miguel's restaurant when my cell phone rang. I'd programmed in ringtones, so knew right away that it was Emmaline. "Hey," I said after pressing the button on my car's system that allowed the phone call to play through the speakers. We were a hands-free state, after all, and I wasn't willing to get a five-hundred-dollar ticket for anyone.

"Hey. I have two things for you," she said, cutting to the chase. She was a busy person with a busy job, and it was the middle of the workday. No time for chitchat.

"I'm all ears."

"First, Billy and I set a date."

It took a second for her words to register, and then I screeched. "Whaat! When?"

"Let's go to dinner and I'll fill you in. Baptista's at six o'clock?"

Her demeanor changed instantly, her voice dropping to a low tenor and losing its happy tone. "Ben Nader. I've viewed the bystander video a dozen times. I'm convinced it wasn't an accident."

This sucked the joy over my brother and my best friend getting married right out of me. If it wasn't an accident, it was attempted murder.

"Ivy?"

Em's voice in the car brought me back to her. "Yeah, I'm here."

"But here's the thing. So far, the guy comes across as squeaky clean. He volunteers at the women's shelter and doing handyman stuff. No traffic citations. He and his wife go to church every Sunday. He keeps to himself, donates to the Big Brothers Big Sisters organization. I have to assume that his philanthropy comes from a personal place. The Naders' son and his fiancée died in a car accident ten years ago. They'd been in Europe. Ben and his wife, Tammy, have been raising their orphaned grandson ever since. Tammy, as you can imagine, is a mess. Doesn't know how their grandson is going to handle it. She says the boy and Ben are very close."

"The wife has an alibi for the time of the hit-and-run?" I asked. Possibly a little blunt, but I knew from Em that the spouse was always a likely suspect.

"She was home with the grandson. Phone

records show that Ben was on the phone with her when he was hit."

So she'd heard it all. I couldn't even imagine what had gone through her mind. "Okay, and you have no other suspects?"

"None. According to everyone we've interviewed, he's well-liked at work. We have nothing so far."

I pulled into the restaurant parking lot. "What about the car?"

"Nothing new on that. We know the driver had on a baseball cap and sunglasses. He—or she—held a cell phone at the steering wheel, but it doesn't look like it was in use. Video doesn't show the license plate. Dark-colored sedan is the best we can do right now."

"Can you tell if it's a man or woman?" I asked.

"Nope. I'm telling you, Ivy. There are witnesses, but they haven't given us anything useful. We have nothing."

"Did you talk to Sandra Mays?" I asked as the woman's face flashed in my mind. She was the type of person I could see attempting murder if it suited her in some way. I'd gathered that she and Ben had some sort of history. Did it go deeper than I'd imagined?

"Yeah, I interviewed her, for what it was worth. She's a prima donna," Em said. "Ben Nader's current situation is definitely more about her than it is him or his family."

I knew exactly what she meant. I could see the reality TV host wringing her hands and bemoaning the loss of her cameraman. *He was the best* . . .

The station won't be able to find anyone good enough to replace him . . . What will I do without him? He always made me look so good!

"I have to go," Em said. "Keep your eyes and ears open for me, okay? See you tonight."

"I will," I told her, taking her request as a green light to ferret out whatever information I could. It was only after we hung up that I realized I hadn't told Emmaline about my encounter with the SUV the night before.

Chapter 9

Out of sight, out of mind. I'd been able to put the incident of the car following me the night before out of my mind, but getting out of my car in Baptista's parking lot in broad daylight, the evidence of the collision was front and center. Instinctively, I turned and scanned the surrounding area. Nothing jumped out at me. No dark scary SUVs were in the parking lot. It didn't offer me any comfort, though. All I could think was that it was ironic that what I was going through with an unidentified car was the same thing that Em was investigating connected to Ben Nader. For a fleeting moment, I had the thought that maybe I was the intended victim yesterday, and not Ben. But that idea went as fast as it had come. Not even someone with cataracts would mistake me, with my long spiral-curled ginger hair and curvy figure, for Ben Nader's trim and authentic male form.

Two different automobile incidents, with two different targets. I just had no idea what the motive could be for either one.

I stared at the smashed bumper of my car, looking up only when I heard footsteps approaching. My heartbeat ratcheted up a notch in response, but calmed again when I saw it was Miguel striding across the asphalt toward me. Although we were back together again after too many years apart, a charge of electricity still went through me whenever I saw him. His years in the military had given him broad shoulders and a lean body that I was slowly getting to know again. He was a year older than me, and dang if he didn't wear his thirty-seven years really well. We'd found each other again, and he looked at me with the same adoring eyes I had for him. Young-ish . . . and falling in love again. It was a great feeling.

"Hey, whatcha doing?" he asked, but stopped when he saw the car. "Holy sh—What happened?"

As I told him about the drive to Olaya's the night before, he slipped his arm around me and pulled me close. We stood side by side, looking at the damage to my car. "You're okay?"

I waved away his concern. "I'm fine. Just a little spooked. I was at the wrong place, wrong time, that's all."

He looked down at me skeptically. "You're saying it was just some crazy person acting out?"

That was what I was saying, but I didn't know if I actually believed it. "It must have been. I can't think of anyone who'd do that to me on purpose"

The pads of his fingertips tapped against my shoulder. "You've been involved with some sketchy characters lately."

"What, you mean with Marisol's funeral?" I asked, talking about a local investigation we'd both played a part in—and had helped solve.

"That, and the poker room, and—"

"I'm sure it was nothing." I rotated my body to face him. I'd planned on his arms circling around me as I stretched up to kiss him. Instead, he moved his hands to my shoulders and looked me square in the eyes. "Ivy, this is not a joke. Someone rammed into you last night. You could have been hurt."

I'd tried to make light of it and ignore the niggling concern in my gut, but Miguel was right. The car on my tail, right on the heels of Ben Nader's hit-and-run, had me spooked. "I know it's not. I just don't know what this is," I said.

Chapter 10

My visit with Miguel was quick. A sous-chef had up and quit, which meant he was filling in and looking to hire a replacement. I'd passed on his offer for a bite to eat, telling him that I'd be back later for a dinner date with Em. I left for home to take a nap, cuddling with Agatha as I snoozed. I awoke with a jolt two hours later. Waking up at four in the morning had crashed down on me like a piano falling on me from the sky. If my plan was to help Olaya more at the bread shop, which it was, I'd have to completely recalibrate my internal clock. Early to bed, early to rise.

I had time before I was to meet Em and I couldn't sleep the day away, so I piled Agatha in my car and drove to Cambria Street. I parked by the Lutheran church, strapped Agatha into her harness, and started walking. Past a local brewery, past a new Thai restaurant, past a kitchen store filled with knickknacks I couldn't afford and didn't really need—but sorely wanted. The antique mini-mall was across the street. A new boutique had opened up right next to it, the juxtaposition of the old and the new a perfect example of Santa Sofia's quirky character.

Agatha trotted along beside me, her ears back and her tail curled, two signs she was utterly content. The breeze off the ocean had kicked up, pulling strands of my hair free from my hairband. I did my best to contain them, tucking them behind my ears, as I kept walking. I approached Yeast of Eden, looking inside as I got to the awnings. I hadn't planned on going in, but that was before I spotted Sandra Mays going into the kitchen. What was she doing here?

I stepped up to the window, cupped my hands, and peered in to get a better look. No Olaya. No Mack. Just Maggie cleaning up after what looked like a great day for the bread shop. Not a loaf or scone or baguette remained.

Maggie spotted me. Her face lit up with a smile. She threw jazz hands up, waving at me, then beckoned me in. I picked up Agatha. I couldn't have her in the bread shop roaming around, but if I carried her in . . .

"Oh, she's so cute!" Maggie rushed around the counter and held her hand out for Agatha to sniff. Agatha didn't have an aggressive bone in her body. She crinkled her flat nose and licked.

"Why is Sandra here?" I asked, my voice low as if it was a whisper.

Maggie shrugged, matching my cadence. "She

wanted to talk to Olaya, but she's out sick. Crazy, right? Olaya's *never* sick!"

"So why did she go into the kitchen? Is Mack here, too?"

Maggie waggled her eyebrows at me. "Look at you, calling them Sandra and Mack."

I leaned closer, whispering like we were sharing confidences. "They're just people, Mags."

"But they're celebrities! They're on TV!"

"You're going to be on TV, too." I scooted behind the counter and pushed through the swinging door to the kitchen, not waiting for her to answer either of my questions.

"I heard her say she wants to film today," Maggie called after me.

"Then Mack must be here," I said, remembering the scene between the two of them and Mack's stern reminder that he was the showrunner and she needed to remember her place.

"Not that *I've* seen," Maggie said.

Oh boy. So maybe Sandra hadn't learned her lesson. I knew show business was cutthroat, but Sandra seemed to be pushing the boundaries far and wide. The kitchen was empty. Where had she gone?

At that moment, Sandra Mays strode out of Olaya's office. "Oh good, you're here!" Her voice seemed to echo off the stainless steel counters.

"I am," I said. "But why are you here? What were you doing in there?"

Sandra threw her head back and laughed. "I like you, Ivy. You say what you think. Just looking for Olaya." Her smile dropped and she became instantly serious. "I imagine you think it's in bad taste to be here, what with Ben's, uh, situation, but the show, as they say, must go on. We have some excellent footage so far. We still have a lot to do, though."

"But we don't have the Bread for Life class tonight. And what about Mack?"

She had her cell phone in hand and quickly tapped her thumbs on the screen, composing a text. "Taehyun will be taking Ben's place."

"Who is Taehyun?" I asked.

As if on command, there was a quick knock on the back door. It opened and a young Korean man stepped in carrying what looked to be the same camera equipment Ben Nader lugged with him. Sandra swung her arm toward him. "Right on time. Taehyun Chu."

The man couldn't have been more than twenty-five. His dark hair was parted and neatly swept to one side and his long sideburns gave him a slightly edgy look. With his black coat, an open-at-the-collar white button-down, and black twill pants, he could have been ready for a night out with friends, but he was here with Sandra Mays instead, seizing the opportunity that fate had presented him with—an opening as a camera-man. I guess I didn't blame him.

"Hey," he said a little sheepishly and with a quick wave. "Call me Tae."

Sandra waved her arm wide. "Taehyun has seen Ben's footage so he's familiar with what we've been doing," she said, ignoring Tae's request. Sandra, it seemed, wasn't willing to give up any of her power, not even with a green cameraman. Ironic, since she insisted on being called Sandra, and not Sandy as Mack had done several times.

"But is this okay?" I asked. "What about Mack—"

Sandra spun around, eyes blazing. "We. Do not. Need. Mack."

I grimaced from her tone, not liking the way it had turned on a dime. Sandra ran hot and cold. "Get some test shots of the kitchen," she told Tae. An order, not a request.

Tae set up his equipment and did as he was told. His sheepishness had morphed into something else. Anxiety? Hesitation? Out-and-out fear?

Maggie came into the kitchen from the front. "Closing's done," she said, stopping short when she saw Tae swing so his camera was directed at her. She took a step back. "Oh, uh, sorry—"

Sandra strode to her, taking her arm before she could disappear to the front of the bread shop again. "We don't have any tape of you," she said. She clasped Maggie's chin, moving it this way, then that, as if she were evaluating Maggie's bone structure. Maybe that was exactly what she was doing. "The camera will love you," she said.

Maggie stammered. "Oh, I, uh—"

"She's right," Tae said, lowering the camera and raising his eyebrows.

Maggie blushed and Tae gave her a shy smile. Ooo, a little love connection was happening right here in the kitchen of Yeast of Eden.

Sandra clapped her hands, drawing the attention back to her. "This afternoon, Tae and I are going to work on an intro and some transitions. We really don't need you."

It wasn't her bread shop, so that seemed pretty ungracious.

"Your bread is amazing," Tae said. "I came in for the first time yesterday. I'm already addicted. This is going to be a great show."

The moment he started to speak, Sandra's jaw tightened. "Ben did his job, Taehyun. They already know it's going to be great," she sniped.

Tae glanced down to avoid Sandra's glare and Maggie's wide eyes, but I thought I detected a faint smile on his lips. Maybe he wasn't quite as green as I initially thought.

I hung back and watched Sandra run through an opening just like she'd done, then she and Mack had done. Take after take, she changed her words around, changed the cadence of her voice, changed where she stood.

"I think we have it," Tae said.

I could see the blood boiling just under the surface, but before Sandra could put Tae in his place, her phone rang. She took the call, immediately putting on a "phone" voice. "Tammy! Any news?"

As she listened, her expression shifted and her tone grew serious. Real. "So I heard."

Tammy, on the other end of the line, said something, and Sandra replied. "Ben has always said, choices have consequences—"

She stopped abruptly. Listened. Turned her back on us. "You'll let me know how he's doing, won't you?" she said, then followed up with a curt, "Great. Talk to you later."

"Is everything okay?" I asked as I adjusted Agatha in my arms. I couldn't put her down in the kitchen. Pugs had two layers of hair and shed a lot. A. Lot. I was not going to risk dog hair in a single bit of Olaya's bread.

"That was Ben's wife. There's no change."

"Do you know her well?" I asked. "Is there anything we can do for her?"

"Ben will be fine, and Tammy needs to be strong. She's scared, that's all."

So Sandra was a tough love kind of woman. I wondered what she'd meant when she'd said that choices have consequences. Definitely not sympathetic words to lift up the spirits of a scared wife whose husband was in the hospital in a coma.

Chapter 11

Later that night, as I was still digesting the overabundance of food Em and I had eaten, I sat on my back patio and opened my laptop. Emmaline had mentioned to me in passing that Ben Nader volunteered at the women's shelter in town. I'd become fixated on that detail of his life. The shelter, dedicated to women and children, was apparently one of Santa Sofia's best-kept secrets. I'd never even heard of the place, which was shocking since I'd grown up here and the sheriff was my best friend. Its existence was a well-kept secret and I had no clue where it was located. Olaya had never mentioned it, either, which meant she probably didn't know it existed. If she did, I felt sure she'd be donating bread to the people who took solace there.

It stood to reason that the secrecy was connected to the reason women would need a shelter for themselves and their children. Most, I assumed, were escaping abusive situations. The way I saw it, I could *a*) ask Emmaline for details—the place was secret for a reason, though, so I didn't think she'd offer up much; or *b*) use my detecting skills to ferret out the information on my own.

I went for option *b*.

I was no expert and didn't have the resources of a police detective—or any other kind of detective for that matter. So I started at the logical place. I opened a browser and typed in *Santa Sofia Women's Shelter*. The first listing that popped up was: *Crosby House—Investing in Safety, Hope, Healing, Justice, and Prevention for Victims of Sexual and Domestic Violence.*

Huh. Not so secret after all.

I clicked on the link and scanned the website, zeroing in on their motto: *Partnering with our community to provide compassion and comprehensive services, and promoting safety, hope, healing, justice, and prevention to women and their children in need.*

I kept reading. The statistics were startling: One out of four women is a victim of domestic violence. Nearly twenty people are abused by a domestic partner every single minute. One in seventeen women is stalked by an intimate partner to the point that they feel fearful or believe they would be hurt or killed.

A shiver wound through me. It was hard to fathom that so many women suffered in this way. I was suddenly so thankful places like Crosby House existed and were a haven for women and children who needed a safe place.

Clicking on the volunteer link took me to an

application. I scanned it, homing in on the volunteer opportunities. The pulldown list ranged from adopting a family to working at the food closet or the children's program to helping with the Thanksgiving drive—and everything in between. Anyone with a special project idea was encouraged to submit a proposal for consideration.

I experienced two things at once: a pull in my gut and an unexpected need to be part of this organization, as well as the strong desire to find out why Ben Nader volunteered with the organization. Could it lead to some answers? Had he tried to help a woman at the facility, pissing off a violent partner? It wasn't outside the realm of possibility. Or maybe he knew someone who had been a victim of domestic violence or rape. Knowing why he spent time there might help me understand the man I was hoping and praying would come out of the coma he was in. I wanted to walk in his footsteps, and to do that, I had to do what he did. Crosby House was a place to start.

It was an online application, which was easy to fill out. A background check would need to be completed and I had to schedule an orientation date and time. I selected one three days from now. The last section of the application was a disclaimer for those seeking to work directly with Crosby House clients. It warned of the sometimes tragic circumstances, distress, and chaotic lives of the shelter's women, and something called "vicarious traumatization," a phenomenon where a volunteer may begin to feel victimization similar to the client's after hearing their story. It also warned of triggering unresolved issues and pain from past abuse or trauma. I thought of Luke, my ex-husband, and how fortunate I was that our split had been relatively amicable, despite his infidelity. A person really did have to count their blessings.

A bundle of nerves opened up inside me as my finger hovered over the SUBMIT button. Was I going in under false pretenses? I wanted to dig around about Ben, but not at the expense of the women who took shelter at Crosby House. Would I make a good volunteer? Would I take on the trauma of the victims? I answered the questions in my head. Yes, I was compassionate and caring, so I'd make a good volunteer. At least, I thought I would. And yes, I probably would internalize some of the stories I heard, but I'd try hard not to let them get me down. The purpose of volunteering at Crosby House, as I saw it, was to be a positive force in the lives of people who needed someone to listen, lean on, or just to be present for them.

I could do that—while I hunted for clues about Ben and who might have had it out for him.

I pressed ENTER and instantly received a message saying that my application had been successfully submitted. I sat back and breathed out, any trace of anxiety drifting away as the form traveled to someone else's computer.

Now I just had to wait.

Chapter 12

The next three days passed in a blur. Felix and I did the early morning baking at Yeast of Eden while Olaya continued to recover; I worked on the bread shop's website and blog, posting up-to-date photographs from the last Bread for Life session; and at home, I baked far too many macarons, a delicate cookie I was determined to master. Add to that a little personal time with Miguel, walks at the beach with Agatha, and visiting with my father. I'd had little to no time to think about what had happened to Ben Nader.

Or, I guess to be more accurate, I had nothing to investigate. I had no natural way to dig into his life, and so I'd waited. Let me tell you, waiting is not all it's cracked up to be. I felt anxious and restless and useless, all at the same time.

After another early morning at the bread shop, I'd spent the afternoon in my kitchen, which was

one of the things I'd loved most about the old
Tudor house I'd recently bought. With its pale yellow cabinets, warm honey-colored wood floors,
perfect work island, and a stovetop framed by a
red brick arch, it had quickly become my happy
place. I'd finished making yet another batch of
macarons when my cell phone rang. It was an
unknown number and for a second, my heart
skittered. I hadn't had any more road rage en-
counters, but I was still on edge.

The woman on the other end of the line introduced herself as Vivian Cantrell, Crosby House's
volunteer coordinator. "Oh! I figured I'd speak
with someone tomorrow after orientation," I
said to her. Finally, maybe I'd have something to
do in regards to Ben Nader.

"Before a prospective volunteer spends his or
her time at orientation, I like to have a conversation," she replied. She had the hint of an accent,
which I couldn't place.

"Makes sense," I said. I imagined that she could
suss out quite a bit about a person through a simple
phone call. I know I could. For example, Vivian
Cantrell came across as incredibly professional
and no-nonsense. I supposed those qualities
were important when you worked in an emotionally charged environment.

"Is now a good time?"

I'd just finished piping small rounds of the
macaron meringue onto parchment-covered
baking sheets. I'd lifted and dropped the trays
several times, eliminating the air bubbles.

Now, I set the trays of macarons aside on the

counter and turned to look out the window behind the cooktop. It overlooked the front yard,
the leaves of the old tree in the center rustling
from the light coastal breeze. "It's the perfect
time," I said.

"Ivy Culpepper. That's an unusual name. I
feel like I've seen it before." The woman's voice
held an almost accusatory note, but that, of
course, didn't make sense. I didn't know her, so
it stood to reason that she didn't know me.

"My mother was a school teacher at Santa
Sofia high school," I said, "and my dad is the city
manager?" My voice lifted at the end of the sentence, posing it as a question in case it triggered
a recollection for her.

"Mmm. Maybe." She paused. "It'll come to me.
Anyway . . . is it Miss Culpepper? Ms.? Or Mrs.?"

"I'm not married," I said, adding a silent *anymore* at the end. "And please call me Ivy."

"Okay then, Ivy. Thank you. Tell me, what
made you complete the volunteer application
for Crosby House?"

I turned away from the window and moved to
one of the stools on the other side of the island.
I'd given a lot of thought to how I'd answer this
question. I wanted to be straightforward, but I'd
decided to leave Ben Nader's name out of it
until I'd seen the place for myself. "To be honest, I just learned about the shelter recently. I
did a little research and, I don't know, I guess I
felt the need to help. I'm fortunate enough to
have some wonderful people in my life. Not

everyone has that, I realize, but if I can be that for someone in . . . need, well, I'd . . . like that."

My back straightened at the sound of a pen or pencil scratching against a sheet of paper. Vivian Cantrell was taking notes. "In what capacity do you see yourself volunteering?" she asked.

I knew Olaya would want to help through the bread shop, but I didn't want to broach that subject yet. Not until I'd mentioned it to her. Instead, I focused on my strengths and what I thought I had to offer. "I'd love to read with some of the children. I can help with anything that needs doing. Laundry, cooking, cleaning. I can bring supplies, shop, or work on any special projects you have."

"Do you garden?" Vivian asked.

I didn't, not really, although I had a lemon tree and a pot of basil on the back patio. Still, I cleared my throat and nodded. "Absolutely."

"That's good to hear. We have a garden here in terrible need of tending. After the orientation—you are planning on attending that?"

"Yes—"

"I'll show you the garden and we'll set up a schedule that works for you."

"That sounds great," I said. I wasn't sure if I spoke with too much enthusiasm, or not enough. Either way, Vivian Cantrell didn't seem to notice. She thanked me for my interest in volunteering, told me to be prompt to the orientation, said goodbye, then hung up the phone.

I looked at Agatha, who was sprawled out on the cool floor. "I guess I passed," I said.

She looked at me with her bulbous eyes, but didn't bother to lift her chin. She snorted heavily as her eyelids fluttered closed again. She didn't show it, but inside, I knew Agatha was super excited for me.

Chapter 13

"How long will it take to get used to getting up before five a.m.?" I asked Olaya the next morning. It was 4:49, and we were already hard at work. It had felt like the middle of the night when I'd awoken. To Agatha, too, who'd grumbled when I'd carried her sleepy body outside so she could take care of business. Back on the bed, she'd curled up and had fallen right back to sleep. I was jealous. I craved my bed and another two hours of z's, too.

Felix manned the heavy floor mixer and was making the day's sourdough bread, which would be shaped into *bâtards* after the rise, then baked to a golden crusty brown. Olaya rolled out the buttery layers of croissant dough, shaping them into the traditional crescent shapes. She had chocolate paste in a bowl at her station, so I knew she'd be making chocolate croissants today, too. It wasn't something she baked consistently, focusing mostly on the traditional breads rather than pastries, but I could see the bounce in her step and the color back in her cheeks. She was back after weathering the illness that had taken her out of commission and she was thrilled to be back in her kitchen. Baking chocolate croissants was her way of celebrating.

"It depends," Olaya said. "If you establish a routine of going to bed early enough, your body clock will adjust. *Pero*, if you keep your old routine and go to bed late, you will be always be tired."

"It's an adjustment," Felix said over the sound of the mixer. "If you're like me and struggle with the going-to-bed-early thing, naps will be your best friend."

I stifled a yawn just thinking about the warmth and comfort of the bed I'd left in the dark this morning. A nap was already calling, but it wasn't in my immediate future. When I was done here, I'd be heading to Crosby House.

We worked silently, the strums of classical guitar music playing in the background. Olaya changed the music daily. Some days smooth jazz played through the speakers into the bread shop. Other days it was all Etta James. Sometimes it was opera. And sometimes it was Earth, Wind & Fire or the Doobie Brothers. You never knew what you were going to hear at Yeast of Eden.

Today I could have used a little 70s disco pick-me-up, but I absorbed the soothing sounds of the guitar and kept working on the Hawaiian rolls currently in process. The secret ingredient was pineapple juice. They baked up soft and supple. The simple tactile act of pulling apart these rolls fresh from the oven was so satisfying. That promise was keeping me going at the moment.

The three of us worked in companionable silence, ticking each item we baked off the day's master list. The core offerings were always the same, but Olaya changed it up once in a while by adding specialty items that were not the normal fare. These we advertised on a chalkboard display sign on the sidewalk outside the bread shop, and on the blog. I'd done the intro post for the blog, but hadn't gotten much further than putting up photographs and an accounting of the day's special baked items each morning. It was enough for now.

I helped man the front counter while Olaya, Felix, and the late-morning crew continued in the kitchen. The minute hand on the analog clock over the counter ticked over to the new hour. Nine o'clock. The bell on the door dinged and the *America's Best Bakeries* team piled in. What the . . . ? I gave myself a mental head slap. I'd completely forgotten. Ben was still in a medically induced coma, but, according to Emmaline, the doctors were cautiously optimistic.

I smiled faintly as the crew lined up and we served them complimentary coffee and croissants, morning buns, and banana-walnut bread. My skin, sallow from lack of sleep, combined with the blackened-marshmallow bags under my eyes, made me look the worse for wear. Honestly, I'd forgotten about the filming today. The last thing I wanted to do was be in front of a camera.

Mack Hebron strode in a few minutes later looking every bit the TV star. His skin glowed and his eyes were crystal clear. His messy hair was perfectly coiffed and his rolled-up shirt-sleeves and open collar gave him an air of ease. He was tan, fit, and knowledgeable—the perfect trifecta for a reality-show host. He waited his turn in line, making sure the crew members had all gotten their fill before he stepped up. "Maggie, right?"

Maggie nodded, her eyes wide and starstruck.

"It's great to see you again," Mack said, meeting her gaze head-on. She blushed, the rosy afterglow of a television star knowing her name.

Next he looked at me. "And Ivy. You're looking lovely as always." Liar, I thought—maybe a little ungraciously. "You ready for our last day of filming?" he asked.

God, I was so ready. Being on camera was a worry I didn't want to think about anymore. "I think we all are," I said, handing him a disposable coffee cup, the top sealed with a lid made of recycled materials. Olaya did her part to minimize the bread shop's carbon footprint.

"Is Sandra in the kitchen?" he asked, coming around the counter, following the crew through the swinging doors.

"I haven't seen her yet. She may have come in the back door, though."

"We'll be doing some filming in the front today." I felt his gaze roam over my messy topknot and settle back on my face. My face, which was free of makeup. "I'll have someone come help you, um, spruce up."

My eyes pinched involuntarily. I knew I looked like I'd been through eight rounds in a boxing ring, but I didn't like that he'd felt the need to comment on it. "Great, thanks," I said through a forced smile.

After Mack disappeared into the kitchen, Maggie put her hand on my shoulder. "It's not that bad, Ivy," she said, but I caught a glimpse of my reflection in the display case glass. It most definitely was that bad.

I left Maggie to the short line of customers and went into the kitchen. The crew was already in action with Mack and Olaya both mic'd up. No one mentioned Ben Nader, but his absence was like a storm cloud hovering over the building.

Mack looked around the kitchen, then once again asked about Sandra Mays. "She has not been in this morning," Olaya said matter-of-factly.

Mack pulled out his cell phone and dialed. "No answer," he said a moment later. He opened the back door, peeking into the parking lot. A second later, he opened it wide, looking back over his shoulder at us. "Her car's here. You sure she didn't come in?"

"I have been here since four thirty," Felix said. "She has not come in."

I hadn't thought there was any love lost between Mack Hebron and Sandra Mays, but a decided look of concern came over him as he went outside and let the door close behind him.

"I'll walk around the building," I offered. "Maybe she took a walk to the beach or something."

Olaya nodded and continued her baking. Felix had gone into the walk-in refrigerator and the rest of the crew immediately drew out their phones, heads lowered, shoulders hunched in that familiar twenty-first-century posture. I grabbed my sweater from the hook by the door and slipped it on. April in a coastal town could be pretty chilly, and today it was particularly cool. Mack was walking back toward me, shaking his head. "She's not in her car. Engine's not warm, so it's been here a while."

I pictured him laying the flat of his hand against the cold metal. Interesting that he thought to check that, I thought.

He still held his phone and now dialed again. Even with the handheld device to his ear, I could hear the faint ringing on the other end.

I did a double take. Or could I?

I pointed to the curb on the edge of the parking lot. It overlooked a lower lot in the back of the collection of stores next door to the bread shop. "Go over there and dial again."

He looked at me like maybe my elevator didn't go all the way to the top, but I insisted, jabbing my finger in the air in the direction I wanted him to go. Finally, he walked away from me. I watched him dial and once again hold the phone to his ear.

At the same time, I cocked my head to one side, listening intently. There it was! A faint ringing sound coming from . . . from where?

"I hear her phone ringing!" I said.

Mack jogged back over to me. "What?"

"When you dialed, I thought you had your volume way up because I could hear the ringing, but it wasn't coming from you. I hear her phone. She's—or at least it—is around here somewhere."

He looked skeptical, as if I had spun a tale and he couldn't figure out why. "It probably was just her phone ringing from mine—"

He stopped as I shook my head. "No. That's why I had you go over there. I couldn't have heard it from here. Call her number," I said, all traces of sleep pushed aside. I loved a good puzzle, and tracking down Sandra by her ringing phone was like a step in a scavenger hunt. Maybe she was in some clandestine embrace in someone else's car. Or maybe she was playing games, trying to irritate Mack.

Mack did as I asked, dialing, but this time he held the phone down by his side, moving his head this way and that while he listened. I heard it. It sounded far off, but I heard it nonetheless. I walked away from Mack. A moment later, the ringing stopped. I turned back to him with raised eyebrows.

"It went to voicemail."

"Call again," I said. Sandra wasn't declining the call if it rang a number of times before it clicked over to her mailbox message. We wouldn't hear it ringing if she was talking to someone else and just wasn't clicking over. Another scenario came to mind. Maybe she'd dropped it and hadn't realized it yet.

Mack dialed again. I walked, following the sound, with him right behind me. Over and over, he dialed. I turned left, wandering through the nearly empty parking lot, but the ringing grew fainter. I turned right, heading to the bread shop planter beds that ran along the perimeter of the building and the sound grew louder. "This way," I said, walking along the side of the building and turning right at the corner. "Dial again."

Mack did, and we both listened. We kept walking. The ringing stopped, but Mack hit redial and it started up again, this time loud enough to know we were right on top of it. I had a moment of déjà vu as I stepped into the foliage. I'd done this a few days prior when I'd been out here with Ben Nader. Instead of looking up toward the hidden ladder as I'd done with him, I crouched down and pushed away the leaves and flowers until I found it. Sandra's phone was under the wide leaves of a hydrangea next to the bricks that created a barrier for the bedding plants.

I started to pick it up, but stopped myself just in time. Something didn't feel right. The phone was face-side up and the screen was a splintered roadmap of cracks. Like it had fallen from a great height.

My heartbeat slowed. No, it definitely didn't feel right. I stood and backed away from the building. Like it had fallen from a great height, I thought again. Slowly, I looked up, my gaze following the ladder Ben Nader had shown me. All the breath went out of me at the same moment that Mack spotted what I'd already seen. A limp hand hung over the edge of the top of the building.

A limp hand that had let the phone it had been holding drop.

A limp hand that presumably belonged to Sandra Mays.

Chapter 14

Owen Culpepper was Santa Sofia's city manager and my father. He'd come a long way in his grieving process since my mother had passed unexpectedly, and for the first time, I felt like I could go to him for some comfort without adding too much of an extra burden to his already loaded shoulders. I wouldn't call my meeting him midafternoon on a Thursday a father-daughter date. That conjured up memories of roller skating, a special dinner out with just the two of us, a trip to the library, and the annual Father-Daughter Valentine's Day Dance.

Today? This was me needing a shoulder to lean on. His shoulder specifically.

I turned up at his office unannounced, hoping he'd be available and not tied up in meetings or even out in the field. The city offices were flat-roofed, boring buildings on the west side of Santa Sofia. During the summer months, the town was overrun with tourists, and even in the off months, places like Yeast of Eden kept people coming. But over in this area of town there were no souvenir shops or trinkets stamped with *Santa Sofia: A Beach Town with Style*, or *Live, Laugh, Love in Santa Sofia.*

The parking lot was filled with cars. I found a spot in front of one of the annexes, backtracking to the front entrance of the main building. I'd spent a good amount of time at my dad's office throughout my childhood. It was as familiar to me as Baptista's and the schools I'd attended or Santa Sofia High School where my mother had taught. Sally O'Brien, the office manager, sat at her desk, her fingers flying over the keyboard. She stopped only so she could move a hand to her mouse, navigate somewhere, then start typing again. She'd worked with my father for almost the entirety of both their careers and were friends as well as colleagues. She'd been there for Billy and me after our mother died, and she'd been an anchor for my dad throughout the years.

She looked up from her computer. As she laid eyes on me and recognition hit, her smile lit up her face. She was ten years older than my dad, a little shorter than me, and was probably stronger than any American Gladiator—physically and emotionally. She would always be our rock. "Ivy. Darlin', you're a sight for sore eyes."

I felt the same about her. I caught her up on my new hours at the bread shop, my photography freelancing, and my romance with Miguel before giving her a hug and heading down the hallway to my dad's office. I knew he'd be willing to drop everything to find out what was on my mind.

I wasn't wrong. He canceled a meeting he'd had on his schedule and shepherded me out to his car. Minutes later, we stood side by side ordering at Two Scoops, our favorite ice cream parlor. The classic striped awnings, the long malt shop bar inside, the checkerboard floors, and the long case of homemade ice cream. This place took me back to my childhood and brought up good memories and warm feelings. Coming here had been a good decision.

My usual go-to was a scoop of strawberry in a cup, but today felt like a hot fudge kind of day. I went for the cappuccino chip with extra hot fudge while my dad had two scoops of vanilla bean. We sat across from each other on old-fashioned bistro chairs at a slightly sticky table. It was all part of the experience.

"What's going on, Ivy?" my dad asked after we'd both taken our first spoonful. He'd aged after my mother's death, his salt-and-pepper hair turning solid gray. He'd taken up running as a way of exorcising his demons. The result was that he was lean and fit in a way I don't remember him ever being. People dealt with grief differently. He handled his ongoing loss by moving his body. The more he ran, the less he had to think. At least that was my theory about it.

There was no need to beat around the bush with my dad, so I cut to the chase. "You've heard of Sandra Mays?"

He put his pink plastic spoon in his mouth,

pulling it out again, half the vanilla ice cream left behind. "From TV?" he asked.

"Yeah."

"Okay. I know who she is," he said, finishing the ice cream that remained on his spoon.

"You know the reality show I told you about? The one doing the feature on Yeast of Eden?"

"*America's Best Bakeries*, right?"

Owen Culpepper absorbed a lot of information in that vast brain of his. If I'd told him about it, he remembered every last detail. "Right. She and Mack Hebron, the celebrity chef, are the co-hosts." *Were*, I corrected myself. They *were* the co-hosts.

My dad's eyes grew wide. "That's impressive. Good for her."

Only not. "She's dead, Dad."

He'd been about to take another spoonful of his vanilla, but froze, the spoon stopping midway to his mouth. He dropped it back into the cup, interlaced his fingers on the table, and waited for me to go on.

"She didn't show up this morning. Mack and I went out to the back parking lot to look for her. Her car was there, but she wasn't. When he dialed her number, we heard her phone ringing. And then we found her. She was on the roof of the building." The image of her hand casually flung over the edge was emblazoned in my mind. "It appears that she met someone up there, had an argument, was knocked down, and her head slammed against the roof."

He ran his palm down over his face as he took in everything I'd said. "How did she get on the roof?"

"There's a ladder. It's kind of hidden behind the vines. I just learned about it the other day from Ben Nader—"

"The man who was hit outside the bread shop?"

I nodded. "I don't know who else could know about the ladder, Dad. Olaya didn't even know about it."

"Okay, here's another question. Why did she climb the ladder to go up to the roof?"

That was the first question I'd asked myself when I'd seen the dangling hand. I felt pretty sure that if we were able to figure out the why, we'd learn what had happened and who was responsible. Because someone was definitely responsible. Sandra Mays had been murdered.

"Emmaline and her team have processed the crime scene. She said it looked like no one had been on the roof in years and years except for the cluster of footprints and disturbance connected to Sandra being up there. They've got forensics looking at some fibers they found both on the roof and gathered from Sandra's body. That's the only physical evidence they have to go on."

"Ivy." My dad's brow furrowed with his concern. "It's enough that your brother's soon-to-be wife—"

"And my best friend, don't forget—"

"How could I? I've always loved that girl like a daughter. It's enough that Em lives in the dangerous world of law enforcement. You don't need to get involved in this."

He was right, of course, but how could I not

when it had hit so close to home? Something dark was going on, and though I couldn't prove it, I was convinced the attack on Ben and the murder of Sandra were related.

"If I can help, I want to."

"Let Em and her people do their job."

"Dad," I said, pushing my half-eaten ice cream aside. "There's something else."

He looked at me, waiting for me to continue.

"Ben Nader showed me the ladder to the roof the day he died. Miguel was there, too. Other than us, who else could have known about it? How did Sandra Mays know about it? I'm worried—"

He took one of my hands and squeezed. "If this guy Ben showed you, he probably told other people about it, too. The police have no reason to think you had anything to do with this woman's death."

"I don't want it to affect Olaya or the bread shop, either. A murder right there on the roof, and so soon after her friend Jackie was killed in the parking lot? It doesn't look good. I have to help if I can," I said.

He nodded, tight-lipped. "Be careful, Ivy."

I squeezed his hand. "Always."

Chapter 15

My eyelids drooped with exhaustion as I drove my pearl-white Fiat crossover down Maple Street. It had been my mother's car, which my dad had passed on to me after she died. It wasn't as if the car represented her or made me feel closer to her, exactly, but I did always think of her, even for the briefest moment, when I drove it. She'd loved it, which meant I loved it.

Right now, as I pulled into my driveway, I felt comforted by the memory of her presence in it. I pressed the programmed button to open my garage door, waited for it to open, and pulled in. Moments later I'd let Agatha into the backyard, leaving the French door open a crack, had kicked off my shoes, and collapsed onto the sofa.

Sleep came almost instantly. I drifted off, a dream settling in. A giant loaf of bread. A cell phone with a cracked screen. A hand rising up through a bowl of proofing dough. I felt myself turn cold. I had to save her—whoever it was. Sandra. Was it Sandra? I grabbed ahold of the hand, recoiling at the clammy feel of it. A bell sounded. I let go. Saw it dangling, the fingers directed downward toward the inner wrist. I was too late.

The bell rang again, startling me out of my slumber. I pried my eyes partway open. The room had grown dark. How long had I been asleep? I pushed myself halfway up, peering into the room as my vision adjusted to the darkness, calling for Agatha.

She squirmed at end of the couch, then gave a put-upon snort.

I'd heard something, hadn't I? Or had I dreamt it?

The doorbell rang, followed by Miguel's voice calling for me. "Ivy, are you home?"

That's what had woken me up. I pushed myself up and shuffled to the entryway, releasing the dead bolt and opening the front door. Miguel stood there, concern worrying his face. He stepped in and wrapped me up in his arms. "Thank God you're okay," he said, exhaling with relief.

"Why wouldn't I be okay?" I asked, my voice muffled against his shoulder.

He pulled back and retrieved a reusable grocery bag he'd set on the front porch. "I heard what happened at the bread shop. You found her?"

He shut the door behind him and we walked to the kitchen. "Me and Mack Hebron. He dialed her phone and I heard it ringing. That's how we tracked it." I stopped to look up at him. "Miguel, it was in the flowerbed by the ladder Ben Nader showed us."

He set the grocery bag on the butcher-block island, giving me his full attention. "So Sandra climbed that ladder?"

"Along with someone else, who then killed her up there."

He shook his head, as stunned by the whole thing as I was. "What does Emmaline think?"

"She doesn't have any leads yet." He started unloading the bag, pulling out a head of napa cabbage, two carrots, a bunch of green onions, a red bell pepper, and something wrapped up from the butcher. "What's all this?" I asked.

"With your new schedule at the bread shop and after the trauma of today, I thought I'd make you dinner then put you to bed early." I flicked my eyebrows up at him suggestively. He just smiled and got to work. "First things first." He pulled a bottle of white wine from the bag, got two stemless glasses from the cupboard, withdrew the cork, and poured us each a glass.

I sat on one of the stools at the counter and watched while he found a cast-iron skillet in my pots-and-pans cupboard, setting it on a burner to heat up. Next, he undid what turned out to be chicken thighs from the brown paper wrapping. He seasoned them with paprika, garlic, and onion, spritzed the pan with olive oil, and laid the chicken out to grill.

Next, he washed the vegetables, got out a clean cutting board, and set to work chopping the cabbage, shredding the carrots, dicing the bell pepper, and chopping the green onion. I hopped off the stool to find him a wooden salad bowl, then went back to my wine.

He checked the chicken before moving on to the dressing. In a coffee mug, he measured seasoned rice vinegar, sugar, soy sauce, and sesame oil, stirring it together with a mini whisk.

"That's all that goes into it?"

"Less is more, love."

I lowered my chin but looked up at him sheepishly through my eyelashes. I liked that little endearment.

A few minutes later, he added sesame seeds and the dressing to the chopped salad, plated it for us in shallow wooden bowls, also from my cupboard, and laid the sliced chicken on top of the greens. He set one bowl in front of me, sat down on the other barstool with his, and we dug in.

I didn't say a word for a full minute as I ate. "Oh my God, this is so good," I said, my mouth full.

He laughed. "I figured you'd be hungry."

How right he was.

I had the leftover tail end of some French bread I'd baked the day before. I got it from the plastic baggie it was in, tearing off a hunk for him as I returned to my seat and my salad. He used a bit of it to sop up the remaining dressing at the bottom of his bowl.

It didn't take us long to wipe out the entire salad. If there had been more, I would have eaten more.

We cleaned up together and a few minutes

later, we were sitting on the sofa. I reclined with my feet stretched out on his lap. He draped one arm across the back of the couch, lazily resting his other hand on my crossed ankles. "Be careful, Ivy."

I eyed him. "Have you been talking to my dad?"

He shot out a quick breath. "No, but I know you."

"What do you know?" I asked.

"Oh, all kinds of things, but about this specifically?"

"Yeah," I said, not having the energy to go anywhere else with him tonight. Another time, though, and I wanted to hear everything he thought he knew about me.

"I know that you are going to put on your amateur sleuth hat and see what you can find out about Sandra. I know that you're going to try to figure out who went up to the roof with her, and how she even knew about the ladder going up there. And I know that you won't stop until you have the answers."

"God, you're good," I said.

He cracked a smile. "I've seen it before."

"So you have." We'd amateur sleuthed together, in fact, so it should have come as no surprise that he'd know my mind. "It can't be a coincidence that Sandra's dead and Ben is in a coma. They have to be related."

"Were they friends?" he asked.

"More like frenemies, I'd say. She was a little hard to take."

"Who else was she frenemies with?" he asked. "Or just straight-on enemies?"

Names flitted through my mind like stocks on a ticker tape. Mack Hebron was in bold print. Maybe Ben's wife. If there had ever been something between Ben and Sandra, she'd be a woman scorned. Unbidden, Tae, Ben's replacement cameraman, came to mind. He had a motive for Ben, but did he have one for Sandra? Finally, I answered Miguel's question with an exhausted, "I don't know."

I couldn't keep my eyes open anymore. Miguel moved my legs off the couch and helped me sit upright. "Come on, Ivy," he said. "Up to bed."

"Wait. Agatha—"

"I'll walk her around the block. No worries."

After I kissed him, he turned me around by the shoulders and gave me a little shove toward my bedroom. "I'll be back," he said, already crouching down to harness up Agatha.

I got myself ready for bed, slipping into sleep shorts and a tank before heading to the bathroom to brush my teeth and clean my face. I reached for my toothbrush, but it wasn't in its normal spot. Weird. Had I been so out of it this morning at four thirty that I'd stuck it in the drawer? I checked all of the drawers. No toothbrush.

Downstairs, I heard a faint clicking sound. A door? Was Miguel already back from walking Agatha? I called his name.

Silence.

The hairs on the back of my neck stood up. I

spun around, suddenly more alert. The hand towel and bath towel, both of which had been neatly hanging from their towel racks when I'd left this morning were reversed, the hand towel hanging where the bath towel had been and vice versa. My breath caught in my throat.

Someone had been in my house.

"Miguel?" I called again.

Still nothing.

My skin felt hot, my nerves frayed. My heart dropped. I dropped to my knees and speed-crawled from the bathroom, through my bedroom, to the window overlooking the backyard. I'd left the patio lights on and solar lights dotted the landscape. From my vantage point, it didn't look like anyone was lurking nearby.

Still, my heart thundered. Someone had been in my house! Were they still here, or did the click I'd heard mean whoever it was had already left? I hoped for the latter.

I stood and pressed myself against the wall and moved slowly from down the hallway to the kitchen, feeling like an FBI agent searching for a suspect. Only I was without a weapon or any backup. Where was Miguel?

My mind raced, circling around until it landed on something. The tailgating car. The impact as it hit me. Was it the same person?

Another thought careened into my brain. Luke. He'd warned me about Heather's death wish for me. I hadn't taken Luke very seriously when he'd shown up at my dad's house during Billy and Emmaline's engagement celebration to tell me that the woman he'd cheated on me with, and who he was still in a relationship with, wanted me dead. I was rethinking my cavalier response to that bombshell now. I inched closer to the kitchen. "Heather?" I called, then froze, scarcely breathing so I could listen.

I couldn't explain why, but I felt sure there was another presence in the house. Not a ghostly presence, but a real live human being. The air seemed to carry the breath of someone else. "Heather?" I said again.

A click. The sound of the front door opening. Silence.

I bolted toward the entryway, skidding to a stop when I saw the door was ajar. I grabbed ahold of the blown-glass Galileo thermometer Miguel had given me as a housewarming gift. It was not a good weapon, and I didn't want to destroy it, but it was something, and right now I needed something. Anything. I edged up behind the door and peeked my head around, my elbow cocked, my hand clutching the glass.

No one lurked on the front porch. No one ran across the lawn. I stepped onto the porch and peered around the corner to the driveway. The street was deserted. I heaved out the breath I'd been holding. Whoever it was, they were gone now.

Back inside, I sank to the floor, my back against the wall of the entryway. How had someone broken into my house? And why? I didn't want to believe it was Heather, but I couldn't think of anyone else who'd be stalking me. On the heels of Ben Nader's accident and Sandra Mays's murder, I was fully freaking out.

The handle of the front door jiggled. I jerked back, lifting the Galileo thermometer again.

"Come on, Agatha." Miguel's tone was light and coaxing as he led my little fawn pug inside. He stopped abruptly when he spotted me. He went on instant alert. "What's going on?"

I fell back to a sitting position, the beautiful glass piece shaking in my hand. He reached out and took it from me, setting it back on the little table where I kept it. It took three tries before I managed to speak without my voice trembling. "Someone was in the house."

One of the things I'd come to love about Miguel Baptista as an adult was that he was no-nonsense. He didn't look skeptical or question whether or not I had imagined it. He simply believed me and went into action. "Are they gone?"

"Yes. At least, I think so."

He made sure the front door was locked, then quickly circled the house, checking the rooms, doors, and windows, making sure no one was hiding and that everything was secure. Back in the entryway, he took hold of my hands and pulled me to standing. "Are you okay?"

I thought about how to answer that. "I'm shaken," I finally said. I told him about the missing toothbrush and the rearrangement of the hand and bath towels, then about the sound I'd heard cluing me in to the fact that I hadn't been alone.

"Any sign of forced entry?" I asked, pulling myself together and slightly surprised at how easily the investigative jargon came out of my mouth.

"The back window in your office is open. The screen's off."

I slapped my hand to my forehead. "I opened the window last night when I was working on my website. I must have forgotten to close it." I supposed it was possible that it was a random breaking and entering. A burglar seizing an opportunity.

Miguel's thoughts had gone in the same direction. "Your computer's there. Nothing looks amiss."

I hadn't checked to see if anything was missing, but I didn't really have many valuables. My laptop was probably the most expensive thing I owned, if you didn't count the baking supplies. It had all added up to a pretty penny, but really, who would break in to take any of that? Add to that the fact that the toothbrush was missing, and the rearrangement of the towels. Breaking into a house to steal a used Sonicare was not something any burglar worth his salt would do. I dismissed the idea of it being random. The toothbrush and towels made it personal.

"I'm staying here tonight," Miguel said.

I worked to control my still trembling hands. I thought about refusing. Insisting that he go home. That I was old enough and strong enough and independent enough to manage on my own, thank you very much.

Instead I nodded, because who was I kidding? I did not want to be alone tonight. Not even for a second.

Chapter 16

Early the next morning, I awoke to my alarm. My anxiety from the night before had settled into a mild worry, which I pushed aside. Instinctively, I checked my phone to see if Emmaline had texted with an update on Sandra Mays or Ben Nader. She had not. Or if Penelope Branford had messaged me while I slept, about a doctor's appointment she'd forgotten about, asking me to take her first thing. There was nothing from her. Or if Olaya needed me to pick anything up on my way in to the bread shop this morning. She didn't.

The only message I had was from Felix. A friend is coming into work with me today. She'll be here to help, so take the morning off and sleep in!

I lay back and processed this. Felix had a female friend who wanted to see what life running a bakery would be like. Was I jumping to conclusions to assume it was a girlfriend? Yes, I decided, I definitely was. I hardly knew Felix, but still. If it was his girlfriend, it made good sense that she'd want to see what the life of a baker would be like, especially if she had any plans to tie her apron strings to his.

I debated whether or not I should go in to Yeast of Eden anyway. I was not experienced, by any stretch of the imagination, but I was probably more experienced than Felix's friend. I lay back to think about it, letting my eyes close.

I woke up to the clatter of someone moving around in the house. That mild worry ratcheted up and my heart seized reflexively. I pushed myself up to sitting, scanning the room. Panic gripped me. Where was Agatha?

I leapt out of bed and hurried down the hallway, a feeling of déjà vu crashing into me. I slowed as I reached the kitchen, peering around the corner. The adrenaline that had been pumping through me suddenly crashed. It was Miguel. He had coffee brewing. A few pieces of kibble remained in Agatha's bowl while she lay contentedly in a sliver of sunlight stretching across the floor. Miguel stood at the stove, manning a frying pan that I could see was filled with vibrant yellow. He slid a silicone spatula around the edge of the pan, loosening the eggs before expertly flipping them. He spooned what looked like sautéed chopped bell peppers, mushrooms, and onions into the pan, added a sprinkling of shredded cheese, then flipped half of the omelet onto itself. He cut it in half with the spatula before sliding each of the two sections onto their own plates. He picked up a bowl, this one with strawberries and blueberries mixed together, and scooped it out onto each of the plates before turning toward the table. He spotted me and a slow smile spread. "Morning, sunshine."

"Morning," I said. Agatha raised her head, her bulbous eyes looking at me for a moment before they closed again and she gave herself to the sunlight. I sat at the table, feeling suddenly self-conscious about the state of my hair and pajamas and just . . . everything. I slept with my mass of curls in a topknot to prevent an onslaught of tangles, my sleep shorts and tank were rumpled, at best, and I was sure I looked worse for wear after not bothering to remove any traces of makeup before I'd crashed the night before. A weaker man might have turned and run for the hills, but Miguel poured us both coffee and sat down.

"I made you breakfast," he said.

I laughed. "So I see."

Food was his love language, I thought. He'd taken care of me last night, but his care went beyond simply being present. Neither one of us had been in control of the situation with the break-in, but he was in control when he cooked. Maybe I was reading more into it than was actually true, but I felt that Miguel making me breakfast was his way of starting the day off with him in driver's seat, and was a way for him to usher me right alongside him. He didn't want me spooked. He wanted me empowered to take the bull by the horns and face the day.

We ate and cleaned up together. After getting dressed,we drove the short distance to the shoreline walking path for a little jaunt with Agatha. He brought me back home before heading off to the restaurant for the day. I triple checked to make sure every window and door was locked before showering. Cleaned up and ready for the day, I spent the next hour mixing dough for a loaf of rosemary bread, then cleaning up the kitchen again. While it went through its first rise, I worked on the bread shop website and blog in my little office, and did some photo editing I'd been putting off.

After the bread had baked and I'd had an end piece—my favorite—slathered with butter from a local farm, it was time to head to Crosby House for the orientation meeting with Vivian Cantrell. The email confirmation gave the address of the women's shelter, which had been bothering me. I guess the phone call was the first line of vetting, but it was concerning that I knew the location of the shelter after only filling out an online application and having a brief phone call with the director. How did they keep the women safe from their abusers if the place wasn't as top secret as I'd initially thought? Unless I was missing something, that sounded like a pretty big flaw in security to me.

The address led me to a nondescript building located in Santa Sofia's business district. The fact that *Crosby House* wasn't emblazoned on a sign gave me a little bit of comfort. There were no windows. The door was closed and locked. A doorbell with an intercom was to the right of the door. I knew enough about such systems to know there was wireless video monitoring going on, probably streaming live video of whatever happened out here on the stoop to whoever monitored such activity, ultimately storing it on the cloud. A security system sticker was adhered to the top right corner of the door. I let out a relieved sigh. Okay. So no one was getting into Crosby House without permission.

My ringing of the bell was quickly followed by a staticky click and a voice saying, "Crosby House. Can I help you?"

I bent down and spoke right into the speaker. "I have an appointment with Ms. Cantrell. I'm Ivy Culpepper."

The voice came back at me with a clipped, "Just a minute."

Less than a minute later, I heard the click of a lock on the other side of the door and it swung open. The woman standing before me was rail thin, had fine blond hair pulled back into a ponytail, and looked to be in her late fifties. Her phone voice, with its deep tenor and slight accent, had left me with he impression that she was much taller than she actually was. It felt a little strange to be looking down at her. She held her arm out to me. "Vivian Cantrell."

"Ivy Culpepper," I said, shaking her hand. In my experience, you could tell a lot about a person by the grip of their handshake. Vivian Cantrell was no exception. Her natural strength came through, but she had control at the same time. She didn't hold on for too long, so it wasn't about exerting her power over me, but rather just long enough to show she was a force to be reckoned with if it came right down to it.

As she ushered me inside, I caught her scanning the parking lot, her gaze narrowing and holding for a split second on something. I turned in time to see the taillights of a dark SUV drive away. My blood ran cold as my mind flashed back to the incident with the car ramming into my bumper. Surely it wasn't the same vehicle.

Vivian closed the door, sliding the dead bolt into place. "We must always be vigilant," she said.

I nodded, swallowing hard. "Absolutely."

She led me through the center hallway, turning right into a small office where she waved me into a chair before taking a seat behind the office desk. "Thank you for coming, Ivy, and again, thank you for your interest in volunteering at Crosby House."

"I'm ready to help," I said, surprised at how true that statement was. I'd come because of Ben Nader, not realizing how much I also wanted to be an anchor for the women and children here.

"Let me tell you a little more about what we do, then I'll show you around. There's no one else here for orientation today, so it's just you and me."

I smiled and nodded, wondering how many times she'd given this same spiel. "Sounds great."

She launched right into it, starting with the

background of Crosby House, which had been in existence for going on thirteen years, and ending with a large donation they'd just received from the CEO of a Silicon Valley tech company, a Santa Sofia native whose sister had died as a result of domestic violence and who was trying to make a little bit of difference, one donation at a time.

After a moment, I chastised myself for thinking Vivian Cantrell's words might sound hollow or rehearsed. Every single sentence she spoke rang with truth and passion.

She leaned forward, laying one forearm over the other and looking intently into my eyes. "I lost my mother at the hands of my father. They say history repeats itself. My daughter and I escaped a similar situation. The women here, they've lost so much. We take our safety, a roof over our heads, food in our children's bellies, for granted. One woman here lost her boyfriend and her son at the same time. She's still fighting her demons. Too many women don't have a voice, or a safe place to run to. Crosby House is that place. We depend on volunteers like you to help us, so again, Ivy, thank you for being here."

My eyes had turned glassy at her story, but I quickly blinked them clear. "I'm honored to be part of this."

She tilted her head to one side, considering me. "Is your interest in helping personal?"

I recalled the question and statements on the volunteer application about victims of abuse volunteering and the need to complete counseling first, so I knew what she was asking. "No," I said.

"I'm fortunate not to have been a victim. No one I know personally has been, either. I think that's part of the reason why this opportunity resonates so much with me."

She raised her eyebrows slightly and nodded in a way that encouraged me to continue.

"I want to be able to offer my support to other women who have not had the same good fortune I've had. In a way, I guess I want to give back."

As she pushed back in her chair and stood, I felt her strength, almost as if it shone from inside her like the rays of the sun. "We're lucky to have you, then," she said, picking up her cell phone and coming around to the front of her desk. "Let me show you around."

I followed her out of the office and back down the hallway the way we'd come. She turned right at the entrance, which led to a community room with several couches and overstuffed chairs forming seating areas; three square game tables, each with four rail-back chairs; bookshelves scattered with adult and children's books; and a pile of board games neatly stacked on a table in one corner. The back wall had two windows looking out to a grassy backyard dotted with a few small trees that looked to have been planted fairly recently. Two stakes anchored each tree to the ground, tape loosely connecting the stakes to the skinny trunks. From my view at the window, there was no garden to be seen—presumably the reason Vivian Cantrell had asked me if I gardened. If this was my volunteer assignment, I'd be starting from scratch.

Several women and a few young children, no more than five or six years old, sat in different areas of the room. Every single eye turned to the shelter's director and me when we entered. "Ladies," Vivian said, "this is one of our newest volunteers, Ivy Culpepper. You'll be seeing her around."

I smiled warmly and waved. The response was a low murmur from one or two of the women, but none of them made eye contact, and most directed their gaze downward or at the TV hanging from an arm on the wall. A noon news show played. The volume was low, but subtitles were on.

Vivian turned to me, speaking softly. "It'll take time."

I understood. They'd been hurt. Betrayed. They certainly didn't want to be gawked at, and they certainly wouldn't be blindly putting their trust in some stranger who'd just walked into their safe world.

Vivian led me through a door tucked into the back left corner of the room, which led to the backyard. She folded her arms over her chest as she directed her attention to the overgrown raised planter beds. "That is where we currently need the most help. The beds haven't been tended to in more than a year. We had a volunteer who loved to garden, but she moved to the Central Valley. No one else has been inclined to take on the project."

She let the last sentence hang there between us like an invitation. I hesitated, realizing the scope of the task. Tall grass and weeds sprouted thickly from each of the raised beds. They'd need to be removed. I'd done some reading about gardening in preparation for meeting Vivian, so I knew we'd need to amend the soil before anything could be planted. Unless I had an entire crew of women helping me, and if I only planned on volunteering once a week, we'd never get the job done.

"How does it work?" I asked. "I come two or three times a week and some of the women will help me in the garden?"

Vivian nodded. "Basically. We ask that everyone here help out around the house if they are able. We ask that the women take care of their own laundry, and that of their children, if they have any. They take care of their personal spaces, of course. And then there are communal tasks like cooking and cleaning. We've wanted to get the garden going again. There is something so rewarding and empowering about cooking with produce you've grown. It's important that we incorporate it back into Crosby House. If you're willing to take it on."

"I'd love to," I said, not hesitating for a second. I wasn't sure how I'd find chunks of time, and it would take some research to figure out exactly what it meant to amend the soil and how to do it, as well as what to plant and how, but I was up for the challenge, and I was especially up for contributing to Crosby House in whatever capacity they needed.

I'd have to build some trust to get anyone to talk about Ben Nader, but I was patient. There was nothing, however, stopping me from asking Vivian Cantrell about her other volunteers. "I work at Yeast of Eden," I said, staying focused on the yard so I sounded nonchalant. "I met a man there who volunteers here. Ben Nader?"

"He does," she said. Had she tensed when I'd said Ben's name, or had I imagined it? "He's very handy, although I don't believe we'll see him for a while."

"Right. The accident."

She walked toward a free-standing shed. "Some of the girls were talking about it. And about the woman from TV. A double tragedy."

"It's been a shock," I said truthfully. "We're all hoping Ben pulls through."

She opened the door to the shed, revealing garden tools, bags of soil, chicken wire, stacks of old newspapers and magazines, and who knew what else. "Do the doctors think he will?"

"They are optimistic," I said. "Was he, mmm, close to any of the women here? Maybe someone would like to visit him?"

"There are one or two," she said, "but I don't know how they will handle seeing a man they know in a coma. They're all so fragile."

That was a good point. "I was there," I said, "so I'd be happy to talk to them about what happened."

Vivian fell silent, considering. "We can arrange that," she said after a moment. "I'd like to be there to support them, but Ben has been a constant presence here. Some of the women would like to see him, I think."

Vivian gestured to the contents of the shed. "Use whatever you like. When you're ready to buy seeds or plants, just let me know."

Vivian's cell phone rang. She checked the screen, held up one finger to me, turning her back and walking a few steps away. A few seconds later, she was back, her hand clutching her phone. "If you'll excuse me, Ivy. There's a . . . situation that requires my attention. Feel free to look around. I'll find you when I'm done."

"Of course," I said, but she'd already turned on her heels and was walking across the patchy grass to the door.

Well, well. The director of Crosby House had given me leave to explore. It probably wasn't a typical situation for a new volunteer, but I'd take it. I slowly turned in a circle. Where to start?

Ben may very well have worked outside in the yard, but I didn't think that would help me any. It wasn't as if he'd known he'd be attacked and left a clue in the shed, convenient as that would be. No, if there was any connection between his accident and this place, I'd find it courtesy of one of the women inside.

I followed in Vivian Cantrell's footsteps, back across the grass and through the door. The same women and children I'd seen were still sitting in the room. I let my gaze travel over them. Just like before, most of them avoided looking at me. Only one looked up and met my gaze. She had shoulder-length wavy dark hair, her skin was as pale as Snow White's, and her full cheeks just as rosy. I couldn't tell how tall she was while she was seated, but her feet barely touched the ground, which told me she was definitely on the short side. I turned and strode over to her like an arrow heading straight for a bull's-eye. "Mind if I sit down?" I asked.

She scooted over, taking the pillow that had been by her side with her, making room for me. "I'm Ivy," I said.

"Yeah, I saw you earlier," she said, her voice quiet. She didn't offer her name. We sat in silence for a minute before she spoke again. "What are you going to do here?"

"Ms. Cantrell asked if I'd work on the garden."

She looked surprised. "I didn't know we had a garden."

"I guess there used to be one? I'm going to get it started again."

She gave a little nod, but didn't say anything else. I guess gardening wasn't a big priority for someone who was escaping domestic violence of some sort. This woman probably had bigger things to worry about.

Another woman in the room suddenly sat forward and pointed at the TV. "Hey. Turn that up."

Someone directed a remote control at the television.

The volume suddenly increased. A local noon newscaster sat behind a desk, only her red top and black blazer visible. She was mid-sentence and talking about the death of local celebrity Sandra Mays on the heels of another tragic accident that nearly killed local cameraman Ben Nader.

A low chatter started on the opposite side of the room as the women listened to the television host give the details about Sandra's body being discovered on the roof of a local business.

"Tell me I'm not the only one who thinks that's way too much of a coincidence," the woman who'd asked to turn up the volume said. She sat on the edge of her seat. Thanks to the light shining through the windows, I could see freckles dotting the dark skin of the bridge of her nose.

"What do you mean, D'anna?" It was the woman holding the remote control who spoke this time. She had a pixie haircut and her narrowed eyes held suspicion.

"That they're connected, girl. No way a reality TV star is murdered and her cameraman is run down and those are two different events. No way," she said again, emphasizing the words.

My thoughts exactly, D'anna. I thought about agreeing out loud, but although the women in the room were talking with me around, I was still a stranger and this was still a safe house. It was better for me to listen and observe.

"You think there's a killer in Santa Sofia?" A third woman spoke this time, her voice shrill and nervous. "Like the Golden State Killer? Or Son of Sam?"

D'anna put her straight right away. "No, Jasmine, not a serial killer. Relax."

But Jasmine, poor thing, couldn't relax. "My ex, he could have done that kind of thing. I could be dead right now. I could totally be dead right now."

D'anna moved from her chair, taking the spot next to Jasmine. "But you're not. You're fine, and that crazy man doesn't have a clue where you are. Remember that. You escaped."

Jasmine's nose flared. She blinked her eyes, holding back her tears. "But Ben—"

"We don't know what he was involved with, Jasmine, but it has nothing to do with you." D'anna, it seemed, was the glue holding poor Jasmine together.

The other young woman who manned the remote joined D'anna on Jasmine's other side. She put her hand on Jasmine's shoulder. "Come on," she said. "Let me take you to your room."

Jasmine allowed herself to be guided out and once again a haunting silence took over the room. "It sounds like she knows this guy Ben Nader," I said to the nameless woman I sat next to.

She just shrugged. It seemed these women, probably with very good reason, kept things close to the vest. Vivian Cantrell returned just then, gesturing for me to join her. "I'm afraid I must tend to some things, Ivy, but I'll see you tomorrow?"

I agreed. I left Crosby House excited and ready to dig in, both with the gardening, which I'd research tonight at home, and with Ben Nader's connection to the place. Something, I was sure, would eventually bloom.

Chapter 17

My alarm went off before dawn the next morning. I planned to keep helping Olaya with her early morning cooking to take the pressure off. The last thing she needed was a relapse. I'd texted her that I'd be in soon. My cell phone rang almost immediately.

"Go back to sleep," she said when I answered.

"You've been sick. I want to help—"

"Pfft. I am, as you say, fit as a fiddle."

"I don't think I've ever said fit as a fiddle," I said.

"I am relieving you of your morning duties. Felix and I can handle it."

"It's too much for you to do alone," I argued, but the truth was, I wanted to be there with her. She hadn't actually signed off on my coming in for the early baking shift. Maybe she didn't actually want that.

"That is why I have Felix," she said.

"But—"

"I will work with him today," she interrupted, "and see how it goes. Then you and I will work out a new schedule. *Sí?*"

I fell back onto my bed. Agatha snuggled up next to my leg, exhaling with a snuffled snort. "Are you sure?" I asked, only half reluctantly. I still hadn't fully recovered from the early morning shift I had put in, and I welcomed another hour or two of sleep.

"Positive. *Gracias por todo*, Ivy. Felix said you made a good team, *pero* now I am back."

I had to admit, she didn't sound like she'd relapse anytime soon. Alert. Bright. Excited. I'd come to know Olaya well, and the indisputable truth was that she loved the bread shop more than anything. It was her home away from home. Being back was good medicine for her.

"I'll stop by later," I said, "and please don't overdo it."

"I will take things slow. Now go back to sleep."

She didn't have to tell me again. I hung up, sank back into the warmth of my bed, and drifted off. Three hours later, I awoke to the sound of my phone ringing. My conversation with Olaya notwithstanding, it was too early for a phone call. I wouldn't be surprised if it was Mrs. Branford. She was an early riser, had her pulse not only on our neighborhood, but on the town of Santa Sofia as a whole, and didn't care a whit for convention. *I'm old enough to not concern myself with what other people think, Ivy*, she liked to say to me, and it was 100 percent true. If it was her style, she'd wear giant black-framed glasses, red lipstick, and a vibrant boa, just like Iris Apfel.

I lifted the phone, prepared to see her name. I didn't. Instead, it said UNKNOWN CALLER.

"Hello?" I said, hearing the grogginess in my voice.

Silence.

Maybe it was a bad connection. "Hello?"

Still nothing.

And then . . . a rustling. "Hello?" I tried again, my skin prickling. After the break-in two nights ago, I was on edge. I listened intently to see if I'd imagined the sound.

I hadn't. The hairs on the back of my neck stood on end as I registered faint whispering. "Hello," I said, more forcefully this time. "I can't hear—" I started, stopping at the sound of a click. The line went dead.

I stared at my phone, immediately scrolling to recent calls. There was no point. No number or name was listed. Just UNKNOWN CALLER, with no location given. Who had been on the other end of that phone call?

Once again, my first thought was my ex-husband's girlfriend, Heather.

A hour later, after my walk with Agatha, a shower, a stop at the nursery to pick up a variety of vegetable plants to start with, and a stop at the Habitat for Humanity ReStore for supplies, I arrived at Crosby House. The phone call was still on my mind. Someone had definitely been on the other end, breathing loud enough for me to hear and moving around in a disconcerting way. I tried to talk myself out of believing it could be Heather. She lived in Austin. She wouldn't have uprooted her entire life to come to California to stalk me. It just didn't make sense. And yet . . .

I parked and texted Luke. Is Heather in Austin with you?

The three little gray dots blinked and his response appeared a second later. We're on a break.

Not what I wanted to hear, because if they were on a break, Heather had a lot of potential emotions she needed to direct somewhere. But is she in Austin? I typed.

Another message appeared. Why?

I turned my phone sideways, my thumbs tapping rapidly against the keyboard. Bc someone broke into my house, some car stalked me the other night and hit me, and I just got a weird phone call.

What kind of weird phone call?

I stared at the phone. After I told him about the break-in, the scary car incident, and a weird phone call, the call was what he wanted more information on? The kind with heavy scary breathing and nothing else.

Luke didn't respond. I waited. Surely he would say something. Anything. Instead, he said nothing. Hello? I typed.

The dots blinked again and I waited. They disappeared, showed up again, then vanished. No message came.

I threw my phone in my purse, cursing Luke under my breath. How dare he drop a bombshell about Heather wanting to kill me like he did, only to ignore me when I wanted more information because maybe, just maybe, the crazy adulteress was acting on her threat.

As I got out of the car, an image of Vivian Cantrell staring at a car that had been lurking in the shelter's parking lot came to mind. Why had that vehicle raised suspicion for the director? I had yet another feeling of unease. SUVs abounded in California, and everything surrounding the women's shelter would have the director on high alert, but the more I thought about it, the more I thought it was my stalker. My. Stalker. Those were two words I never thought I'd utter, but here I was. I had a stalker.

I pushed it out of my mind—as much as I could, which meant it was still there lurking and making me anxious and aware, but I tried not to think about it—as I deposited the array of tomato, zucchini, pepper, and eggplant seedlings next to my work area. I was on a mission. It was going to be a work-heavy garden day, but I was getting these plants in the soil. And I'd find out something about Ben Nader and his volunteerism at Crosby House. This was my day.

I sorted through the garden storage shed Vivian Cantrell had shown me and waited for Miguel to arrive with the crates I'd bought at the Habitat store. The Crosby House property was like a little fortress. A stucco wall ran around the perimeter. A driveway on the back end of the property was closed off by an electric iron gate. Inside the gate was a row of tall shrubs obscuring the yard from the outside. I'd gotten permission for Miguel to drop off the crates, but he wasn't allowed on the property unless he completed the volunteer application process like I had. There was no time for that, so another resident, Angie, said she'd help me move the crates from Miguel's truck to the garden area. "What are you going to do with them?" she'd asked as we waited for Miguel to arrive. I noticed the yellow remnant of a bruise just under her eye. It underscored the reality of the lives these women were running from.

"Keyhole gardens," I said, keeping my voice upbeat. She stared blankly, but I'd done my research and was only too happy to explain. "It's a garden that uses an integrated composter to continually amend the soil—"

Her eyes had glazed over from either her lack of interest or lack of understanding. Either way, I stopped and just thanked her for her help. A moment later, a pickup truck pulled up alongside us. The driver's side window rolled down and there he was. Miguel Baptista. "Hey there, Ms. Culpepper. You having a good day?"

I grinned at him. "It just got a little bit better."

Angie was tentative at first, watching warily as Miguel backed the truck into the driveway, stopping with the bed just inside the gate. "You sure I can't help you unload them?" he asked, dropping the tailgate.

"Yeah, you can help get them off the truck,

but Angie and I will move them to the garden area. They're very strict about allowing people on the property here."

"As they should be," Angie said. "I'm surprised Ms. Cantrell let you deliver these things."

Her tone made it clear that she didn't think Ms. Cantrell should have. "Getting the crates now means we can start the keyhole gardens today, rather than waiting," I said. I'd explained my need and solution to the director and she'd allowed Miguel to come this far only after I'd given her his entire background, showed her his history from the opening of his father's restaurant when he was a kid, to his time in Santa Sofia High School, to his military career, and finally his grand reopening of Baptista's Cantina and Grill. He was clearly not one of the Crosby House women's estranged violent partners disguised as a local man.

The square crates were four feet on each side and about three and a half feet tall. Over time, the wood slats would deteriorate, but I figured they'd last a good couple of years. Maybe at some point we could use them as a base and create a stone frame around them that would be more durable. I could see myself volunteering at Crosby House long after my sleuthing ended.

Together, Angie and I carried one of the three crates Miguel off-loaded for us past the shrub barrier and across the yard. We set it down in one of the areas I'd prepared. After we lugged the other two over, Angie strolled back inside, throwing me a backward glance that seemed to say, "I'm tapping out, you're on your own."

"Thanks for your help," I called to her. Maybe she was great with the women in the shelter, but I wasn't sad to lose her company.

Without turning around, she threw up her hand. At least she'd acknowledged me.

By the time I trudged back to the driveway for the fourth time, Miguel had moved his truck to the curb and was against the passenger door, deep in conversation on his cell phone. He cut the conversation short, hanging up and tucking his phone into his back pocket when I slipped my arms around him. "Let me thank you properly," I said.

"Mmm, I like that." He wrapped his arms around me. "Any more favors you need?" he murmured as he brushed his lips over mine.

Somehow, I managed to pull away. I gave him a coy grin, saying, "I'm sure I can think of something, but it'll have to wait. I'm on volunteer duty."

He reluctantly dropped his arms to his sides. "Until tonight, then."

My dad had planned a family dinner tonight at my childhood home. I nodded. "Can't wait."

He lifted the coil of chicken wire from the bed of his truck, handing it over to me, along with a pair of wire cutters. "Let me know if you need anything else," he said before driving off.

I waited until he was out of sight, then entered the code to close the gate behind me.

I'd brought a staple gun and heavy-duty plastic sheets, which I used to line the crates. As I continued to work on the keyhole garden boxes, a woman watched me from just outside the door to the house. She stood in front of the window, her arms folded across her chest like a barrier. I recognized her from the day before. I smiled at her, but stayed focused on my work. Vivian Cantrell came up to her and they talked for a long moment. Vivian handed her something. I craned to hear, but caught only a few words, then the young woman said, "Thank you, ma'am." After another moment, Vivian patted her on the arm and left the young woman to watch me. After another ten minutes, the woman moved a little closer to me, stepping to the edge of the small cement patio. Arms still crossed, a set of keys hanging from one hand, her other tucked tightly under the other side. Lips curved down. Guard still up.

She was small and willowy with blond hair in a short pixie cut, a small bow-shaped mouth, and deep gray-blue wary eyes. She had a small scar above her lip that was accentuated when she frowned, but that I bet would disappear when she smiled. I had a big smile, and long ginger locks that spiraled this way and that, inherited from my mother. I was freckled and had a fair complexion. This petite woman, who couldn't be more than five three, seemed opposite of me in nearly every way.

I smiled again, then gave it another ten minutes before waving at her. "Would you like to help?" I asked.

She looked over her shoulder as if she wasn't

sure I was speaking to her. She looked back to me, but didn't budge.

"They're called keyhole gardens," I said, continuing as if she'd answered me with a resounding *Yes!* I'd created three large cylinders, placing each one in the center of each crate. I touched one of the chicken-wire cylinders. "All the compost generated from the kitchen goes in here, along with brown compost like paper bags and leaves. We'll plant the vegetables in the soil around it. As the compost breaks down, it'll feed the soil of the garden." I stood back, arms folded, and admired my handiwork. "They'll be our own little organic gardens."

"What else do you have to do?" she asked, her voice quiet. She had the faintest accent. Welsh, I thought. Or Irish or Scottish.

"We have to collect newspaper and cardboard first. Anything compostable. We layer all that in the bottom. After that, we put in leaves and twigs. Grass clippings. Things like that."

My gaze scanned the yard. Piles of leaves left from the fall were heaped against the fence. It was clear that keeping the yard manicured wasn't a priority. Not surprising, since I imagined that, like having a garden, it would come down to volunteers. I couldn't see Vivian Cantrell hiring a random lawn service to come onto the property, not when her priority was keeping the women here safe and protected.

"There's a rake and wheelbarrow," the woman said. "I can get it if you like." Her accent came out a bit more the more she spoke.

I tempered my reaction, not wanting to come

across as overly thrilled that she'd sort of agreed to help me. "That would be great, thanks."

She tucked the keys she'd been holding into her front pocket. I caught a glimpse of a scar that ran from the top of her hand, up her arm, and disappeared under the sleeve of her shirt. God, what these women had been through.

She disappeared behind the shed, returning a few seconds later pushing a rickety and rusted wheelbarrow. She stopped in front of the shed, stepped inside, and came out again with a floppy-tined rake.

Without a word, she set to work. It didn't take long for her to fill up the wheelbarrow with the natural mulch in the yard. She brought it over next to the garden boxes. "Cardboard and paper?" she asked.

"Right." I wasn't sure how much we'd find inside the house. It seemed unlikely that any newspaper was delivered to Crosby House, and any empty boxes had probably been thrown away already. With any luck, we'd be able to gather enough to get the layering started, though. "Do you have any?"

"One of the girls, Mickey, is obsessed with the *Santa Sofia Daily*," she said, "and she never throws anythin' away."

That sounded promising on two levels. Another person to meet and potentially talk with, and a newspaper hoarder.

She nodded. "This is her second time being here," she said. "Her guy cried and apologized and swore up and down that he'd changed. Mickey believed him and went back, but . . ."

DOUGH OR DIE 163

She trailed off, so I finished for her. "But he hadn't changed." It wasn't lost on me that she'd referred to Mickey's abuser as *her guy*. It almost felt like ownership of the abuser, which translated to fault.

"Beat her worse than I've ever seen anyone beaten. The way I see it, she's lucky she survived."

If that was what another abused woman thought, I believed her. "Will she let us have some of the newspapers?"

She shrugged.

I held out my hand to her. "I'm Ivy, by the way. Ivy Culpepper."

She looked at my outstretched arm, hesitating. I didn't think she was going to shake, but then she did. Her grip was loose and her hand smaller than mine. For a second, I thought I might shatter the bones if I squeezed too hard, but then I realized that, of course, I wouldn't. This woman, who looked to be about my age, had gone through something difficult and challenging, but she was still here. She'd gotten herself out of whatever situation she'd been in. She was a fighter. If whoever had abused her hadn't broken her, I certainly couldn't.

She looked back at the house as if she sensed we were being watched. Angie and Vivian Cantrell stood at the window. The woman waved to them. They waved back before turning their backs to us and going off in different directions.

"I'm Meg McGinnis," she said, looking at me again.

"That's a pretty name," I said. The slight lilt of

her accent made more sense. She was an Irish girl.

"Okay," she said. "Come on then." She dropped her arm, turned on her sneakered heels, and went back into the house. I followed, brushing my hands on my jeans and stomping my feet before stepping inside. Meg didn't stop to see if I had followed her. She walked straight through the living area, not acknowledging any of the women or kids there, turned right at a hallway, and followed it to what I assumed were the living quarters for the women and children.

She stopped at a door on the right and gently rapped her knuckles against it. Someone called from inside, and Meg opened the door, sticking her head in. She spoke too quietly for me to hear, but a second later, she opened the door all the way and stepped inside, ushering me in behind her. "Mickey, this is Ivy. She's making vegetable gardens for Crosby House," Meg said.

Mickey lay facedown on her bed, propped up on her elbows, a magazine opened in front of her. Her legs were bent at the knees, her feet crossed at the ankles. Her red hair, which was a solid three or four shades more vibrant than mine, was piled up on her head in a haphazard topknot. She looked up and I started, registering the yellowed remnants of a bruise under her right eye. My gaze skimmed over her and I saw more bruises on her arms and legs. One finger on her left hand looked permanently crooked, and her wrist was wrapped. In that moment, I realized that knowing Crosby House was a haven for abused women was vastly different from seeing the evidence staring me in the face. The very existence of this place meant women like Meg and Mickey had a place where they could feel safe.

"You need some of my newspapers for a garden?" Mickey asked. Her voice was monotone. Even though she'd asked a question, I didn't get the feeling she cared all that much about the answer.

"We're making keyhole gardens," I said.

Meg smiled at being part of the *we*. "That means a compost system is built right into the garden. We have to layer green materials, like leaves and grass, with cardboard and newspaper, then the stuff we compost from the kitchen will go on top of all that."

Mickey dampened her index finger with her tongue before absently turning the page of her magazine. "So I won't get them back."

She said it as a statement, not a question. "No, they'll become part of the garden."

She didn't move for a few seconds. I began to wonder if her parting with any of her copies of the *Santa Sofia Daily* was too much to ask. Just as I was about to move on to plan B, she rolled over, swung her legs off the bed, and bent over, taking ahold of something underneath her bed. She sat up with a stack of folded newspapers in her hand, *Santa Sofia Daily* emblazoned across the top paper on the stack. She held them out to Meg. "Take 'em. I don't even want 'em anymore."

Meg gave Mickey an encouraging smile as she took them. "Good for you. He's not worth it."

The *who* she was referring to had to be the guy Mickey'd been in a relationship with . . . the same one who'd given her those bruises. But what did he have to do with the *Santa Sofia Daily*?

Meg seemed to anticipate my unasked question. "Mickey's ex works for the paper," she said once we were clear of the hallway. She kept her voice low as she continued. "She's always rereading his articles like there's going to be some coded apology in them or something." She shook her head. "It's sad, really, how she can't quit the guy."

"Do you think she'll go back to him?" I asked, stunned.

Meg nodded solemnly. "Probably. It's a struggle most of us deal with."

"With going back to . . . whoever you're all running from?"

"Yeah, definitely. It's twisted as all—. It's messed up, but it is what it is. If I could turn back the clock and do things differently, maybe I'd still have . . . the things I lost."

Her voice trembled with emotion and I didn't want to push her beyond her comfort zone or make her shut down. Maybe in time she'd come to trust me and open up more. If I could help her, I would, but it had to be on her terms, not on mine.

There was nothing more to say at the moment about Mickey and what her future held. Meg led me into the kitchen. Crosby House did not have any sort of open concept floor plan. The kitchen was completely separate from the living space in the center of the house. Cabinets and

counters ran around the perimeter of the room.
A long rectangular table and ten chairs took up
one side of the room while a portable butcher-
block island on casters filled another space,
looking disproportionately small for the space.
The stainless steel sink and appliances were old,
but looked to be in good shape. The kitchen was
spotless. Not a single crumb dotted the counters. No cereal boxes, bags of bread, or dirty
dishes were left out. Looking around, I didn't
hold out much hope for finding a lot of compostable material ready to go, but Meg had a determined look on her face. She marched right
over to the garbage can and stepped on the foot
pedal. The lid sprang open, banging against the
wall behind it. She stared into it, plunged her
hand into the cavernous space, then pulled it
out again, clutching a handful of trash.

"I . . . um . . . is there a bag I can get for you?"
I asked, stunned by Meg's determination. When
she decided to help, she went for it 100 percent.

She notched her head toward a door that I
took to be the pantry. "In there on the right."

I fetched a plastic grocery bag from a wad in
the corner of the pantry, holding it out to her as
she dropped in fistfuls of banana and orange
peels, damp paper towels, the remains of a head
of lettuce, and discarded eggshells. I stifled a grimace as she dug further into the garbage. Who
knew what else was in there? Nothing I'd want to
be rummaging through, that was for sure.

Meg kept digging, so I set down the first bag
and grabbed another, holding it open for her
until it, too, was filled. We headed back out to

the makeshift keyhole gardens, each of us holding a bag of the kitchen scraps. We tore up the *Santa Sofia Daily* newspapers, adding the pieces to the chicken-wire containers, then divvied up the produce and paper scraps between the three garden compost cylinders. "We'll need to add soil to the boxes to get them ready for planting," I said, wishing I'd thought to ask Miguel to bring some bags when he'd brought the crates. I took my phone from my back pocket and pressed the HOME button to power it on to find the nearest garden center, but clicked on a text from Miguel instead. Soil delivered. ✓

I looked around the yard, wondering what in the world he meant. I texted him back. What?

Three flashing dots appeared on the screen. A message gray box showed up a few seconds later. Threw it over the gate.

I laughed. Miguel Baptista, you sly fox, I thought. He'd assumed I'd need soil and had taken it upon himself to make sure I had everything necessary to finish the garden boxes. You didn't!

The dots flashed again, then his response came. Anything for you, Ivy.

I sent back a heart emoji before putting my phone back in my pocket and heading to the gate with the wheelbarrow. I'd expected a few bags of soil, but the pile was thigh high. Miguel had filled up the bed of his truck and one by one, he'd tossed them over the gate. It took three trips with the wheelbarrow to haul them over to the keyhole gardens. With Meg's help, we filled each crate, using every last crumb of the soil. All the while, I tried to figure out an organic way to bring up Ben Nader. So far, there wasn't one.

"Last thing to do is plant them," I said, pointing to the seedlings in their thin black plastic containers.

Meg arranged them by kind, with all the tomatoes in one box, the zucchini and yellow squash in another, and the peppers and eggplants together in the third. "If these do well, we can add more boxes," she said, smiling for the first time since I'd met her. There was something powerful and rewarding about growing your own food and I could see that she felt the same sense of accomplishment that I did. "We depend on volunteers like you. Thank you."

And suddenly, there it was. An opening. "Are there very many others who help out here?"

"There are a few steady ones, but most come and go."

"Yesterday, when we were watching the news, it seemed you all knew of the guy who was hit by the car the other day."

She stood up straighter, as if she had a depleted battery inside her that had suddenly been recharged. "He's one of the good ones."

I wanted to pump my arm in victory. "So you know him?"

"If you tell me what to do for the gardens when you're not here, I'll take care of them." It was an abrupt shift back to our original subject.

"That's great. Just pull any weeds, make sure the compost goes in, and water."

We bent to gather up the discarded bags of

soil, taking them to the garbage can. "What do some of the other volunteers do?" I asked, circling back around to my snooping.

She shrugged. "Sometimes people bring groceries, or they clean the windows. One guy did a lot of painting recently. There's a woman who likes to knit. She's made a few blankets and baby hats. Things like that. Oh, and there's a woman who does a story time for the kids. All different stuff, I guess."

We gathered up the crushed black containers that had held the vegetable seedlings and dumped them in the garbage cans. As we worked, I wondered what type of tasks Ben Nader would have taken on. "Did Ben do the painting?"

She met my gaze, her eyes flat and sad. "Yes."

"He seems like a good guy," I said, keeping the brakes pumped on my questioning. I had to take it slowly.

"Yeah, it's pretty shocking when someone you know was fine one second, then gone the next." Her eyes turned glassy. In this place, emotions were raw and on the surface.

"Did you see him recently?"

She looked to the sky, her lips moving slightly as she thought. "He came every week, so yeah."

Strands of my hair had slipped from the hairband I'd used to hold my ponytail. I pulled it off, gathered up all the loose strands of hair, and wound it up again, this time into a topknot. "How much longer do you think you'll stay here?" I asked.

She stared off over my shoulder for a long

moment before answering. "I don't know. Till everything's right again, I guess."

I supposed one person's "right" was different from another's. "You'll get there," I said. "It just takes time."

We worked in silence as we finished cleaning up. Finally, I broached another question. "Meg, why did Ben Nader volunteer here?"

She looked at me, her eyes narrowing. "Do you know him or something?"

"A little bit," I said. I couldn't very well tell her that the sheriff had asked me to keep my eyes and ears open about a potential attempted murder that had happened right outside of the local bread shop. "I worked with him briefly."

"But he's a cameraman," she said, trying to make the connection.

"I work at Yeast of Eden. The accident happened right outside."

Her eyes opened wide. "And that's where the other woman was found, right?"

"That's right."

"Is that why you're here? Because of Ben?"

I debated how directly to answer her question. "It's how I found out about Crosby House and once I learned about it, I really wanted to volunteer like he did."

"You mean like he *does*," she corrected.

"Right. I hope he'll recover and be back here soon."

"Do you know anything more about what happened to him?" she asked.

I swallowed, a sudden bundle of nerves climb-

ing my throat. If Ben's accident was connected
to Sandra Mays like I thought it must be, then by
digging around I was potentially exposing myself to a killer. Meg would surely tell others
about our conversation. If there was a connection between Ben's accident and Crosby House,
I was drawing a pretty direct line between the
two.

I hesitated before answering her question, finally saying, "The authorities aren't quite sure.
They're investigating."

"The news hasn't said much. What does that
mean?"

Even as I exposed myself as being somewhat
in the know, I decided to be evasive. "It happened outside Yeast of Eden, the bread shop
over on Cambria Street. He was part of the crew
doing a piece on the bread shop's Bread for Life
program—"

"Right."

"We were taking a break and he was crossing
the street. The car came out of nowhere, but it
was like it was gunning for him."

The color drained from her face and she muttered to herself inaudibly. I put my hand on her
shoulder. "Are you okay?" I asked.

"Esmé," she murmured. "Does Esmé know?"

I was sure the surprise I felt clearly registered
on my face. "Do you mean Esmé Adriá? Is she . . .
does she *stay* here?" I asked. After all, how many
Esmés could there be?

Meg drew back, but nodded. Her brows
pinched together with suspicion. "Do you know
her?"

"I know Esmé Adriá," I answered. "She's part of the Bread for Life program at Yeast of Eden." I couldn't wait to tell my posse—which consisted of Olaya, Mrs. Branford, Miguel, and Emmaline—that I'd established a link between Ben Nader and someone I knew. I was experiencing the equivalent of a runner's high. They'd known each other through Crosby House. Why hadn't either one said anything?

My thoughts immediately went to the moment of the accident. Esmé had said she'd gone down to the beach during the break we'd taken, the same break during which Ben Nader was mowed down. Could she have lied about where she'd gone? Could she have been behind the wheel of the car instead?

But why?

"Is she here?" I asked.

This time Meg shook her head. "I haven't seen her today."

My brows pinched together. I couldn't help the immediate suspicion surfacing in my mind. "When did you see her last?"

At this question, Meg paused. "Day before yesterday, maybe?" She thought for a second then gave a single nod. "Yeah, yeah, it was after dinner. Her room is across from mine. I passed her in the hall when she came in. She went straight to her room. I guess . . . no, I haven't seen her since."

Suspicion mounted. Could Esmé have skipped town after attempting to murder Ben? I followed that thought by playing devil's advocate. Did Esmé know Sandra Mays, too? If she was con-

nected to Ben's accident, could she also be involved in Sandra's death? "What time was that,
do you remember?"

She looked to the ceiling as she thought.
"Around six fifteen, I think. Maybe six twenty."

That was well after Ben Nader had been hit.
Where had Esmé gone after the accident? I had
such a bad feeling about this. The hairs on the
back of my neck stood on end. I'd programmed
the phone numbers for the women in the Bread
for Life program into my cell. I took out my
phone now, looked up Esmé's contact, and dialed. It rang four times before her accented
voice said, *"This is Esmé Adriá. Leave a message to
me and I will call you back."*

"Esmé, this is Ivy. Culpepper. From Yeast of
Eden? Would you give me a call when you get
this? Thanks." I turned back to Meg. "You're
sure you haven't seen her since night before
last?"

"Positive." Her brow furrowed. "I hope she's
okay."

Me too. "Could she have been here, but you
just didn't see her?"

She didn't even hesitate a second before saying, "No. I haven't gone anywhere, and yesterday I spent the whole day in the game room."

"The game room—"

She pointed in the general direction of the
main living area where the TV was and the
women and kids gathered. Anyone hanging out
in that room would have a clear view of the front
door, which was the main entrance to the house.
If Meg had been there all day, she definitely

would have seen Esmé come or go. But, she had to have gone to the kitchen to eat, or used the restroom. I doubted all day actually meant *all day*.

"What about after you went to bed? Could she have come in or left then?" I asked.

But Meg shook her head. "I watched a movie last night till after hours. If any one of us goes out, we have to be back here by seven o'clock."

"Do you think I could see her room?"

I hadn't expected Meg to jump at the request, but she hesitated a bit longer than I'd hoped. "We should ask Mrs. Cantrell about that, I think. Right?"

I wasn't opposed to breaking the rules every now and then, now being one of the optimal times when I'd gladly jump over the line. There were two reasons I'd hoped not to bring Vivian Cantrell into it at all. One, I didn't want to jeopardize my volunteer status by making her question my motives, and two, I didn't want to give her the option of saying that, no, we could *not* have a look in Esmé's room. But now that Meg had brought it up, we probably had to. "Good idea," I said.

I followed her inside. She walked right through the game room and turned left at the hallway, going straight to the Crosby House director's office. The door was closed. Meg knocked and waited. There was no answer.

A scratchy female voice came from behind us. "Mrs. Cantrell is off at a meeting."

We turned as the woman approached us. She was similar in height to Meg, but where Meg was petite and pixie-like, this woman was round like a McIntosh apple. "Thanks, Maxine," Meg said.

Meg and I moved out of the way to let Maxine pass us by. Maxine lingered, as if she wanted to see what we were going to do next, but I bided my time and waited until we were alone again before turning to Meg. "Can I just take a peek?"

She frowned and kicked her foot under her like a petulant child. I thought for sure she was going to say no, but then she sighed and gestured for me to follow her. We headed back the way we'd come, once again passing through the living area into the bedroom hallway. Meg stopped at the room just past Mickey's. She knocked softly, glancing around to make sure no one, like Maxine, was lurking. I didn't know what the rules actually were, but I felt pretty sure that going into someone else's room without their knowledge wasn't allowed. Meg was being bold, bless her heart.

There was no answer from inside the room and the coast was clear. Meg slowly turned the knob and gently pushed the door in. She poked her head inside, making sure Esmé wasn't sleeping or simply ignoring us. "Esmé?" she called, her voice soft.

She glanced back at me before stepping in and holding the door open for me to follow, but she stopped short. I bumped into her, and she lurched a step farther into the room.

I hadn't been nervous about looking in Esmé's room when I'd suggested it, but Meg's tentative actions had made my heartbeat skitter and I was having second thoughts. Was the knowledge that she and Ben Nader were connected through Crosby House enough of a reason to look for a deeper connection?

I debated with myself. We could turn around right now and leave the room before we'd invaded Esmé's privacy any more. Or we could take a look and see if anything in the room raised any suspicions, because, after all, a man was in a coma—and Sandra Mays was dead.

The fact that Esmé may have known Ben Nader was enough for me to push aside the anxiety I had at being in her room without her knowledge. I reminded myself that Emmaline had asked me to keep my eyes and ears open.

Several boxes sat on the bed. The bedside lamp was on and one of the dresser drawers was open. The window overlooked a long-limbed tree and the keyhole gardens we'd been working on. "Oh wow," she said.

"What?"

Meg turned herself in a circle, looking around, her expression strained. "Esmé didn't want to have a window to the backyard. She says the shadow of that tree freaks her out. I told her I'd switch with her. I didn't realize they'd be moving my stuff for me."

"So this was Esmé's room, but now it's yours?"

She peeked in the closet, then looked through the dresser drawers before nodding.

"So her stuff is in your old room? Can we go see it?"

"It's across the hall," she said. I followed her out and we repeated the same cautious entry process into the room across the hall. Once we were inside, she quickly closed the door behind us. "What are we looking for?" she whispered.

If only it were that easy. "I don't know. Anything to show us where she might be, I guess. I'm worried about her." It was a true statement. I was very worried—especially if she was on the run.

The room was stripped of personality, much like Mickey's room had been. Just like Meg's new room, a few boxes sat on the bed. The bed was made and everything seemed to be in order for the most part. Probably all the rooms were on the barren side, I thought. The battered women being helped here had most likely escaped their dire situations without the opportunity to bring decorative items along with them. I imagined most had suitcases or duffel bags filled with clothes and toiletries, maybe a few personal items and mementos, and that's about it. It seemed to me that a little artwork on the walls could go a long way to bringing some positive mojo into the rooms. "Are all the rooms the same?" I asked.

"Everything's donated, but they all have pretty much the same things. A bed, a dresser, a nightstand." She looked around, frowning. "Same room, different person," she said softly.

"What do you mean?"

"Mickey was in this room when I first got here. They moved her and they put me in here. Now it's Esmé's. It's strange. So many of us here don't have many personal belongings. Same room, different person. You can hardly tell them apart."

It was true. I'd now seen three rooms and they

were each as depressing as the last. Esmé's twin bed was covered with a simple light gray bedspread—donated by someone, I felt sure. A dresser sat against the back wall under a window. The accordion closet doors were open, revealing a few dresses, pants, and tops hanging on the closet rod. Two pairs of shoes—sneakers and black flats—sat on the floor of the closet. "Esmé's stuff?" I asked.

Meg glanced in the closet and at the nightstand where several books sat. "Yes."

I started at the closet, pushing the clothes aside. A single box sat in the back corner of the closet, taped up, the letters KM written on the side. Her boyfriend? Husband? The person she was here hiding from?

I turned and strode to the bed. The two boxes stacked there were open, the flaps directed outward. I could see inside them without touching anything, which was some comfort. It made the invasion a little less . . . invasive. The boxes held clothes. Bras, T-shirts, shorts, a pair of pajamas. No great clue, I thought.

I quickly pulled open a dresser drawer.

Meg took a step toward me, arm outstretched. "You shouldn't—"

She was right. I shouldn't. But I kept going, quickly looking through each drawer.

Her anxious gaze darted to the door every few seconds, but the coast remained clear.

Esmé didn't have much more in her dresser drawers. Some underwear. A few more T-shirts. A belt and several fashion scarves, as well as a pale pink cardigan. The bottom drawer held a single picture book, a sketchbook, and a pale green knitted blanket. I moved the blanket aside and took out the sketchbook, taking a moment to flip through the pages. There were still-lifes of fruit and vegetables artfully displayed on a platter, individual pieces of fruit drawn to perfection, just the stem and a single leaf sketched out. The same male face was drawn over and over again—sometimes just the lips, sometimes the eyes, and even just an ear or the curve of a nose. There were other collections of people—a child's face, a father and child, and the back of a head. The art transitioned to a series of trees, with studies on leaves and flowers. If Esmé was the artist, she was incredibly talented. To know every last detail of someone or something? It was astounding. The attention to detail and in-depth study of each subject portrayed in the pages of the sketchbook had taken skill and time and determination and practice.

I put the blanket back the way it had been. It was soft and delicate, like the blanket for a newborn. "Does Esmé have a child?" I asked.

Meg stood with her back to the closed door. "I don't know. I don't think so. Come on, we need to leave. This isn't right."

But I couldn't leave quite yet. Two books lay open on the little nightstand next to a small table lamp. The first, *Tuesdays with Morrie*, was creased along the spine. I'd read Mitch Albom's book in high school and knew it was a comfort for a lot of people. It was rife with life lessons and bits of wisdom. For someone going through a trauma, like the women at Crosby House, I could see why it might resonate. The cover was frayed and worn. This was a well-loved book.

I used one finger to peek at the book underneath. *Looking for Alaska.* I knew a few of the novelist's other books. I'd never read this one, though. I didn't know what Esmé's story was, but if it were me and I'd come out of an abusive relationship, I'd have gone for something uplifting rather than a John Green tearjerker. To each her own, I thought.

On the floor, just out of sight under the bed, was a journal lying open and faceup. I picked it up and glanced at the open page.

> It's eating me alive. I can't keep quiet anymore. I'm going to talk to them. They can't do this to me. To us. They cannot keep him from me.

Meg gasped when she saw me. "You can't read that! It's personal." She strode across the room and snatched it away from me. She closed it and put it on top of the other books on the nightstand. "She's going to know. We shouldn't be here."

I gave a backward glance at the journal, a thread of guilt weaving through me. Meg was right, I had no right to be invading Esmé's privacy like this, but I couldn't help but wonder who she had been talking about in her journal. I quickly looked back at the labeled box in the closet. Poor Esmé.

"Come on," Meg prodded.

My guilt multiplied. I had no valid reason to

suspect that she had anything to do with Ben Nader, and other than the reality TV show, nothing at all to link her to Sandra Mays. I was grasping at straws. Esmé had her own troubles without me adding to them by suspecting her of being involved in something unsavory. More than anything, I just wanted to find her and make sure she was okay.

Meg and I left the room just as we'd found it. We exchanged cell phone numbers before I thanked her for her help with the garden and told her I'd be back in a few days to check on it. "Make sure you water tomorrow, and compost!" I called. She stood at the door and waved at me. No smile. She was still freaked about sneaking into Esmé's room, and I didn't blame her. I hadn't only had her help me with the garden. I'd led her down the garden path and the guilt was already turning black inside her.

I felt the same way.

Chapter 18

I went straight from Crosby House to Yeast of Eden. Olaya had said she didn't need help, but I wanted to check on her all the same. Felix, his friend Kimi, and Olaya, along with her regular morning crew, had managed all the baking for the day, and had prepped the long-rise dough for tomorrow. The kitchen was spotless and the day's bread was nearly sold out.

I needed to feel productive, and distract myself from the guilt I felt from snooping in Esmé's room, so I worked in the front of the store, cleaning the display cases and tidying the local Yeast of Eden merchandise and other bread-making supplies and knickknacks Olaya sold. The bread shop's phone rang, jingling from its place on the wall behind the cash register. When someone called Yeast of Eden, you were never sure what to expect. Some of the most common questions were What time do you open? What time do you close? and Do you have sourdough bread? The answers to those questions were: seven a.m., whenever we run out of bread for the day, and yes.

We also got an array of more specific questions, too. Do you have gluten-free bread? Answer: We're in development now and will have it soon. Question: What kinds of grains are in the multi-grain loaf? Answer: Wheat, millet, flax, oats, sunflower seeds, amaranth, barley, rye. Question: What type of olives are in the olive loaf? Answer: Juicy kalamata and oil-cured olives. Question: How many skull cookies are hidden right now? The answer to that is always: I have no idea.

I reached for the ringing phone and answered with a cheery, "Yeast of Eden, how may I help you?"

Emmaline's sheriff voice came back at me, short and clipped. "Heads up. Tammy Nader is on her way to the bread shop."

"The wife?"

"She's upset. She wants to know how it happened."

Of course she's upset, I thought. Her husband was hit by a car. But none of us at the bread shop had any extra information that she didn't already know from the incident report and police. "What does she think we can tell her?"

Em sighed. Heavily. "I wish I knew, Ivy. She's a little unhinged, to be honest. What she wants is for you to suddenly remember some elusive detail that will reveal who did this to her husband.

The reality is that you're going to have to suffer through a conversation with her, trying to get her to understand that you don't know anything."

I cupped my hand to my forehead and dipped my head. I'd seen plenty of people grieving, and I'd had up-close-and-personal experiences with my own, so I knew what Tammy Nader was feeling. With luck, her husband would come out of his coma and be okay. That fact, however, didn't alleviate the pain and helplessness Tammy Nader was feeling right now.

It was only after I hung up that I realized I hadn't mentioned my discovery that Esmé and Ben Nader knew each other through Crosby House. I'd tell her at the family dinner tonight at my dad's.

Ten minutes later the bell on the front entrance to Yeast of Eden dinged. The woman who entered looked to be in her mid-fifties, with slightly saggy jowls and eyebrows that had faded and thinned with age. Her face was drawn, her eyes red-rimmed. From the looks of it, she was barely keeping it together. She didn't even so much as glance at the display cases, which were empty anyway, but which reinforced the idea that she was not here to buy a loaf of bread.

"Can I help you?" I asked, although there was no doubt in my mind about who she was.

"I hope so," she said, her voice stronger than I thought it would be given the way she wrung her hands and clutched a wad of tissue. "I'm Tammy Nader. Ben's wife?"

I gave her a sympathetic smile. "I'm so sorry

about what happened." I gestured to one of the bistro tables. "Would you like to sit? Can I get you some tea or coffee?"

Her eyes glazed as she looked around the empty bread shop. For a second, I thought she was going to refuse the offer to sit, but then her feet shuffled forward and she lowered herself into a chair. "Some water would be good."

I left her to fetch a glass of water from the kitchen, returning with it a minute later. "The sheriff called and said you might be stopping by," I said as I sat down in a chair opposite her. "I was here when you called and spoke to Sandra Mays the other day."

She looked at me like I had horns growing from my head. "You were?"

I nodded. "It's such a tragedy, her death. And on the heels of Ben's accident—"

"Sandy and I went way back," she said.

"I had no idea," I said, not that I would have, but I wasn't sure what else to say. "I'm so sorry for your loss."

She gave an irreverent shrug. "We weren't close anymore."

"Oh . . ."

I left the word hanging there. I'd learned that silence often compelled people to fill it. She didn't disappoint. "We had a falling out years back. Ben always thought he could still trust her, but she changed." She sighed. "As people do," she added.

Had Sandra betrayed Tammy's trust in some way, I wondered, or was the implication that she could no longer be trusted more of a general observation? The thing that screamed out at me was: Motive! "Celebrity can do that," I said.

"Hmm."

It sounded to me like she thought it was something other than Sandra's celebrity that made her untrustworthy. "Do you have any ideas about what happened to Sandra? Who she fought with?"

"I didn't know her anymore."

"What happened between you two?" I asked, hoping she wouldn't think I was prying too much.

She shrugged. In a different situation, it would have been nonchalant, but given everything else, Tammy's shrug was tortured. "You know how it can be. I confided in her, and she betrayed that confidence."

"Did you know her separately from Ben?" I asked, curious about their relationship. Sandra and Ben hadn't seemed close, but Sandra had become unglued when she'd seen him laid out on the road. Was that reaction simply based on their working history together, or something more? Could the betrayal Tammy mentioned have to do with a romantic entanglement between her husband and Sandra? But no, she'd said she'd confided something to Sandra, so that couldn't be it.

She stared out the window, her eyes glazing over like she'd gone into a trance. Then she started talking. "Our kids were the same age. We met through a mom's group. Ben already worked at the station. When Sandy got the job, she got a nanny and dropped out of playgroup. She became a career woman, whereas I was just a mom. Just a mom, as if that's not the hardest job on the planet."

Tammy looked to the ceiling as if she had the superpower of seeing right through to the rooftop above. "I heard she was on the roof here . . . where Ben used to go as a kid."

So she knew about her husband's childhood secret. "Did Sandra know about the rooftop access?" I asked, hoping my voice didn't pull her out of her narrative.

Tammy gazed right, then left as she thought. "I don't know. Ben took our son up there once or twice when he was little. It was a big thrill for Grant. Maybe Sandy was around at that point? I really can't remember. She must have known about it, though, if she was up there."

"Right," I agreed, unless someone else had arranged the meeting up there. But who else knew about it?

"How's your husband doing?" I asked. "Any change?"

She wrapped her hands around the water glass, gripping, releasing, gripping, releasing. She was trying to control her distress. My heart went out to her. It took her another minute to gather her thoughts before she finally spoke. "The swelling on the brain is going down. The doctors are watching him closely. They are"—she paused— "cautiously optimistic."

I nodded encouragingly, knowing there was nothing I could say to make things right for her. It was going to take time, and all we could do was hope for the best.

"I just . . . I don't understand who would want to hurt Ben like this." As she continued, her voice grew shrill. "He doesn't have any enemies. He keeps to himself. He's just an ordinary man. My ordinary man." She looked up at me. Met my eyes. "We just had our anniversary. Twenty-seven years together. That's a long time. You get to know a person in twenty-seven years. I know Ben. He doesn't have secrets from me. He didn't have enemies. I was on the phone with him, and then suddenly . . ." She broke down as she said, "Suddenly I wasn't." She pressed her hands to the sides of her head as if she was hearing the sound of the impact replaying in her mind and wanted desperately for it to stop. Finally, she looked up at me again. "Wh-who c-could have done this to him?"

"Mrs. Nader, I wish I had some answers for you, but the car, it just came out of nowhere. It didn't slow down. He didn't see it coming."

"The doctors say he didn't feel any pain, but I don't know if that can be true. Can it? Can you get hit by a car and not feel pain? Did you see it? Do you think it's true, that he didn't feel anything?"

My own mother had died from a hit-and-run, and I often wondered the same thing. Ben, when and if he recovered, would be the only person who could answer that question for her. "Like I said, the car came out of nowhere and it hit him hard. I think the sheriff is probably right. Once his head hit the ground . . ." I trailed off.

"Nobody saw it coming? Nobody screamed for him to get out of the way?"

"It came out of nowhere," I said again.

A pained sob escaped her lips. I put my hand on her shoulder to comfort her. It was all I could do. After a minute, I spoke again. "Mrs. Nader, do you have anyone to help you?"

She turned the glass in her hands, focusing intently on it as the water churned from the movement. "Our son is gone. He died in a . . . in a car crash," she said, barely holding in her emotions. What a horrible coincidence, I thought, and prayed, for her sake, that her husband would survive his ordeal. "Kevin—" She stopped. Collected herself. "That's our grandson. He's staying with a friend. My parents live in the Northeast. Ben's parents are gone."

"And your daughter-in-law?"

She balked. "Margaret? No. She was in the accident."

Poor Kevin. "Can I call someone? A friend?" I knew that without Emmaline, my brother Billy, and my father, I wouldn't have made it through the grief of losing my mother. People need other people. It was a simple truth. We grieve alone, but we process through the events of our lives with the people we are closest to. We are stronger because of our villages. Our communities. Without them, we wither. I firmly believed that, and I hoped Tammy Nader had a village of her own on which she could rely while her husband fought for his life.

She stood and moved to the window overlooking the street. It was exactly where I'd been standing when Ben Nader had been hit. "That's where it happened," she said, pointing. It wasn't a question, but a statement of fact. A cross and collection of flowers had appeared on the side of the road. Prayers for his speedy recovery.

"He's going to be okay," I said, coming to stand next to her. I only hoped I was right.

She looked at me with her watery eyes. "He has to be. I don't know what I'd do without him. He lights up a room." At this, her tears spilled over her eyes, streaming over her cheeks. "He has to be all right."

I placed my hand on her shoulder in what I hoped was a gesture of comfort. Of camaraderie. "If I can do anything to help, please let me know," I said.

She suddenly looked up at me, her eyes wide and full of . . . terror? Or was it shock? "You don't think . . ."

"What?" I asked, prodding her.

"Could the same person that ran Ben over have killed Sandra?"

It was my working theory, but I played innocent. "Why would you think that?"

"They happened, one after the other. They worked at the same place. It makes sense, doesn't it? Except . . ."

"Except what?" I prodded.

"I can see plenty of people wanting to hurt Sandra. She was a piece of work. But not Ben."

"You can't think of a connection?" I asked.

"No. But like you said, anything's possible."

"Ivy," a woman's voice said. "You should go home now." Olaya came through the swinging door, stopping short when she saw the two of us standing side by side. "*Lo siento.* I apologize. I did not mean to interrupt."

"It's okay. I'm just walking Mrs. Nader out."

Olaya rushed forward, her multicolored caftan swinging behind her, her arms wide. Before Tammy Nader knew what was happening, Olaya had her wrapped up in a hug. She held her tight, and after a moment Mrs. Nader succumbed to the embrace. From where I stood, I could see her glassy eyes and quivering lower lip. She was barely hanging on.

"Your husband, he is a very nice man," Olaya said. "He made all of us here feel very comfortable in front of the camera. He did not deserve what has happened to him."

As Mrs. Nader pulled free, Olaya said, "If you give me your phone number, I'd like to check on you."

Mrs. Nader nodded. Olaya looked at me and I understood. She didn't carry her cell phone around with her, but I did. I took mine out and opened the Notes app. Mrs. Nader rattled off her number and I typed it in. I'd write it down for Olaya later.

Mrs. Nader offered her a sad smile before heading to the door. "Thank you for saying that. You've both been very kind. Thank you."

Olaya joined me at the door and together we watched Tammy Nader walk slowly toward the curb, staring at the street where her husband had been hit. She turned to look at us, as if she'd felt our eyes on her back. She lifted her arm in a brief acknowledgment before gathering herself together and continuing on down the street, her hand and the wad of tissue I knew was clutched there pressed to her face.

"Very sad for her," Olaya said, "but she will be all right."

After Mrs. Nader melted into the sea of pedestrians walking down the street, I locked the door and we retreated to the kitchen. Since I'd been back in Santa Sofia—and maybe before, since Luke had been unfaithful to me—I'd developed a suspicious mind and tended to question things that I used to take at face value. The question that came to mind at the moment was all about Tammy Nader. What had she really hoped to learn by coming to the bread shop? None of us had any more information than the sheriff did, and Emmaline had given the woman everything she could. Was it part of her coping process, that she needed to hear firsthand from someone who'd witnessed what had happened? Did she question the sheriff department's ability to do their job and get to the bottom of what happened? She hadn't said so. Maybe on some level, she wanted to take matters into her own hands.

It bothered me. What had she been after?

Chapter 19

I spent the rest of the afternoon hunkered down in Olaya's office at Yeast of Eden, working on the blog and website. Even with a user-friendly interface like WordPress, I got stuck and frustrated. By the time four thirty rolled around, I was ready to hurl the computer out the window. I needed a break. And a snack.

I opted for a hunk of sourdough, one of the few loaves left at this late hour. I slathered on a healthy pat of butter, got some grapes from the fridge to go with the bread, and poured myself a glass of iced tea. Miguel and I were going to dinner at my dad's tonight, so I didn't want to overdo it.

Four thirty. I had a solid two hours to kill before I needed to go home to change. I let my thoughts return to Esmé and Crosby House. The next Bread for Life class wasn't for a few days—far too long to wait to see if Esmé turned up.

I'd been thinking a lot about the books she had on her nightstand. They were tied together, but I couldn't quite make out how. I opened a new browser and typed in *Tuesdays with Morrie.* It was a tribute to a dying man and lessons on life that he passed on in his last moments. I searched *Looking for Alaska* next. The blurb didn't give me much information, so I scrolled down to the reviews, zooming in on the idea that the book was about life, death, and moving on.

The bottom drawer of Esmé's dresser. The green knitted blanket. The sketchbook. The box in the closet. The books on Esmé's nightstand both had to do with loss and grieving. The box in the closet had been marked with the initials KM. Had something happened to him or her? Was Esmé mourning a loss?

Anxiety crawled through me like the legs of a spider scurrying over my skin. I had to find her. To make sure she was okay.

Olaya had a spreadsheet file with the names and information of all the people who'd taken her classes. Each class had its own tab. She archived each year's classes on December 31st with the new year's classes ready to go. Olaya Solis had run a successful business not only because of the magical properties she baked into her breads, but because she was an astute and incredibly organized human being.

I already had Esmé's number, but didn't have the others'. It took only a few clicks of the mouse to find the spreadsheet with Claire's, Esmé's, Zula's, and Amelie's information. I dialed Esmé first, hoping she'd answer, but not surprised when it went to voicemail. I left a message, asking her to call me, then used the info sheet to dial Claire.

"Hello?" Her voice was tentative, as if she was baffled that she'd gotten a phone call.

"Claire, it's Ivy Culpepper. From Yeast of Eden?"

It was as if a switch flipped. She became instantly animated. "Ivy! Hi!" Then a pause, followed by, "Oh my gosh, do we have class tonight? Did I blank on it? I can be there—"

"No, no. Not at all. Class Tuesday."

She exhaled with relief. "Oh, good."

"You're fine. I was just wondering if maybe you'd heard from Esmé. She, uh, hasn't been home for a few days. Since we saw her after Ben Nader's accident, actually."

"I haven't seen her." Claire hesitated before she said, "Do you think something's happened to her?"

"I admit, I'm a little bit worried. I didn't realize it, but she knew Ben Nader outside of the bread shop. I'm concerned that she's taking the accident hard."

"She knew Mr. Nader before?"

I didn't want to reveal that Esmé was staying at Crosby House, so I phrased my response carefully. "Apparently they crossed paths when he did some volunteering."

"She never mentioned that."

No, she hadn't. That in itself troubled me. Why had she kept it quiet that she knew Ben Nader in a different context? Was it because the connection was through Crosby House and she

didn't want to open up that can of worms? Or
was it something else entirely? Or again, maybe I
was drawing a connection where there was
none.

"Have you seen or heard from her, by any
chance?"

I sensed her shaking her head. "No, sorry."

"Claire, has Esmé ever talked about a boyfriend . . . or husband? KM?"

"Not to me. Why?"

Why indeed? "I was just wondering. I got the
feeling that maybe he died?"

"Wow. I don't know, Ivy. Poor Esmé. I hope
you find her."

I thanked her, hung up, and made the next
call, this one to Zula. The phone rang three
times before she answered with a vibrant,
"Hallo!"

My own tone changed in response to her natural enthusiasm. "Zula! It's Ivy Culpepper. From
Yeast of Eden."

"Hallo, Ivy! How wonderful that you have
phoned me. What can I do for you?"

I launched into the same spiel I had with
Claire, ending with, "Have you seen or heard
from Esmé?"

"Sadly, no, I have not."

I asked her the same question about a husband or boyfriend, but Zula had the same response Claire had. Esmé had never mentioned
her relationships, and Zula had no idea who KM
was. "Do you think we should be worried?" she
asked me.

That was a good question. In my gut, the answer was a resounding yes, but I didn't have rhyme or reason why I felt that way. "I don't know, Zula. Let me know if you hear from her, okay?"

"I most definitely will do that, Ivy."

I called Amelie next. She answered right away with an out of breath, "Hello?"

"Hi, Amelie. It's Ivy Culpepper, from Yeast of Eden. Do you have time to talk?"

"Yes, sure. Wait one minute, please."

There was a clank followed by a rustling before she came back on the line. "Sorry about that," she said, still breathing heavy. "I just finished a run. A mile for every piece of bread we eat!"

"That's why I do it, too," I said, although I didn't think I was as committed as Amelie.

She sighed happily. "The beach is so lovely. I think I will never leave here."

I understood her sentiment completely. I'd left my hometown after high school. Looking back now, I wondered why it had taken me so long to come back. Santa Sofia was a small town with a lot of charm. The historic district. The Bungalows. Cambria and Main Streets. Beach Road. The pier. Every little corner had character to spare.

I got to the point of my call, asking her if she'd heard from Esmé.

"Yes! I saw her at the beach just now," she said.

I practically fell off my chair. "Really?"

"Really, yes. I like to run on the paved path between Cambria Beach and Rockway. It is two miles there, and two miles back."

I knew that stretch well. The city council had
done an amazing job of creating a beach-to-
beach paved walking path that started at the
northernmost beach and went all the way down
to Rockway, the southernmost beach in town.
Cambria Beach started a little ways south of the
pier where Miguel's restaurant was. We didn't
have a boardwalk with rides, like Santa Cruz, but
we had a lot of artisan shops and a stretch along
the beach where vendors set up to sell their
wares, sketch caricatures, and perform for the
tourists. And we had the beach-to-beach path.
"And Esmé's there right now? Where exactly? I
need to talk to her," I added quickly.

"She was at a table at the Shrimp Shack."

The Shrimp Shack! The Shrimp Shack was a
beloved Santa Sofia institution. The restaurant
was a converted house with seating inside and a
deck that ran along the sides and back, afford-
ing spectacular views of the coastline. Celebrities from all over made it a point to visit, take
pictures with the owners and staff, and sign
menus. Unlike a lot of places, the Jacobs family
didn't hang up those photos in the dining
room. Instead they used the space in the hall-
ways and in the kitchen, making sure that the
people who worked the hardest to make their
restaurant a success could bask in the memories
of the celebrity visits. I liked that about the
Jacobses. They understood the importance of
the people who worked for them, never taking
them for granted.

I logged out of Olaya's computer, grabbed my
purse and what was left of the sourdough bread,

and raced to my car in the back parking lot. "I have to run. Thanks, Amelie!"

"Sure. What's go—" she started, but I hung up and tossed the phone in my purse. Minutes later, I was on Beach Road heading south. Traffic was thick with tourists and locals heading to the beach for Friday evening activities. I crawled along, impatiently tapping my fingers against the steering wheel, starting and stopping, starting and stopping.

Out of nowhere, an SUV heading north in the oncoming lane veered left. I jerked my steering wheel to the right, barely escaping a head-on collision. "Hey!" I yelled, but the driver's head was angled down. She was intent on her cell phone, I realized. I laid on the horn, but by the time I saw her look up in my review mirror, I was already past her.

This, on top of the incident the other night, made too many close calls for comfort. My hands shook as I signaled, slowed, and pulled into the parking lot at the Shrimp Shack. The distracted driver was long gone and probably never fully realized what a close call we'd just had.

I shook away my frustration and calmed my nerves. I had no time to waste and could only hope that Esmé was still here. The board-and-batten white siding of the Shrimp Shack was crisp and fresh. The contrast of the charcoal shutters, window trim, and a thin black trim at the roofline made the place welcoming. It was a restaurant you couldn't wait to get into, knowing the inside would make you feel as happy as the outside did. This, I thought, was the type of restaurant that Guy Fieri would go crazy for and celebrate in his *Diners, Drive-Ins and Dives*. It had always been owned and operated by the Jacobs family. The atmosphere was addictive and the food was spectacular. Fried prawns with a delicate buttermilk batter that literally melted in your mouth. Thick homemade potato chips. Fresh crab salad and coleslaw. Cod fish-sticks in a beer batter. These were the standouts, but everything was delicious. They also served sautéed portobello mushrooms and spinach with browned butter, braised artichokes with garlic aioli, and grilled asparagus that tasted like it had just been picked from the most fertile patch of earth. The homemade tartar sauce had just the right amount of zing to tickle every last taste bud.

My stomach rumbled. God, if I wasn't going to dinner at my dad's, I'd grab a menu and order one of everything. I might be the first person ever to leave the Shrimp Shack still hungry.

I didn't think to ask Amelie where she'd seen Esmé sitting before I'd hung up on her. Had Amelie been heading down to Rockway, or on her way back up to Cambria when she'd spotted Esmé? Either way, it was logical to assume that Esmé had been on one of the porches. I went inside, told the hostess I was meeting someone, and walked right on through to the back. The Shrimp Shack had a primo location. The porch wrapped around the house on the north, south, and west ends, each with a stunning view of the water that rivaled what Baptista's Cantina and Grill offered. Basically you couldn't go wrong with a restaurant near the beach in Santa Sofia.

There was no time for soaking in the beauty of the place, though. I searched the porch, fearing I'd missed Esmé, heaving a relieved sigh when I spotted her. There she was, sitting at a tall café table along the railing on the south side of the building, her elbow on the table, one hand spread across her forehead, her fingers and thumb massaging her temples.

"Esmé!" I exclaimed, coming up to her table and in full theatrical mode. "What a surprise running into you here!"

She jumped out of her skin, staring at me wide-eyed. And, I thought, slightly terrified.

"No one has seen you for a while. I've been so worried," I said, dropping the overenthusiastic tone I'd forced into my voice and sliding into the chair opposite her.

Her eyes instantly teared, as if the mere question itself turned on a faucet. "I am staying with a friend."

"Are you okay?" I asked.

"No. I don't know." She looked up at me. "I do not know what to do."

I rested my arms on the table and leaned in, wanting to take her hand, but not sure if she'd appreciate the gesture or eschew it. "You don't know what to do about what?"

She dropped her hand, folding her arms on

the table in front of her, and raised her gaze to mine. "Maybe it is not that I do not know what to do, but more that I do not know what to think?"

"Do you want to talk about it?" I asked.

She sighed, her breath tremulous from whatever was bothering her. "I can't," she said, her voice scarcely more than a whisper.

Could it be guilt that had her so distraught? "Esmé." She looked at me, watery-eyed. "Are you upset about KM?"

Her jaw dropped and her eyes opened wide. "Wh—" She stopped. "What?"

"I was with Meg at Crosby House. We were looking for you and I . . . I saw a box in your closet with the initials KM. I just—I wondered if he was your husband or—"

She froze. Stammered. "My husband? N-no. I am not . . . w-we were never m-married. *Ay Dios, mi amor, lo siento,*" she murmured.

I summoned my rudimentary Spanish, translating what she'd said. *Oh God, my love, I'm sorry.* What was she sorry for? Hadn't he driven her to Crosby House? "But did he hurt you?"

Her head jerked up and her eyes flashed. "Who?"

"KM?" I repeated.

"You have it wrong, Ivy."

"Then help me understand," I said.

"No, no. Eduardo. He is the one . . . *Pero* KM—no, that's not . . . no . . ."

She trailed off and I read between the lines. Whoever she'd been with after KM—this Eduardo . . . that was the person she had escaped from. That was why she was in Crosby House.

The books on Esmé's nightstand flashed in my mind. Was KM dead? It made sense. I thought about the open journal on her bed, the words fresh as if they had just happened. This time I did reach for her hand. "I'm so sorry."

"Life is not fair, you know." She looked at me, imploring me to understand what she was saying. "I have tried to make a life. I came here to do that. To make a life, but now I cannot. There is too much—" She stopped abruptly. "Everyone has a story. Everyone has heartache."

Never was there a truer statement. "You're right."

She looked at me. "Why are you here?"

"No one has seen you since Tuesday night. I was worried about you."

"I have been staying with a friend. I told Mrs. Cantrell." She paused, then asked, her eyes suddenly guarded, "Ivy, how do you know about Crosby House?"

I went with the partial truth, leaving out that I'd wanted to snoop. "I heard that Ben Nader volunteered there and I wanted to . . . to help. So I volunteered. Meg and I worked on gardens in the backyard. Your name came up and we realized that we both knew you."

She seemed to take me at face value, but didn't ease up. "Why were you in my room?" she asked with a hard edge in her voice.

"To look for you," I answered, my guilt mounting. "I knew I should have waited, but—"

"Meg should have known better. Our spaces are private."

I kicked myself for even mentioning Meg's name. The last thing I wanted was to get her in trouble. "She tried to stop me. I was worried about you—"

"He was in my room there, do you know that?" She paled. "I got back one day after work and he was in my room."

"Who was in your room?"

"Ben Nader."

A memory of the first day of filming at Yeast of Eden came to me. "Esmé, is that why you were upset when you came out of the interview room that first day at the bread shop?"

She nodded.

"Can you tell me why? What happened?"

"I did not expect to see him . . . there. Crosby House, it is a safe haven. Protected. It was . . . was strange to see him somewhere else."

"Why was he in your room?"

"He was painting, but not my room, so I do not know. He played it off like it was a mistake, but it felt wrong."

Every nerve in my body zinged. It sounded like maybe Ben Nader wasn't quite as squeaky-clean as he came across.

"No one should be able to come into my bedroom without my permission," Esmé said.

The statement was directed at me as much as at Ben, and I couldn't blame her. She was right. Crosby House was supposed to be a space for the women and children who were there. We'd both violated that rule.

I held my hands up to stop her. She knew something, but she seemed scared. Of what? Or of who? "Wait—"

She stood abruptly, her chair nearly toppling over from the force of her shoving it back. "I have to go."

She grabbed the key ring from the table and without a backward glance, she disappeared.

Chapter 20

After my encounter with Esmé at the Shrimp Shack, I'd gone home to shower, change, and let Agatha out. I couldn't shake the fear that had clearly coursed through her and her abrupt departure. I needed to give her time. Hopefully she'd come around and be willing to tell me what had her so spooked.

A text from Emmaline came in just as I was leaving for dinner at my dad's. Ben Nader is awake.

Okay! If I couldn't get Esmé to give me anything more, maybe Ben could fill in the gaps. I took Agatha with me in the car, calling Billy along the way. It wasn't hot out, but I didn't like to leave Agatha alone in the car for longer than five minutes or so, and I didn't know how long I'd be inside with Ben. He agreed to meet me so he could take Agatha and I'd be free to visit Ben.

I stopped at a florist to pick up a small arrangement, then hightailed it to the hospital. Mercy Hospital of Santa Sofia was located inland on the north side of town. Billy was already there waiting for me when I arrived. "I'll be at Dad's in a little while," I told him as we transferred the pug from my car to his arms.

Billy took after our father, with gentle waves in his dark hair, his fit stature, and nary a freckle in sight. I was the spitting image of my mother. The topknot was currently my best friend.

Billy was five eleven and with his broad shoulders, Agatha looked a lot smaller than she was as he cradled her. "Why are you going to the hospital?" he asked.

"That hit-and-run that happened outside Yeast of Eden? The man is here at Mercy. I want to check on him."

He cocked a brow at me. "The case Em's working?"

"Well, yeah. One of them." Emmaline was the sheriff, so technically she worked every case.

"Why do you need to see the guy?" he asked, tucking Agatha into the extended cab of his truck.

"Em asked me to keep my eyes and ears open. That's what I'm doing."

"Did she deputize you or something?"

"Or something," I said. "There's not a single lead and, I don't know, there's something off about him and a woman I know from the bread shop. I just want to talk to him."

He didn't ask any more questions and a minute later, he'd driven off with a wave of his hand and I was heading to the information desk inside the hospital. The volunteer directed me to the elevator that would lead me up to the fourth floor. Since I wasn't family, I'd have to ask at the nurse's station about Ben Nader and whether or not I could see him.

Turns out there was not a nurse in sight. I waited for a few minutes before registering what was going on. Someone was in crisis. Nurses and doctors streamed in and out of a room down the hall, each focused on their specific task. Everything else could wait.

Visiting Ben Nader in his room was not the same as looking in Esmé's room without her knowledge. Presumably Ben could tell me to leave if he wanted to. A huge whiteboard hung in the nurse's station with columns for the last names of patients, abbreviations for what ailed each one, the attending doctor . . . and the room number. That was convenient.

A moment later, I knocked on the door to the room in question. The response was a low sound—not exactly a *come in*, but I took it as one anyway. The man lay in his hospital bed hooked up to an IV drip, a steady beep coming from the monitor he was tethered to. "Mr. Nader?" I tiptoed in, keeping my voice low so as not to startle him. "Ben?"

He slowly turned his head to me. Even with his head wrapped with bandaging, I could see that he had less hair than I'd realized. Not bald, but definitely headed in that direction. Without his signature ball cap on, he looked older. More frail. I supposed that was true for most people lying supine in a hospital bed. "Ivy?" he croaked as he tried to push himself up to elevate his head. He lay back, cleared his throat, and tried again. "Ivy."

"Let me help you." I gently propped his shoulders up and fluffed up a pillow, helping him scoot backward slightly so his head was raised. He found the remote control and pressed a button. A motor kicked into gear and the head of the bed rose.

A wooden chair with a blue padded-fabric seat and backrest sat between his bed and the window. A lightweight sweater was draped over the back of it. "Do you mind if I sit?"

He gestured vaguely to it.

"How are you feeling?" I asked once he'd gotten the bed where he wanted it and laid the remote down again.

He managed a wry chuckle. "Like I've been hit by a car."

"We're still trying to understand it," I said. "Do you remember it happening?"

"I remember talking to my wife on the phone. And waking up here. Today."

"Your wife was home with your—?"

"Grandson," he finished.

Right. "You've been through a lot. I'm so sorry."

"And Sandy," he said softly.

I wasn't sure he'd know about that yet. My surprise must have shown on my face because he said, "Tammy—my wife—told me. And the sheriff was here earlier."

"I'm so sorry. I know you had a long history with her."

His eyes glassed, but no tears materialized. I imagined he was in shock over everything that he'd awakened to. "A very long history. We started out in this business together when we were both pups."

"Your wife said your and Sandy's kids were in a playgroup together."

"You talked to her?"

"She came into the bread shop today. She said the doctors were cautiously optimistic. I'm so glad they were right."

He closed his eyes for a long second. "Me too."

"Did you help Sandra get her start at the station?" I asked, still trying to understand the complexities of the Naders' relationship with Sandra Mays.

"I didn't get her an in, if that's what you mean. I was brand-new myself. I had zero clout. But we grew up together there. Into seasoned old dogs. That's what I liked to say. She hated that expression, though. *I am not an old dog,* she'd say. But really she was. We both were. Been around a long time and seen a lot of things."

I settled back, relieved he was in the mood to talk. "What kind of things?"

"This business makes you jaded, Ivy. Cynical. It's sad, but true. I was perfectly okay with finishing out my career here in Santa Sofia, but Sandy still felt like a little fish in a little pond."

"But she was a Santa Sofia icon. She *was* a big fish here."

"Preaching to the choir. She didn't see it that way. Tammy never wants to move from here, and why should she? Her friends are here. Our grandson's life is here. To start over at our age . . . it's not what Tammy wanted, and it's not really what I wanted."

I understood that sentiment. The move back to California from Texas had been tough for me on a lot of levels, one of which was the starting-over part. "Tammy said she and Sandra had had a falling-out of some sort. Was it over that?"

He looked surprised. "Sounds like she spilled her guts to you."

I shrugged. "I was a shoulder to cry on, so to speak."

I fell silent, waiting to see if he'd answer my question. It took an awkward minute before he spoke again. "Tammy always felt . . . judged . . . by Sandy. Sandy thought women like Tammy made the wrong choice by staying home—first with our son, and then with our grandson."

That was the same thing Tammy had said. "They fell out over that work-versus-mom philosophy? Seems extreme. Why did Sandra even care?"

Ben thought for a moment about how to answer that question. "Sandy had a pretty big self-importance meter."

Yeah. I'd witnessed that firsthand. "Ah, like she was always right?"

"Exactly. Anyone who deigned to disagree. Bam!" I jumped when he clapped his hands suddenly, the sound loud and echoing in the hospital room. "You were cut off."

"Do you think she was happy?"

I don't know why it mattered exactly, but she

hadn't seemed happy to me and it made me sad that she'd died the way she did—alone and on a rooftop, but Ben rejected that notion. "She's been pissed at me for a year. She wanted to move on and I didn't. But she finally got what she wanted, so yeah, she was happy now. At least as happy as her genetic makeup allowed her to be. *The Best Bakeries in America* show with Mack Hebron as her co-host was going to put her on the map."

"Was the show her idea?"

"According to her it was. She said she pitched the idea and the network loved it. They're always looking for the next big thing, and who doesn't like baked goods? They got Mack onboard. Trouble was, in case you didn't notice, Sandy and Mack were like oil and water. They did not gel."

"Yeah, I noticed that. Seemed like she couldn't stand him, and he tolerated her." I'd considered him as her possible killer. What I didn't see so far was why he'd be behind Ben's accident, and I was still operating under the theory that the two incidents were connected. I thought about the dynamic I'd observed between them, though. She pushed his buttons and defied his authority as the showrunner. Could he have had enough of her? Could he have been the one she'd met on the roof of the bread-shop building?

"Here's the thing I'm stumped about, Ben," I said, deciding I just needed to cut to the chase. He looked at me expectantly. "You'd just rediscovered the ladder to the roof. How did Sandra know about it?"

His chin dipped, and I thought I saw a wash of guilt slipping onto his face, but then he lifted it again, shook his head, and said, "I don't know."

If I believed Ben, there hadn't been much love lost between him and Sandra Mays. That supported the idea that he had no reason—or occasion—to have told her about his recent rediscovery of the ladder to the roof. So either he told someone else—presumably the killer—or someone else already knew about it. Either way, it made the most sense that Sandra was lured up to the roof for a private meeting that turned deadly.

"Did you tell anyone else about the roof?" I asked.

"My wife, of course, but that's it."

Tammy hadn't mentioned that Ben had told her about his rediscovery. Curious, I thought, but I let it go since she seemed to have an iron-clad alibi. I moved back to Sandra and Mack. "The other day, Sandra said something to Mack about what happened in New York. What was that about?"

He scoffed. "A love affair gone wrong. Mack is notorious for his little . . . dalliances, shall we say? Sandy thought she'd be more than that. When it turned out she wasn't, she went a little Glenn Close on him. If he'd had a rabbit, I'd have told him to watch out for its safety."

Wow. That was an old reference. My mom had loved Michael Douglas, and *Fatal Attraction* had been one of her go-to rainy-day movies. "Could Mack . . ." I trailed off, unsure if I wanted to voice my question aloud.

Ben snapped his gaze up at me. "Could Mack have killed Sandy, is that what you were going to ask?"

Sandra Mays had done nothing to hide her frustration with Mack. I leaned forward, resting my forearms on my knees. "Do you think it's possible?"

Ben laid his head back against the pillows, letting his eyes drift closed. "You're full of questions. Why are you so curious?"

"First you were hit by a car outside the bread shop, then Sandra was killed on the roof. It doesn't bode well for business. I care about Olaya and don't want this to affect her."

He didn't say anything for a beat. Finally he sighed. "I wouldn't have pegged Mack Hebron as a murderer, but it sounds to me like it was a crime of passion. If they met up there on the roof and argued, maybe she got his goat. Maybe he snapped. Or maybe it was someone else."

Maybe. I wanted to explore the other thing that had been on my mind since my talk with Tammy Nader. There wasn't a delicate way to ask him if he and Sandra had had an affair at any time during their working relationship, but it was something I needed to know. "You and Sandra were just . . . friends?"

He gave a harsh laugh. "That's right. Just. Friends. And barely that toward the end. I couldn't help her get ahead the way Mack could."

"But she did want you to go to New York with her, to bigger and better things."

"She did, but me not going wasn't going to hold her back. I was just a familiar thing to her, nothing more. We were kids when we started out at the station. We didn't know what we were doing and we grew up together there. But her aspirations were not my aspirations. I just want to stay here in Santa Sofia and raise my grandson with my wife. Sandra didn't understand that."

"Could she have done this to you?" I asked, glancing at his bandaged and casted body, hating to even ask the question aloud.

"Sandy? Try to run me down?" He laughed again, but this time it was decidedly amused. "No way. She took her anger out on me passive-aggressively. Sandy is not the kind of person— sorry, *was*. Was not the kind of person to get her hands dirty."

Ordinarily I would take that to mean that she'd have other people do the dirty work for her, but his meaning was that it was too much of a stretch to think she'd been involved in Ben's accident. I switched directions. "I heard you volunteered at Crosby House."

His brows pinched together. "How did you hear that?"

"You know the police. They had to gather all kinds of background information on you after the accident. Word just got around."

"But that place is off the record. Secure."

I couldn't help but roll my eyes. "Not that secure. You inspired me, so I signed up to volunteer, was accepted, got the address in my confirmation email, and started this week."

He worked to sit up a little straighter, flexing

his hand against the mattress, wincing as he tweaked the IV catheter taped into the vein on the top of his hand. "What?"

If I didn't know better, I'd say Ben looked a little panicked. Interesting. I kept my voice nonchalant. "I started volunteering there. We set up keyhole gardens in the backyard so now the women can compost and grow vegetables."

"Oh," he said, sinking back to his pillow again. "Oh, that sounds good."

"Everyone was really nice. I met a few of the women. Vivian Cantrell, of course. Mickey. Meg. A few others." I paused for emphasis. "And then, of course, you know Esmé."

His skin turned sallow. "Who?" he asked, but I didn't buy his innocent question.

"You know, Esmé Adriá. From the Bread for Life classes at Yeast of Eden."

"Oh. Right. The Crosby House is a shelter. It's private. It's not for me to say I recognize someone. That's part of the volunteer code, if you will."

He had a point. A good point, actually, but Esmé's story about catching Ben in her room at the shelter and my memory of her leaving the little conference room at Yeast of Eden after she'd gone through one of her personal interviews with Mack, Sandra, and Ben told me that Ben had something to hide. Esmé's face had drained of color and she'd looked spooked. Completely, entirely shaken. It had been an extreme reaction. I'd thought so then, but now, in retrospect, I felt it even more. There was something Ben wasn't saying, but did it have to do with the hit-and-run, or with Sandra Mays's death? "She said she caught you in her room."

Ben angled his head slightly, peering at me through his tired eyes. "I'm a volunteer there. The director wanted the bedrooms painted. I was measuring when the young woman came in."

He rattled off the response a little too easily, I thought. As if it had been well rehearsed.

"Is there anything else, Ms. Culpepper?" Ben asked suddenly. "I'm tired. I need to rest."

Which meant my unofficial interview of the victim—who felt oddly like a suspect, but of what?—was over. "Of course. I'm so glad you're doing better."

"If you see my wife, please ask her to bring me some water."

"Of course." I didn't see Tammy in the hall-way, but I found a nurse and passed along the message. As I left, I focused on the fact that Ben had called me Ms. Culpepper at the end. That was a change from the way he'd greeted me ini-tially, so something had definitely gotten his hackles up. Something, I was sure, that had to do with Esmé Adriá.

Chapter 21

The house where I'd grown up was at the top of a small hill on Pacific Grove Street. Billy and I had spent our summers outside playing with the other neighborhood kids. Whether we rode bikes, played hide-and-seek, or hiked down to the beach, we moved in a pack like a swarm of bees. When one turned, we all turned. They were good memories, if bittersweet without my mother around now, and I treasured them.

I parked alongside the curb and let myself in the front door. I was the last to arrive, but I focused on the fact that I'd made it on time. Everyone else, however, had gotten there early. I could see Miguel and Billy through the open French doors sitting at the patio table, Billy with a bottle of beer and Miguel swirling a glass of red wine. Their backs were to me and they looked deep in conversation.

I dropped my purse onto the hall table and

headed straight for the makeshift bar someone had set up. There were stemless wineglasses, two bottles of red, two bottles of white, and a little galvanized bucket filled with ice and bottles of beer. "You made it," my dad said, coming up behind me and busing my cheek as I poured myself a glass of Chardonnay.

"Did you ever doubt me?"

"I wondered if you'd be late," he said, leaving off the part about that being a pet peeve of his.

"Never, Dad."

He scoffed at that, because I'd been late plenty in my life, and as kids, Billy and I had made a habit of it. But I was a lot older now and understood the importance of arriving at a place when you were expected.

"Did you get what you needed?" he asked. I raised a questioning eyebrow at him and he clarified with, "Interviewing the guy at the hospital."

No secrets in the Culpepper family. "Oh. Well, it wasn't an interview exactly," I said. "More like a, I don't know, a conversation."

The way he pressed his lips together told me that he didn't quite buy my clarification. He rephrased. "So did your conversation yield the desired results?"

When had my dad gotten so sassy? "If what you mean by desired results," I said, using air quotes, "is did I get to the truth, then no, I did not."

"Did you get any closer to the truth?" Emmaline asked, coming up next to me, holding her own glass of wine, her engagement ring sparkling in the light as she moved her hand.

I grabbed her hand and gazed at it. "God, I love looking at this thing on your hand."

She smiled as she pulled her hand free and fluttered her fingers at me. "I do, too."

She had the natural look going on with her hair lately, the fragile tiny Z waves zinging all around her head. "Are you doing a weave for the wedding, relaxing it, or keeping it natural?" I asked. I liked it every single way Em styled it. When she'd been in her teens and twenties, she'd often gone for colorful braids in purple or turquoise. She'd stayed with black braids once she'd entered law enforcement, but had been doing fewer and fewer of them in recent years.

"I'm thinking natural, but depends on the wedding dress, I think."

"Any ideas about dress style?"

"Ivy, we have some shopping trips ahead of us. Get ready."

"Name the day, I'll be there."

"I want Miguel and Olaya to do the catering," she said. "Do you think they will?"

Miguel and Olaya had worked together in a lot of ways. Olaya regularly made some of the breads for Baptista's Cantina and Grill, and they'd catered the local Art Car banquet, as well as a funeral not so long ago. They complemented each other perfectly. Miguel would do anything for Billy and Emmaline, and Olaya would do anything for me. "I know they will," I said, and I did.

My dad had already joined Miguel and Billy on the patio. Em and I headed out there, too, me carrying one of the bottles of red to refill

Miguel's glass and Em handing Billy a new bottle of beer. As I bent to kiss Miguel, Billy set his bottle down and grabbed Em around her hips, gently pulling her onto his lap. She swatted at him. "Billy. Your dad," she said, stifling her giggles.

My dad waved his hand. "Don't mind me."

Emmaline pried herself free of Billy and moved to her own chair. We settled into a comfortable conversation about the wedding plans, Billy and Emmaline waiting to adopt a rescue dog from the humane society, a newly approved city park that my dad was working on, my new schedule at the bread shop, Miguel's hiring of a new chef . . . everything *except* Ben Nader's accident and the death of Sandra Mays. Finally, Billy brought it up. "So, did you find out anything from the guy in the hospital?"

All eyes turned to face me, as if I suddenly had the complete answer to stop global warming and turn climate change on its heels. I gave the abbreviated version of my chat with Ben Nader, ending with how abruptly he'd terminated it. "So, what about Esmerelda Adriá?" I felt horrible—guilty, even—suggesting Esmé as a possible suspect, and I had absolutely no motive, but something was sketchy about her connection to Ben Nader.

"Other than the Bread for Life women being part of the show, just like you and Olaya, we have no connections or reason to link any of them to Ben."

"Except there is a link," I said. Emmaline was not going to like that I'd neglected to relay the tie between Ben Nader and Esmé Adriá through Crosby House when I'd first discovered it through Meg. "Remember how you mentioned that Ben volunteered at Crosby House? It kind of lit a fire under me about . . . giving back . . . so I volunteered, too." I paused, feeling sheepish. "And found out that Esmé is a current resident there."

Em stared at me. "What?"

I threw my hands up. "I know. I'm sorry. I guess . . . I just . . . there's something broken about her. I don't want her to be involved, but now . . ." I relayed my search for her when she went MIA and the conversation we'd had at the Shrimp Shack earlier that afternoon. "Neither one of them mentioned that they knew each other—"

"Or knew of each other," Billy said. "Seeing each other at Crosby House doesn't mean they actually know each other."

"Except that Esmé caught him in her room at Crosby House," I said. "When I asked Ben about it just now, he said he didn't know her, but I'm not sure I buy that. There's something fishy going on."

"Here's what I can't figure out," Em said. I sighed, relieved she wasn't going to chastise me for holding out on her about the Crosby House connection. Her posture shifted as she sat up straighter, going into sheriff mode. "The guy seems well liked, and so far, there aren't any skeletons in his closet. Not one. He lost his son and daughter-in-law. He's raising his grandson. He's been with the same job for years. He volunteers and gives back to the community. Happily married, by all accounts. Even if there's a double connection between him and this Esmerelda, so what? What's the motive? And that's what it comes down to. Who has a motive?"

"Do you have a list of possible suspects?" Billy asked. Being around Emmaline meant he'd picked up law enforcement lingo and spouted it like he was talking to his subcontractors about the latest house they were building.

Emmaline answered. "Like I said, the guy doesn't seem to have enemies. We're looking closely at the usual: wife, who has an alibi, although the grandson is the alibi and he was playing video games, so . . ."

"Not solid, then," Billy said.

"But there's no obvious motive, either. Like I said, by all accounts, a solid marriage. No affairs that we know of. We even looked into an affair between Ben and Sandra, but nothing. Old family friends through their kids and a strictly professional relationship. Tammy and Ben Nader have been together since college.

"Sandra Mays is a suspect for the hit-and-run, but of course she's dead now, which poses its own set of problems. Are the two incidents—his accident and her death—related? If they are, then it seems possible, if not probable, that the same person who hit Ben also killed Sandra. But what's the connection between the two? What do they know that someone was willing to kill for, and does that mean Ben is still in danger?"

That was a very good question.

"But they might not be connected," Billy said.

"Did this Sandra woman have a reason to want to run down this Nader guy?"

"According to Ben, she was upset that he wasn't willing to hit the big-time with her," I said, "but is that reason enough to try to kill him? And she seemed genuinely upset when she saw that it was him lying in the middle of the street."

"So she wanted to leave Santa Sofia and he didn't," my dad said, "but she didn't need a cameraman to hold her hand with a new job, did she?"

"I wouldn't think so."

"And she'd already landed the Mack Hebron collaboration," Miguel said. "He's a pretty big name. The fact that Ben didn't want to uproot his life didn't actually affect her."

My thoughts exactly. "So why would she bother being upset with Ben if he didn't want to move on past the pilot episode?"

"She wouldn't," Miguel said. "Not enough to exact revenge."

Em set her wineglass down on the table. "From what I hear, there wasn't much love lost between Sandra Mays and Mack Hebron."

"That's true," I said. "Nothing she did seemed to faze him, except when she started taping without him. He was pissed about that, but he took her to task, made her restart the taping, and it was like it never happened. But her? He got on her nerves big-time. It was like she was trying to prove herself worthy of the new position she had. Or there was some personal issue between them. Ben told me Sandra and Mack had a *thing* once in New York. A dalliance."

Emmaline angled her head as she considered what I'd said. "Mack Hebron doesn't have an alibi for the hit-and-run or for Sandra's estimated time of death. He was at a ball game in San Francisco, but the time of death is midnight to three a.m. Plenty of time for him to have gotten back here to meet her on the roof."

"But how would either of them have known about the roof as a meeting place?" I asked. "Ben said he'd mentioned it to his wife, but no one else."

"Tammy and Sandra were old friends?" Billy asked. "Could Tammy have told her about it after Ben mentioned it?"

"I doubt it," I said. "They had a falling-out going back ten years or so." Unless Tammy was a damn good liar and her story wasn't entirely true.

"Why even meet up on top of the roof?" Miguel asked. "And why in the middle of the night? If Sandra was the one who arranged it, why not choose an all-night restaurant, or some spot at the beach, or at the local studio? It only makes sense if someone like, say, Ben, arranged it because that was a spot that he knew and used to go to. Sandra would have balked, but she would have gone."

That was an excellent point. The one conundrum with the theory, of course, was that Ben had been in a coma. "But Ben is the only person who couldn't have arranged the meeting with Sandra."

"Ben's wife knew," my dad said. "They've been married a long time. Could she have arranged it as his proxy?" Leave it to my dad to home in on the intimacies married couples shared.

Emmaline shook her head. "Of course we don't know for sure, but presumably the meeting was arranged after Ben was already in a coma, so any connection to the meeting and Ben is difficult to make. Barring an affair, why would Tammy Nader have wanted to meet Sandra at all, let alone on the top of a dark roof in the middle of the night?"

We all fell silent, considering this. Just because we didn't know why, didn't mean there wasn't a reason and that it hadn't actually happened in just that way. Maybe Sandra and Ben had had an affair and Em just hadn't been able to suss it out yet. Or maybe Tammy had wanted Ben to have the same aspirations Sandra did and they'd been working on convincing him together. Of course that scenario seemed to lay blame for Ben's accident and Sandra's death on Tammy Nader, but the motive didn't actually work. Why would she run down her husband when she needed him alive and well to pursue the next level of his career? And why kill Sandra when that next level depended on her success?

"Let's look at them as two separate events," I said.

"Yes," Em agreed. "They're too muddied when we try to link them."

Miguel disappeared inside the house, returning a few seconds later with the white wine bottle and a few more beers. He handed my dad and Billy each a bottle, refilled my glass with the white, then topped off Em's red first, then his own. He sat back down, moving his chair closer to mine and taking my hand.

"I keep coming back to Sandra Mays for Ben's accident," I said. "They had history. What if she really did begrudge Ben for not having the aspirations she did? She was pretty on edge. People have killed for less." That was something we all knew too well.

Em picked up the idea. "Okay, so hypothetical. Let's say Sandra left the bread shop during the break, got into the car she'd had at the ready—"

"So premeditation," Billy interjected.

Em nodded. "Right. Then she donned some sort of disguise so she wasn't recognizable—"

"Of course." I snapped my fingers with the realization. "She's a local celebrity, so she would have had to do that." I thought back to when I'd seen Sandra return to discover Ben's body laid out on the ground. I didn't recall her looking disheveled—or anything less than perfectly coiffed and put together as she always was—but that didn't necessarily mean anything. After so many years in front of the camera, she was a pro.

Em continued with her theory. "And then she mowed him down, ditched the car, and returned to deliver a stellar performance as the shocked and distraught friend of the victim."

If Sandra wanted Ben to go with her to bigger and better things, but he refused, she might have taken that as him messing with her career. Was that motive enough for her to have tried to run him down? Had Sandra Mays exacted attempted murder as a vendetta?

"That's one cold-hearted woman, if it's true," Miguel said.

"No sign of the car?" my dad asked.

"None. We've checked the makes and models of cars owned by the Naders, Sandra Mays, Mack Hebron, all the immediate people he worked with. No matches."

Solving crimes, I'd discovered over the past year, came down to a lot of theorizing. Eventually, if you tracked down enough information and gathered enough clues, you landed on a theory that ended up being the truth.

I spent the rest of the evening wondering if we had landed on part of the truth. Had Sandra been behind Ben's accident?

Chapter 22

Sunday night proved sleepless for me. My brain circled round and round a list of suspects. Finally, I hauled myself out of bed, grabbed a sheet of paper, and jotted it all down to get it out of my head. I divided the list into two headings: one for Ben Nader and the other for Sandra Mays. I listed suspects and their possible motives. It was a short list.

BEN NADER		SANDRA MAYS	
Suspect	Motive	Suspect	Motive
Tammy	Was Ben having an affair?	**Tammy**	Same—affair?
Sandra	Retaliation for different career goals	**Ben**	No, he was in the hospital

Esmé	What is the connection between them?	**Esmé**	No motive!
Mack Hebron	No motive!	**Mack Hebron**	Their volatile relationship?

I sat back to study what I'd written. No wonder my mind was mush. Nothing about the situation made any sense. If the two incidents were connected, Tammy was the only one with a possible motive for both, but that was only assuming there'd been an affair that didn't actually appear to have happened—or if there was something else we hadn't uncovered yet.

I came back to Sandra. It would have been risky for her to stash a car, don a disguise, and pray that no one recognized her or got any information on the vehicle when the street was filled with people. It was pure luck that it had played out that way, but I just didn't think Sandra Mays would take the chance and potentially ruin her entire career.

Esmé might have a motive to try to silence Ben, but as of now, I had no idea what it could be. He'd been in her room at Crosby House. Had he been telling the truth that it was to measure for paint, or was there something else? But Esmé had no connection to Sandra.

And then there was Mack Hebron. No obvious motive for the attempted murder of Ben, but plenty of potential motive for Sandra. Was it possible that Mack may have overheard something about the ladder to the roof when Miguel and I had first discovered it with Ben?

Unless this whole thing had to do with Tammy exacting revenge on Ben and Sandra for having an affair—or to do with their opposing aspirations, which was a stretch—then, as we'd done the night before at dinner, I had to look at the two incidents as separate. I felt like I had a bunch of loose ends that led nowhere and I didn't know how to weave any of it together. And it was making my head hurt.

I went back to bed, my mind clear of the clutter. With my thoughts down on paper, I was able to shut down and rest. Still, morning came too soon. Working in my volunteer hours at Crosby House took some finagling of my schedule, but it was a priority, not only because I was committed to helping the women there in any way I could, starting with the keyhole gardens, but also because I knew it was central to the investigation into what had happened to Ben and Sandra.

Olaya had recently started closing the bread shop on Mondays, so today was part of my weekend. Miguel closed Baptista's on Mondays, too. That didn't mean either Olaya or Miguel was not actually working, though. Olaya was probably trying out variations to her tried-and-true bread recipes, while Miguel was most likely tending to the ever simmering batch of *mole* that he used in the same way a sourdough starter operated. He had created the base when he'd re-opened the restaurant. Since then, he kept it at a continual low simmer, adding a combination of chilis, nuts, chocolate, and spices to it as he built in layers and layers of flavor and complexity.

He might be out and about, though. He surfed occasionally, but more often than not, he took his bike and rode for an hour or two. Cycling was his favorite form of physical activity and something he loved to do in the mornings when the air was cool and the world felt fresh against his face.

We'd arranged to meet for lunch at the Shrimp Shack, which never took a day off. After being there Friday afternoon, I'd been craving their shrimp poppers . . . or their shrimp and grits . . . or their grilled shrimp kebobs. Basically, I needed some shrimp and I wasn't going to be too picky.

I arrived at Crosby House ready to pull whatever weeds may have managed to grow in the short time the keyhole gardens had been in place, to encourage more composting—because I figured it would take the women at the facility a while to get into the swing of things—and to suss out what I could about Esmé and Ben.

What I found were the keyhole gardens completely weed-free, with the vegetables we'd planted already taking root and growing quickly, and the compost cylinders layered with kitchen scraps, cardboard, eggshells, coffee grounds, and grass clippings. "It's going great," a voice said from behind me.

I turned to see Angie wearing a pair of garden gloves, her hair pulled back in a ponytail. She'd spent a little time helping the day I'd been here to set up the gardens and had seemed mostly uninterested, but now it seemed she'd taken a robust interest in maintaining them. "I can see that! They look amazing. Everyone's into the composting?"

She smushed her lips together in a strange, frowny expression. "They are. It gives them something to do. Everyone's been out here pulling weeds or watering or bringing things to compost. It's kinda cool to see."

Giddiness washed over me. "It is! So cool."

She gave a semblance of a smile, even though in reality it was closer to her lips being in a straight line. Was she so damaged by whatever traumas she'd endured that she might never be truly happy again? She looked proud, but she definitely didn't share my visible enthusiasm.

"Meg told me you work at Yeast of Eden. The bread shop?"

"I do. I'm kind of an apprentice. Have you been?"

"No. Never had the chance."

An idea cultivated in my mind. If the women at the shelter couldn't—or hadn't—come to Yeast of Eden, I'd bring Yeast of Eden to them. The entire idea behind Olaya's Bread for Life program was to empower women from different backgrounds and income levels. To give them a marketable skill. To celebrate their cultures, their families, and to help them cultivate something real that belonged to them and could never be taken away.

What if, I thought, we expanded the Bread for

Life program, bringing it to Crosby House? Zula, Claire, Amelie, and Esmé could volunteer, if they were interested, to teach the women how to bake. Many, I imagined, already knew how and had their own stories to share. They just needed permission.

The door from the house opened and Meg and Esmé came out to the yard. Esmé, I thought, looked normal—as if she hadn't gone MIA for a few days or had the tense conversation we'd had at the Shrimp Shack.

"I didn't know you were coming today, Ivy," Meg said. She smiled in a way I didn't think Angie could. It was genuine and bright and full of pride. "Can you believe these gardens? They look amazing. Everyone is so into it."

"That's what Angie was saying. I'm so glad." I wriggled my fingers over a basil plant. It had to have nearly doubled in size in the few days it had been growing. "We did good."

She held her arm out to me. I fist-bumped her and she grinned. "We did do good. So good."

Esmé pulled a small basil leaf off, tore it in half, and put it to her nose. "I love this smell. The entire country of Italy must smell like basil, don't you think?"

I'd never been, but it was a great image to have in my head. "If it doesn't, it should."

"Meg," Angie said. "Did you talk to Vivian?"

Meg looked at her, shaking her head. "Was I supposed to?"

"She was looking for you earlier. Something about dinner tonight, I think."

"Oh. Right. Okay." Dinner was a long way off, but Vivian ran a tight ship and Meg scurried off to find her.

I'd been thinking about how to broach any topic with Esmé after the Shrimp Shack Friday night. I'd worried that she'd be put off by me, or, I don't know, hostile. But she wasn't. She acted normal, as if I'd never told her I'd snooped in her room uninvited. The three of us stood together around the keyhole gardens in an awkward silence. I was ready to head back inside to find Vivian Cantrell myself so she could direct me in other ways I could be helpful at Crosby House, but Angie's voice stopped me. "I heard you were there when that guy was hit by a car."

"I was," I said just as Esmé spoke up.

"You know him, Angie. It was Ben Nader. He volunteers here."

"Yeah, I know," Angie said.

"You know Ben?" I asked. It shouldn't have surprised me—after all, the guy had spent time here—but it did. I'd been so focused on everyone else.

Angie played with the loose fingers on her gloves, pinching the fabric, tugging at it, then letting it go. "Yeah, right. He did some painting. I had to leave my room when he came to work."

I felt like a gong had sounded and was now reverberating in my head. "He painted your room?"

"Alabaster white," she said, naming what had to be a designer paint store color. "Took him two days."

"Plus measurement and prep," I said, raising the inflection of my voice at the end to pose it as a question. "I'm sure it's hard to be put out of your space."

Esmé drew in a sharp breath. Why? I wondered. Angie ignored her and asked me, "And you discovered that body? Sandra Mays?"

Once again, I nodded. "That was horrible."

"Do they have any suspects?" she asked.

Esmé hadn't said anything, but I heard her exhale. Sensed her anxiousness as she waited for my reply. "The police have a few leads," I said vaguely. "Ben has come out of his coma, so that's good, too."

"He did?" Esmé's voice rose an octave.

Meg came back out to join us. "Who did what?" she asked, bending over to pick a weed from the garden.

"Ben Nader," I said, watching the nuances of Esmé's reaction. "He's awake."

I thought Esmé flinched. She was seriously freaked out over Ben. I hadn't really thought she could be a legitimate suspect, but maybe she was.

"That's great," Meg said. When she turned around, she held a bundle of basil like a bouquet. She handed Esmé some of the herbs.

Esmé smelled the basil, acting nonchalant. "He's going to be okay then?"

"Looks like it," I said.

"Are the police guarding him?" she asked.

Why did she want to know? I wondered. I spoke slowly. "The police have a guard outside his room."

"A guard?" Angie perked up. "Why does he need a guard? Wasn't it an accident?"

"I think the police aren't quite sure about that. With Sandra Mays's murder right on the heels of Ben's accident, I think they don't want to take any chances."

"So there's a murderer on the loose in Santa Sofia?" Angie's asked. "Is there any news on what happened to Ms. Mays?"

All three of them swiveled to look at me. "There are people of interest," I said, "but that's all I know."

Meg's eyes grew wide. "Like who? The husband? It's always the spouse, isn't it?"

"She wasn't married."

"Oh my God!" For someone who'd been so shy and reserved when I'd first met her, she'd certainly blossomed—into a bit of hysteria at the moment. "Is Angie right? Should we be worried?"

"Sandra Mays's murder was personal," I said, disabusing her of the notion that there was a serial killer on the loose in town.

"She is right," Esmé said. "Someone met her up on that roof. They should look at Mack Hebron. Those two, they did not get along."

Meg gawked. "Really? The chef? You think he could be a killer?"

"Not getting along doesn't mean you're going to kill a person," Angie said. "If it did, we'd all be guilty of murder."

The three women fell silent, but met each other's eyes. They'd escaped similar fates. What had brought them to Crosby House bound them together.

I left them at the keyhole gardens to go find Vivian Cantrell. It was a small thing, but so much about what had happened in the last week couldn't be pieced together in a way that made sense. Confirming the truth of the small things felt like it mattered. "Do you have a minute?" I asked Vivian when I found her at her desk in her office.

She beckoned me in. "I do. Just a few, though."

"I'll be quick. I visited Ben Nader in the hospital the other night. He's awake now."

She'd been only half paying attention, but now her chin lifted and her eyes drilled into me. "I didn't realize you knew Mr. Nader."

"He's actually the reason I came to Crosby House in the first place." I'd left that direct connection out when I'd first spoken to her, but now I needed her to know about it. "He's part of the team working on a reality show here in town. *America's Best Bakeries.*"

Recognition dawned on her face. "I knew I knew you from somewhere. You work there. At Yeast of Eden, I mean."

I thought back, trying to remember if I'd mentioned that fact on the application or during either of my first two meetings with Vivian. I guess I hadn't. "I do. After Ben was hit by that car, I heard he volunteered here. That's why—"

"It sparked an interest in you to give back to those who've been suffering," she said, finishing my thought more eloquently than I'd have been able to.

"It did. He did. I saw him Friday night. He's come out of the coma he was in. He mentioned that he'd been doing some painting for you. Some of the bedrooms?"

Vivian went back to scanning the paper she held. "That's right. He is the best kind of volunteer. He does the prep work, buys the paint, and does the work himself. I don't know if he'll still be able to do that after what happened, but hopefully. Eventually."

"He was going to paint Esmé's room?"

She pulled a file folder from a holder on her desk and flipped it open. She used her index finger as a guide as she scrolled down the information on the sheet. "Here it is. Ben painted Angie's room. Esmé's room. Mickey's. Louise is next. Or, I guess we'll see if he's able to continue."

He'd measured and painted. Come and gone. And, it seemed, his story of being caught by Esmé in her room checked out.

Chapter 23

A week had passed since Ben was run down outside the bread shop. A week, and I was no closer to the truth about why he'd been targeted or who was behind it than I'd been the moment it had happened.

Two more days, and it would be a week since the discovery of Sandra's body. Same story. No real suspects. No closer to the truth. No closer to justice.

The one person I hadn't had the chance to talk to, yet who had a solid link to the victims, and who seemed to have had to have some deep-seated feelings about Sandra Mays, was Mack Hebron. Thankfully, in true Hollywood fashion, the show had to go on. That became clear when Mack showed up with his crew Tuesday afternoon (minus Sandra Mays and Ben Nader). "We have to retape the portions that had Sandra," he informed us.

Esmé, Claire, Amelie, and Zula gathered around him, with Olaya and me slightly on the outside of the little circle. Maggie had sidled up next to Tae and whispered something in his ear. Ah, young love. It looked like they'd gone from zero to sixty in a matter of days.

"I'll just redo the intros and transitions. We'll edit it all together. It'll be like Sandra was never part of it."

That seemed like a coldhearted statement because she had, in fact, been here. She'd leaned over Zula's station when she'd made the hembesha. She'd asked some of the interview questions when I'd been in the hot seat. Surely she had done the same when others had been in the hot seat, too. From their expressions, I could see everyone was turned off by Mack's callous remark, but none of us said anything.

"Go ahead," Olaya said, "but we will continue our session. Today Esmé is taking us through a traditional bread from the Jalisco region of Mexico. It is called *tachigual.*"

Of all the women, Esmé had been the most excited about sharing one of her country's traditional breads with our group. "It's unique there because not many people make it. They mix it by hand. It is stuffed with nuts and raisins. And it is baked in an open oven made of brick and clay, heated by a wood fire. No one else does it that way anymore," she told us before Mack got here.

She'd prepared the starter at home the day before, which we'd all use. "It is a mixture of flour and water. That is all. It sat all of yesterday and for the night. Now it is ready to use. There is a whole-wheat version of this bread that is sweetened only with *piloncillo*."

"Cones of brown sugar," Olaya translated.

"But we will make the type that is made with white flour and white sugar, and then we blend in raisins and many toasted nuts."

Esmé had been halfway through her instructions and we were elbow-deep in hand mixing our dough when Mack showed up unannounced. "I won't disturb you at all," he'd said after telling us what he needed, but he directed Tae to get some close-up shots of the contents of our bowls and the loaf Esmé had sitting at her station.

Meanwhile he tested his mic, someone fussed with his hair, he did a sound check, circled his finger in the air indicating to his crew that he was all set to go, and he was off. He said the same things he and Sandra had said together, ending his new intro with, "We've found it right here in Santa Sofia, California. It's one of the best bakeries in America and is owned by the hardworking Olaya Solis. Today, we are visiting Yeast of Eden."

Mack didn't take long. Time is money, as they say. When he was done, he threw up his hand and turned toward us. "I think we have everything we need. Thank you, ladies. I appreciate your time and help with this."

Olaya acknowledged him with a curt nod of her head. I could tell that she was completely done opening up her bread shop to people who, in her opinion, did not appreciate or understand what she was about. "You never asked me about the history of Yeast of Eden," she said, leaving Esmé to lead the others as they finished mixing their dough. I'd finished mine and had shaped it into the round just like Esmé's. The others still had their hands deep in their dough and it looked like they loved every second of it. I had washed the dough from my hands and now I stood beside Olaya.

Mack rolled his hand at Tae, who immediately hoisted his camera onto his shoulder and began filming. I don't think Olaya noticed. She was in a mood, ready to school the Mack Hebrons of the world about their casual interest in the bread that was her sole passion. "We live in a time of instant gratification and tasteless food. Government subsidizing and low nutrition. My passion for bread represents the opposite of all of that. Yeast of Eden is about taking the time for the long rise, developing taste that is subtle and complex at the same time. It is about farm-to-table quality and ingredients packed with nutrition.

"I started with just six types of artisan breads. The archetypes. Sourdough baguettes, whole wheat, Normandy rye, kalamata olive, rosemary olive oil, and country white sourdough. These breads are the foundation of everything we bake here. We use farm-to-table single origin wheat, all natural ingredients, and wild yeast from organic grape skins. This all results in our signature crusty bread. Every loaf is baked to the highest quality. It is not a mass production. It is a single kitchen filled with energy and love, and it is this energy and love that has given Yeast of Eden the reputation it now holds."

For the first time ever, Mack looked nonplussed. He was startled, as if he'd been given a scolding by a nun at the convent school. He blinked, and just like that, his expression returned to its normal confidence. "And your bread truly is amazing, Olaya. Every loaf is a work of art. What you've created here in this little idyllic town is incredible."

"Yes," she said. "I think so. And it is thanks to women like Esmé and Claire, Zula and Amelie— and to my sisters and Maggie here, who runs the front of the store, and to Felix and Ivy, my apprentices who I am teaching so that the history of my bread goes on—it is thanks to these people that Yeast of Eden is what it is today. That it is here to be featured on your television show."

She stopped, but the unspoken part of her sentence hung in the air. *On your television show that rests on the laurels of someone else's hard work.*

Mack called "Cut." Olaya spun around and returned to the kitchen. I watched her go, the weight of her speech on my shoulders. I'd talked her into doing the show. Now we had an injured cameraman, a dead woman, and a host who didn't seem to understand the significance of the bread shop Olaya poured her heart and soul into. I knew her well enough to understand that what happened to Ben and Sandra was taking a toll on her. She felt as if it had all happened on her watch, at her business. She couldn't have stopped it, and it had nothing to do with her, but I was more determined than ever to get to the bottom of things.

Mack was halfway out the front door of the shop when I decided I wanted to ask him a question. Emmaline had already brought him in for questioning. His alibis were not airtight, and he clearly wasn't in mourning for Sandra. But was he behind her death?

I chased after him. "Mack, do you have a minute?"

He stopped, but didn't turn around until I caught up with him. He kept his head down and his eyes were closed. "Hang on," he said, his voice thick. He shook his head, finally turning to me. His eyes were red. He swiped away a wayward tear. The man had been crying. "Sorry," he said, swallowing hard.

"Are you okay?" I asked after a good thirty seconds. "Can I get you something?" Like a slice of rosemary olive loaf to give him comfort.

"I'm not heartless, you know."

He'd certainly sounded heartless a little while ago, but he looked heartbroken now. I stayed quiet, hoping he'd elaborate. He did. "I actually cared about her. Sandy. Sandra. She wanted more than I did. She knew that upfront, but it still ended badly. I did care about her, though."

"I can see that, Mack."

I guided him to one of the outdoor bistro tables on the sidewalk outside Yeast of Eden and sat across from him. He sank down, propping his elbows on the metal gridded surface and resting his head in his hands. I let him be, giving him time to gather his emotions.

He looked up suddenly. "The police questioned me, you know. Freaked me out."

"It's standard procedure, I'm sure. They'd want to talk to anyone who was close to her."

"Like I could have had anything to do with her death? Completely absurd."

"You knew her well, though."

"And it's usually the boyfriend—which I wasn't, by the way. What we had ended a while ago. I wished her well."

My brain zigzagged to my recent close-calls on the road and in my house, and the jealous-woman scenario. "But she wanted you back?"

Mack scraped his fingers through his carefully mussed hair. "No, not really. I don't think so."

I arched a brow. Was he seeing things clearly? There was no question about Sandra's tenseness around and toward Mack. "She seemed pretty angry at you," I said.

His lips twisted as he shrugged. "She was, but we were over. She knew that." We sat in silence again for a few seconds before he said, "You wanted to ask me something?"

Emmaline had checked Mack's alibi. He could have been the one to run down Ben Nader, and he could have been back to Santa Sofia from San Francisco early enough to meet up with and kill Sandra. But why would he do either of those things? "Do you know Ben very well? He's awake and doing pretty well, I think."

I watched Mack carefully to gauge his reaction. He lifted his eyebrows slightly as an acknowledgment. "That's great news," he said, but that was it. I didn't detect a single trace of concern that Ben was still alive and could reveal something about his would-be killer.

"Did Ben or Sandra mention the roof ladder to you, by any chance?" I asked.

Mack sat up straighter. "No, they didn't. Why?"

"It's just that only Ben knew about the ladder. I'm so baffled about how Sandra ended up on the roof."

"This is starting to feel like an interrogation." He gave me a withering look as he stood. "I'm going to go now."

And he did, without a backward glance.

Chapter 24

I spent the next morning working on the Yeast of Eden website, starting with the history of the bread shop. Olaya's speech the night before had given me the inspiration I needed. It had shown Olaya's vision and passion, so all I had to do was refine it.

The end result, after some editing and fine-tuning, communicated everything Olaya had said succinctly to Mack Hebron, and was in her voice. I moved on to a section about the Bread for Life program, then to the profiles of the core people at the bread shop, starting with Olaya, Felix, Maggie, and myself, as well as the rest of the morning baking crew who worked tirelessly with Olaya to bake every loaf to her standard.

I edited in real time, which allowed me to flip back and forth between the dashboard and the site itself, adjusting spacing, headings, and other style choices as needed. I set up the blog, but skipped doing an entry in favor of focusing on the Bread tab and all the core offerings at Yeast of Eden. Olaya had given me a list of the breads she wanted featured. We'd also spent hours setting up cutting boards, condiments, and knives so I could shoot photos of each variety. The next step was creating hierarchical pages for all the bread, each main page designated by the photos I'd taken. From there, I needed to create connecting pages for each individual loaf, which would include a brief description of it and the photo. It wasn't hard work, but it was tedious and time-consuming.

I started with loaves, adding them one by one. I moved on to petite loaves, then to flat loaves, baguettes, and bâtards, rolls, rounds, and sliced breads. I was just entering the two gluten-friendly options Olaya wanted added. She'd spent six months baking and perfecting them and now she was ready for them to join the weekly menu. We couldn't say gluten-free, since cross-contamination was a thing, and flour powder abounded in the kitchen, but we baked them in a separate section so they were as free of gluten as they could reasonably be in a gluten-filled bread bakery.

My cell phone rang just as I uploaded the last photo. I grabbed it, my stomach instantly clenching as I saw the Unknown Number note on the screen. I debated with myself. I didn't have to answer.

So I didn't.

I hit Decline and set the phone back down. It rang again three seconds later. Once again, I declined the call. We played the game three more times before I gave up and answered with an annoyed, "Hello?"

Nothing. No heavy breathing. No creepy voice. No threat. Just silence.

My hackles were up so I went with my gut. "Heather, you need to back the hell off."

I listened intently. Was that a shallow gasp I'd just heard? Aha! "Heather. I don't have any interest in Luke. You can have him. He's all yours."

Her voice came at me, frenetic and raspy. "I don't believe you, Ivy. He came to see you. He told me you want him back."

Luke Holden, that liar! I sucked in a steadying breath. "He showed up, that's true, but I didn't ask him to come, and I don't want him back. I'm in a relationship with someone else. I have no interest in revisiting the past. With Luke," I added, because I was revisiting the past with Miguel. He was my past, present, and future, whereas my ex-husband was just ancient history.

Heather didn't say anything for a minute. When she spoke again, her voice was softer. Timid even. "Really? You don't want him back?"

I exhaled quietly, but my chest felt tight, like a length of twine encircled it. "I don't want him back, Heather. He's all yours—if that's what you both want. Please stop calling me and following me. And do not break into my house—"

"I didn't break into your house." She sounded indignant, like how dare I accuse her of such a thing, but her words didn't ring true. Now *I* didn't believe *her*. I decided not to push it with her, instead reviewing the stalking incidents in my mind. "Did you rear-end me?"

She sighed. "Don't hate me."

"So you did?"

"I followed Luke out there a while back. When he said you wanted him back, I lost it. It wrecked the rental car."

"And the phone calls."

"Yeah. You swear. You and Luke are over?"

"I swear, Heather." At least she seemed relatively sane, as stalkers go. "No more calls then. You need to back off."

"I will."

"And I want my electric toothbrush back," I said.

"Whatever, Ivy."

My blood ran cold. She'd said she didn't break into my house and I didn't believe her, but what if? If she hadn't, then who had? Like a Ping-Pong ball, my thoughts immediately bounced to Ben Nader and Sandra Mays. I'd witnessed the hit-and-run and I'd been asking around about him by the time I'd discovered Sandra's body. Then there was the slow drive-by when I first went to Crosby House.

I shoved the thoughts away. Murder was getting under my skin.

"Leave me alone, okay?" I said to Heather.

"I said I would. Sheesh."

She was getting attitude? "Bye, Heather," I said, but she'd already hung up. Instantly, she was gone from my mind. I immediately opened a new tab on the computer, and typed in Ben Nader's name. I didn't know what I was looking

for, but something. The most current listings
were all about the hit-and-run and Ben's recovery in the hospital. I skimmed each entry, looking for a clue of some sort. One reporter
likened the accident to the fatal one Ben's son
had been in, mentioning that Ben and his wife,
Tammy, were the guardians of their grandson,
Kevin. I scrolled down through listing after listing of Ben and his work at the local news station,
then on regional cable shows. Eventually, the
listings became years old. I came to one that re-
ported the accident that had killed his son. Like
Em had said, the accident had taken place in
Europe. London, specifically. They'd planned to
be married there, then return to the United
States as husband and wife. The accident had
devastated Ben and Tammy Nader. The police
had no clues and no one was ever charged in the
manslaughter death of Grant Nader. Grant's fiancée and the mother of his child, Margaret
Ryan, had survived the accident.

My brain slammed to a stop. I reread that part
of the article, zeroing in on two points. Ben and
Tammy were raising their grandson, but Margaret Ryan, the mother of the child, had survived. Why, I wondered, was the baby's mother
not raising her child? Had she been too severely
injured? Had she died later? I typed in her
name. The same article popped up, but nothing
else.

I had one thought, and one thought alone.
Could Margaret Ryan have changed her name?

The accident that had killed Kevin Nader's father had happened close to ten years ago. He'd

been an infant, so that put him at nine or ten years old now. I picked up my cell phone and searched the note I'd typed Mrs. Nader's phone number on for Olaya. I dialed it now. Tammy Nader answered right away. "Ben is doing so much better," she told me when I asked after him. She caught me up on his progress. He'll be in a wheelchair for a while, but he's able to get around a little bit. We're so thankful."

"I wanted to invite you and your grandson to the bread shop. Olaya makes these amazing cookies," I said, talking about the skull cookies she hid amidst the loaves of bead for the children of Santa Sofia.

"He'll like that. Kev's been out of sorts since the . . . accident."

"I can only imagine." We agreed to meet at five o'clock. That gave me plenty of time to get Mrs. Branford to help me do a little legwork.

Chapter 25

Penelope Branford was my go-to partner in fighting crime. Today I needed her more than ever. I couldn't shake the importance of the box in Esmé's closet. I thought back to when I'd told her I'd been in her room. She'd said that KM, whose initials were on the box in her closet, had not been the reason she was at Crosby House. But there was something about her face. The way she'd stammered through that conversation.

I knew what I needed to do, and I needed Mrs. Branford to help me.

"It's high time you came around, Ivy," she said from the passenger seat of my car.

"I'm sorry," I said, and I was. With my new hours at the bread shop, the website and blog, and digging around about Ben Nader and Sandra Mays, I'd been neglecting our May-December friendship.

She'd rolled down the window, the ocean breeze not ruffling a single curl of her snowy-white hair. Mrs. Branford had leisure sweat suits in every color of the rainbow. It was a rare occasion to see her in something other than velour. Today she had on a periwinkle number with white stripes running up the side. Her pristine white orthotic shoes kept her balanced as she walked. "What is your plan?" she asked above the sound of traffic and wind.

"I need you to create a distraction."

"And while I'm entertaining the women and children?" she asked.

"I'll be doing something you shouldn't know about."

"Ah yes, plausible deniability." She pressed a button on her door and her window zipped up, shutting out the sounds from outside. She patted her hair. Once she seemed satisfied that her curls were all still in place, she angled her body to the left, turning toward me. "Have you figured something out, then?"

I wish. "Not exactly. But there's something Esmé's not saying, and I feel like it's important."

"To intuit is an itch that must be scratched."

I chuckled. "Is that you or Kevin Shakespeare?"

"Dead as a doornail. Good riddance. What's done is done. Many of our idioms we owe to Kevin, but no, not that. That is all Penelope Lane Branford."

I spun my head to look at her. "Your middle name is Lane?"

The corner of her mouth quirked up. "It is. I spent a summer in Liverpool when I was a young girl."

My jaw dropped and my heartbeat ratcheted up. Was she saying . . . did she meet . . . was she the inspiration for . . . "Mrs. Branford, oh my God. Are you telling me . . . you are Penny Lane?"

She chuckled. Or maybe it was a chortle. "For heaven's sake, Ivy. For such a clever girl, you are far too gullible."

My heart slipped from my throat back into my chest. I exhaled. "Wait. So you're not?"

She had her cane resting on her thighs. She spun it absently. "My name is Penny Lane. Penelope Lane, technically, but everyone—except you, of course, calls me Penny."

My head spun. "So you are . . ."

"I'm not. Of course I'm not, Ivy. Penny Lane is a road in Liverpool."

"But the song . . . ?"

"The song is actually a reference to the Penny Lane bus station."

I thought about the lyrics. Did that make sense? "A bus station?"

"The story goes that Paul was sitting at the station waiting for John. While he waited, he noted things around him. A barber shop. A girl selling poppies from a tray. As Paul was known to do, he turned those notes and scribblings into a song. No girl involved at all. I've just had the good fortune of having the same name."

Which made for a good story. I slapped my hand against my chest. "If you'd met Paul McCartney and he wrote that song about you, I think I would have had a heart attack just now."

She chortled again. "Buck up. Your heart is just fine. Now, back to the plan," she said.

"Back to the plan," I agreed.

I'd called ahead to ask Vivian Cantrell if I could bring Mrs. Branford. "It's highly unusual," she'd said, but after I explained Mrs. Branford's background in education, she reluctantly agreed. I was glad Vivian was a bit loosey-goosey with her rules, but on the flip side, I wished she wasn't. It was a bit concerning.

I parked and led Mrs. Branford in, entering my code on the keyless entry system I'd been given access to. Inside, I gave Mrs. Branford a brief tour, then brought her to the living room. A few moms sat on the sofas while their children put together puzzles, watched *Sesame Street*, or drew at the table. It took all of five minutes for Mrs. Branford to command an audience. She began by picking up a book from a little stack on a side table. Before long, she was embellishing, and soon after that, she was telling a story about a little girl who'd stowed away on a pirate ship. The kids gathered round her, sitting cross-legged. They jumped when she pounded her cane against the floor, the sound mimicking the peg leg of the dastardly pirate ship captain. One of the mothers ran out to tell some of the other women to come listen. Slowly, they trickled in and before long, twelve of Crosby House's residents were

there. Meg and Angie both came in. Angie sat
on one of the armchairs, while Meg perched on
the arm. I hung back, half hiding in a corner,
waiting for Esmé to come.

Five minutes passed. Then ten. There was no
sign of her. Maybe she wasn't here. I debated.
Did I take the chance? The last thing I wanted
was for her to walk in on me searching her
room. But I had to follow my hunch.

I caught Mrs. Branford's eye and nodded my
head. I was going in. She nodded, knocked her
cane against the floor again to keep the attention on her, and I slipped away, racing down the
hallway to Esmé's room.

I looked up and down the hallway. No one was
in sight. I stepped up close to Esmé's door and
rapped my knuckles against it. Three quick
knocks in rapid succession. Nothing. I tried
again. No answer. The coast was clear. I turned
the knob, registering the irony that I was breaking and entering just like someone—maybe
Esmé—had done at my house. Did the fact that
I was trying to solve a murder justify my actions?
I wasn't sure, but I also wasn't going to stop to
think about it right now.

I closed the door behind me, turned, and
leaned back against it. For the second time in
less than an hour, my heart was beating like a
jackhammer. I surveyed the room. The bed was
rumpled. The lamp on the nightstand was on
and the blinds were open to the front. I remembered that Meg and Esmé had switched so that
Esmé could avoid the angular shadows of the tree

limbs in the backyard. That was a good friend. These women did look out for each other.

Something was different in the room. The books, I realized. They weren't on the night-stand anymore. I opened up the drawer to take a quick peek inside. No books on grieving, but there was a book on baking traditions in Mexico. I knew from being with her in the Bread for Life classes that Esmé was passionate about what she baked. I could see her taking the skills she already had, coupled with everything she was learning from Olaya, and going far with them. Maybe she'd decided her grieving was over. Or maybe she'd donated the books to the Crosby House library.

I'd come to get a closer look at the box in the closet. The one marked KM. I strode across the small room, slid open the closet door, and stared. There was no box. Clothes hung in the closet and several pairs of shoes, including the closed-toe black pair Esmé favored when work-ing in the kitchen. Were these the same clothes that had been hanging here before? I rifled through the contents on the shelf above the rod of clothes. Nothing of interest. Poor Esmé had escaped her situation with—what was his name? I thought back. Eduardo. Right. She'd escaped from Eduardo with hardly anything.

I wasn't sure what to make of the missing box. Where had she taken it? I was about to slip out the door again, but stopped at the last second at the dresser. The bottom drawer had held a baby blanket and some drawings. The drawer, when I pulled it open, however, was empty.

Empty. What in the world was going on?

I stood out in the hallway for a minute, trying to understand. Why would Esmé suddenly get rid of what seemed to be the only sentimental things she'd brought with her? I couldn't make sense of it.

Chapter 26

Five o'clock came and went. No Tammy Nader. No Kevin Nader. The bread shop was long closed. Maggie had left a few minutes before five, and Olaya had followed just after that. Now it was just me and the plate of skull cookies. I'd had to go on a little Easter egg hunt earlier to find them to put out, but I'd managed—without alarming Maggie—and had set them aside with a note that I'd be back and not to touch the cookies. I'd taken the fun out of the hunt for some little boy or little girl this afternoon, but it had to be done. I hoped it hadn't been for nothing.

By five fifteen I was beginning to wonder if I'd been stood up. I went out onto the sidewalk and stood under the awning, looking up and down the street. A woman strode down the street holding the hand of a boy, dragging him along with her. I threw my arm up, waving. She hadn't stood me up after all.

Tammy waved back, speeding up. The little guy dragged his feet. "She has cookies for you, Kev," I heard her say as they drew closer. If I'd hoped that cookies would make the boy happy, I was so wrong. He was the unhappiest looking nine-year-old I'd ever seen.

I greeted them and held the door open. Once the boy set eyes on the plate of cookies though, his face broke into a grin. He looked up at his grandmother. She patted his head, moving her hand to the back of his head and nudging him forward. "Help yourself."

Kevin bent over the table, examining each of the intricately decorated cookies. He looked up at both of us again. He was a cutie. Blond hair. Gray-blue eyes that came alive when he smiled. He looked small for his age, but puberty would catch him up. After Tammy and I both nodded at him, he chose a cookie, sat down, and started munching.

Now that I had them both here, I wasn't sure how to bring up the little boy's mother. I pulled Tammy aside. "Would you like something to drink?" I smiled. "Or a cookie?"

"They look good." She dipped her chin, her gaze softening as she looked at her grandson. "I haven't seen him smile like that since his grand-dad went into the hospital."

"How is Ben doing?"

Now her face lit up. "So much better. It's

going to be slow, but he's on the road to recovery, no question now."

"I'm so glad to hear it." I leaned back against the empty display case. "Mrs. Nader, I wonder if I could ask you a question."

She let her gaze leave her grandson. "Sure."

My voice dropped to somewhere just above a whisper. "Where's Kevin's mom?"

She eyed me, suddenly wary. "I told you before, Meg was in the accident with our son—"

"Meg, for Margaret?"

"That's right." Her eyes narrowed. "Why?"

"I was just . . . wondering. I know your son died, but not his fiancée—"

She'd been relaxed, but now she stood up straight, her arms folded over her chest like a barricade. "You looked up my son's accident?"

When she said it aloud, it sounded kind of on the creepy side. Before I could offer up an explanation, though, she snapped at me. "Is that why you asked us here? To interrogate me about my family?"

"It's not an interr—"

I broke off when her glare intensified. *It wasn't an interrogation*, I finished in my head. It was one question.

She strode to Kevin, grabbed him by the arm and yanked him up. "We have to go now," she told him, somehow managing to soften her voice for him.

"Where is she?" I asked again, but she surged out the door, dragging her grandson with her.

Chapter 27

Maybe I'd been wrong. I'd had a suspicion that Esmé had been Grant Nader's fiancée. The one who hadn't actually died in the car accident, but who also didn't have custody of her child. It would give a motive for the hit-and-run Ben was the victim of. Esmé didn't have a firm alibi. She'd gone her own separate way from the other Bread for Life women, returning after the accident. She could have had her car stashed, run him down, stashed the car again, and then gotten rid of it. It was possible.

But maybe not very probable. It wouldn't have been premeditated, and relied too much on being at the so-called right place at the right time to run him down. There was the fact that little Kevin looked nothing like Esmé. And finally there was Sandra Mays. What would the motive be?

Blackmail. I thought about the falling-out Sandra and Tammy Nader had. The timing corre-
sponded with the death of the Naders' son. But
what was at the core of their detonated friendship? That was the unknown.

I had a thought. I went to Olaya's office,
pulled up her contacts, and looked up Mack Hebron's number, hoping he'd simmered down
since I'd seen him last. Pulling out my cell
phone, I dialed him. He was still a suspect in my
mind, but if I stuck with my current train of
thought, I had to figure out how to connect Sandra and Ben through a motive. He answered
right away with a breezy, "Hello?"

"Mr. Hebron, it's Ivy. Culpepper."

"Mack," he said. "We're way beyond Mr. Hebron—if we were ever there."

"Right. Mack. Listen, I have a quick question
for you."

"Another one?"

He sounded normal, so maybe he was over
the so-called interrogation. Maybe I needed to
soften my methods, I thought, since I'd gotten
the interrogation accusation twice now. I'd considered how to phrase my question delicately,
but I decided to just forge ahead, sticking with
the direct approach. "Do you know anything
about the type of relationship Ben Nader had
with Sandra Mays?"

He didn't miss a beat. "Do you mean were *they*
intimate?"

That's not what I meant because I was pretty
sure they had never crossed that line. "No, not
that. I know they'd been friends for a long time.

Their kids were in a playgroup together when they were little."

"That's more than I knew."

Ah. Too bad. If he didn't know that, he wouldn't know about their falling-out. I asked anyway. "Something happened between Ben's wife and Sandra years ago, but I'm not sure what. Do you have any idea?"

"Sorry," he said. "Can't help you."

I sighed. "Thanks anyway."

"Sure thing."

I said goodbye and started to hang up when his voice came at me again. "Wait. There is one thing," he said.

"What's that?" I asked.

"I overheard them talking the morning of the accident. It was before we got to Yeast of Eden."

I was all ears. "Talking about what?"

He was silent on the other end of the line. For a second, I wondered if he was still there, but then he cleared his throat. "I didn't catch it all. She said he wouldn't be able to keep it quiet, and he said he didn't want to anymore. Something like that."

"Keep what quiet?" I asked.

"I have no idea."

I wondered why he hadn't mentioned this before.

"I just remembered," he said, as if he'd read my mind. "I tend to tune out other people's chatter."

He couldn't give me any more information, but what little he did give felt like a thread between Ben and Sandra. There was *something*.

We hung up and I went back to my thoughts

about Esmé. I didn't want her to be involved, but something she said came back to me. Everyone has a story. Everyone has heartache. In a split second, my entire thought process shifted. When I'd spoken to Ben Nader in the hospital, the color had drained from his face after I mentioned that I'd volunteered at Crosby House . . . but not because of Esmé.

I reorganized the information in my head. The baby blanket and picture book in the bottom drawer of Esmé's dresser. The baby blanket and sketchbook had to be very personal to the owner. I'd assumed they'd been hers, but what if—

Esmé had just moved into that room. Meg had been surprised that it had happened without her knowledge. Her words came back to me. They—presumably organized by Vivian Cantrell—moved Mickey. They'd put her in a different room. Esmé had been moved in, but she didn't like the tree. Meg had said she'd offered to switch and they'd moved her there. They'd moved her. Meg and Esmé hadn't moved their own things, they'd been moved for them. And the contents of the bottom drawer had been left behind.

Another image of Meg came to me. When I'd first seen her, she'd been watching me work on the keyhole garden. Vivian Cantrell had come to talk to her about a therapy appointment, but she'd also given her a set of keys and said something about her car being ready.

Her car.

I grabbed my phone and dialed Crosby House. Vivian Cantrell picked up on the second

ring. "What can I do for you, Ivy?" she asked
after the pleasantries were over.

"I have a random question for you, actually," I
said.

"I'll help you if I can."

That was the best I could hope for. Vivian
Cantrell's job, after all, was to protect the women
in her charge. She wouldn't throw one of them
under the bus just because someone asked for
some information. "The first day I met Meg, you
gave her some keys and said something about
her car?"

She didn't hesitate. "That's right. Her car had
been in for repairs. I know the shop owner and
he returned it here for her. Why?"

The hairs on the back of my neck stood on
end. Had it gone in the shop before or after the
attempt on Ben Nader's life? "When did she
take it in for repair?"

Now Vivian Cantrell did hesitate. "What's this
about?"

I'd thought about how to answer this question. I didn't have a good response . . . or at least
one that wouldn't raise suspicion. I went with
something as close to the truth as I could. "I'm
going to be honest with you. I'm afraid that Meg
may have had something to do with the accident
that put Ben Nader in the hospital."

The sentence hung there between us like a
spider web blocking a doorway to freedom. Finally, she spoke. "That's not possible. Meg, she's
a good girl. She's been through so much."

I hadn't asked about Meg's story, and she'd
never offered, but she was at Crosby House for a

reason—just like every other woman there. Everyone here was a victim, but cycles repeated. Victims often became abusers. Maybe murderers in this case. "When did she take the car in?" I repeated.

"She took it in a week ago Monday," Vivian said after a moment.

So before the hit-and-run, I thought. But that didn't coincide with my new theory. I still didn't have a motive, but I was beginning to think that maybe Meg had been behind the wheel of the car that mowed down Ben Nader. How could that be, if she hadn't had her car at that time? "What repair shop was it in?" I asked.

Another hesitation. Just when I thought Vivian Cantrell wasn't going to give me the information I'd asked for, she exhaled. "Bishop's. Ask for Ethan."

My mind circled through the things I knew . . . or thought I knew. "What's Meg's story?"

"I'm afraid I can't divulge the private information of our clients."

Of course she couldn't.

I couldn't even begin to fathom the depths of the holes any of these women had had to climb out of. But that didn't give a person a pass for murder.

Vivian Cantrell exhaled a heavy breath out. "It often happens that after a tragedy, women put themselves into risky situations. They cease to care about what happens to them. Unfortunately, we see a lot of that. Meg's been fighting against that very thing. She's doing well, though."

Not so well if she killed Sandra and tried to kill Ben. I thought about calling Emmaline, but

I had no motive, only a sketchy idea with zero proof. I thanked Mrs. Cantrell, hung up, and looked up the address for Bishop's Auto Body Repair. I plugged it into my GPS and ten minutes later, I'd parked and was inside the lobby of the shop. Ethan Bishop was a small, thin man. I wore sneakers and stood slightly taller than him. He had piercing dark eyes and a pronounced jawline, and a chin that angled to a point. To me, he looked like he should be running a moody basement club in San Francisco rather than a car repair shop, but then I probably looked like I should be a librarian or bookstore clerk. And yet here we both were.

I cut to the chase. "I understand you recently did some work on Meg McGinnis's car."

His eyes narrowed and his lips thinned as he seemed to consider whether or not he should be talking to me.

"It's important," I said.

He tapped on the computer keyboard, bringing up the repair records. "Blue Hyundai Elantra. Needed some front body work."

I felt a rush of electricity zing through my body. "Was there anything . . . unusual . . . about the repair?"

"Mmm. Not really." He paused. "Except . . ."

He stopped, as if he needed prodding to divulge just what was so unusual. "What was it?"

"It came in with some front-end damage. I told her it was going to need a new front bumper. I had to order that, and with the painting, it'd take a good week. She left it here."

"Is that unusual?" I asked.

"No, not that. But when the parts arrived and I brought the car into the bay to start the work, the damage was worse than I remembered."

And there it was. Maybe this whole thing had been premeditated. Bring the car to the shop and leave it, but sneak in to take it for a joyride. It had been a risk. What if the car hadn't been accessible? But the fact was, it had been. I might not be able to prove my theory and it didn't give me a motive, but it was enough to share with Emmaline.

I thanked him and left, immediately calling Emmaline and filling her in on my theory. She'd take over and do her own legwork.

"Nice deductions, Ivy."

I smiled at the compliment and gave myself a mental pat on the back. The next thing to do was figure out if Meg was behind Sandra Mays's death . . . and why.

Chapter 28

I'd spent all day at the bread shop, pondering everything I'd learned about Ben Nader, Sandra Mays, Esmé Adriá, and Meg McGinnis. I felt like I had all the ingredients to make a killer loaf of rosemary bread . . . minus the rosemary. The answer would come to me.

Miguel had taken the evening off from the restaurant. He'd been working himself ragged and needed a little reprieve. I planned to bake us a loaf of bread to go with the soup he'd brought home from Baptista's. I drove, thinking about how much more I appreciated Santa Sofia as an adult versus when I'd been a teenager. Even with the tourist element, it was a quaint, comfortable coastal town that held my heart. It had an eclectic mix of neighborhoods, which was one of the things I loved best about it. My Tudor was part of the historic district. Queen Anne Victorians, Craftsman style homes, a few mid-century moderns, and homes like mine lived on the tree-lined streets there. Cute little cottages defined the Beach Road area. The closer you were to Pacific Coast Highway, the smaller, and more expensive, the cottage. High-end gated communities with massive properties dotted the mountains, and traditional suburban homes sprawled inland, stretching the boundaries of our little coastal town.

One of the most desirable areas was Bungalow Oasis in what the locals called the Upper Laguna District. It was one of the town's oldest neighborhoods and held the highest concentration of traditional bungalow architecture. The area was filled with single-story, low-rise houses with curving roads, verandas, and mature landscaping. Malibu Street sat to the east and Riviera to the south, and an architectural review board was an active part of the Santa Sofia Bungalow Oasis Neighborhood Association.

Miguel had bought his house in Bungalow Oasis as a major fixer-upper. He'd worked painstakingly to restore it to its historical beauty, redoing the stucco siding, landscaping the knoll it sat on, painting the house, along with the single-car garage at the lowest point on the right, and resurfacing the red terra-cotta-tiled stairway on the left leading up to a wrought-iron gate. He'd planted green leafy shrubs on both sides of the railing that led up to the front steps, and he constantly tended colorful flowers in the massive cement pots on the pillars at the top of the steps.

I loved my house, but I also loved his house. What we'd do if we ever broached the subject of spending our lives together, who knew? I couldn't see either of us willingly giving up our respective homes. Miguel's Mediterranean-style house had a courtyard with a single tree, manicured shrubs, and bountiful flowerbeds. The veranda, which gave him a picturesque view of the Pacific, was draped with cascading flowers. The whole place sent a gentle breeze of relaxation through me.

Miguel greeted and kissed me in the doorway, then ushered me in, taking the reusable shopping bag I had slung over my shoulder. I'd brought my preferred flour, a jar of yeast, my proofing bowl, and the rosemary and olives I'd need for the bread I'd be making.

We walked through the entry to the living room. He had the sliding glass doors opened to the veranda, the cool ocean breeze billowing in. Miguel had made the outside a welcoming living area with potted patio trees and more flowers. Miguel, former military man and current restaurateur, loved flowers.

He'd created two distinct areas on the veranda. One had a small bistro table with two chairs on a round sisal rug. The other had a rattan loveseat, two matching chairs, and a small outdoor coffee table. The square sisal rug defined the seating space as separate from the dining space. I breathed in the salty air, feeling it spread through my body all the way to the tips of my fingers and toes.

Downtown Santa Sofia was to the south and was walkable from Bungalow Oasis. Miguel often rode his bike to the restaurant. That was a definite perk of living in this area, but the real gem was the view straight ahead. The Pacific lay vast and wide, a reminder of how small we all are in the scope of our world. I gazed out at the horizon, wishing I'd brought my camera. I wanted to capture every sunset so I could look back on each one and remember the moment.

Miguel came up behind me and wrapped his arms around me. The stubble on his face pricked and tickled my skin, sending a quiver through me. It was a sensation I never wanted to live without. How had we been lucky enough to find each other again?

"I need to start the bread," I said after I'd had my fill—at least for now—of him and the ocean.

He led me through the living area, past his dining table, to the galley kitchen. It was smaller than mine, and shaped differently, but it was efficient. Everything was within reach and there was plenty of counter space. Miguel had spared no expense with his commercial-grade stainless steel appliances. They blew mine out of the water and I loved cooking with him here.

I got to work as Miguel poured us each a glass of wine. He sat at the table, half watching me work, half mapping out the specials for the month ahead.

I pounded down a mound of dough in his kitchen. He watched me with one eyebrow cocked. "Glad you're taking that aggression of yours out on that dough."

It wasn't aggression. It was clarity. With each pound of my fist, I understood a fraction more. "It's Meg. The woman who helped me with the garden at Crosby House," I said.

"The short Irish one or the tall dark-haired one?"

"Irish."

"What about her?"

"It's her car that ran down Ben Nader. I know it is, but I don't know why."

"And Sandra Mays?"

"I keep coming back to Tammy Nader."

"What's her motive?"

I sank my fist into the dough for the last time. "They had a falling out. But Mack Hebron overheard Sandra and Ben talking, with Ben saying something about not keeping it a secret anymore."

My mind circled back to what Miguel had said a moment ago. Meg was Irish. Vivian Cantrell had told me that one of the women had lost her boyfriend and her son. What if—

"What's wrong?" Miguel asked.

I spun around to face him. "Margaret."

He cocked an eyebrow waiting for me to continue.

"Tammy Nader said her son's fiancée died in the crash that killed her son, but the newspaper article I found said she survived." I stopped. Thought back. Had she actually said the fiancée had died, or had I made an assumption?

"Okay," Miguel said.

"The fiancée's name was . . . or is . . . Margaret."

Miguel's expression changed, showing his understanding. "Meg."

"A nickname for Margaret." A chill ran up my spine. Had we figured it out? Were Meg from

Crosby House and Margaret, the mother of little Kevin, one and the same?

Another realization hit me. KM. The K was for Kevin.

I went to the table. Miguel had a lazy Susan filled with condiments. I held up the salt shaker. "Let's say this is Meg McGinnis."

"Okay." He sat down. "Go on."

Next was the pepper shaker. "Esmé Adriá."

He pointed to the little bottle of sesame oil. "Who's this?"

"Tammy Nader."

"And the spicy chili oil is . . ."

"Mack Hebron."

"Let's say that Ben is the soy sauce, and Sandra is the oregano." I looked at the six objects, feeling like there was a missing ingredient.

"What about the other women with the Bread for Life program?" Miguel asked, holding up the garlic bulb. "You're sure none of them are involved?"

"None of them have a particular connection to Ben or Sandra."

"But does this Meg McGinnis have a connection to Sandra?"

I sighed. Heavily. "Not that we've found. Em looked at all their backgrounds. They're all immigrants. Zula's from Eritrea. Claire's from Canada. Amelie is from Germany, and Esmé is from Mexico. Only Esmé has a connection to Ben through the shelter. But it was Meg's car—I know it was—that hit Ben."

"They're friends?" he asked, and just like that, I had an epiphany. I'd seen the bond grow be-

tween the women in the Bread for Life program,
just like the bonds would grow between the
women at the shelter. Except . . . Meg had shown
me Esmé's room. She just hadn't known that all
her own stuff hadn't yet been moved from
Esmé's room to her new one. Or had she? *She
had*, I realized. She had been trying to direct my
thinking toward Esmé and away from anyone
else.

"I'm not so sure," I said, answering his question.

I looked at it from Esmé's perspective. She
had disappeared for several days after Ben's accident. Why? She'd told me she didn't know
what to do, or what to think. Because she'd suspected Meg, which had put her in a conundrum? Had she recognized the blue car? Had
she voiced her suspicions to her friend, or had
she kept quiet?

I suspected that she'd voiced them, which is
why Esmé had become so scattered and distant.
She was completely freaked out, and maybe Meg
was trying to convince her to keep quiet.

Miguel lifted the bottle of oregano and the
soy sauce. "Sandra and Ben were talking about a
secret." He tapped the chili oil. "Which Mack
overheard."

"When I went to see Ben in the hospital, I told
him I'd worked with Meg, and that I knew Esmé.
He turned pale and I thought he'd reacted to
Esmé's name, but it was Meg."

Meg was also an immigrant. Just like Esmé,
she'd come here before, and she'd come back.
It's where she met Grant Nader. It's where she

had her child. Why had she not been back for so many years? Why had the Naders not helped her to be with her child?

I pictured her face. The angles of her cheek. The scar above her lip. And then something Tammy said came back to me and my blood ran cold.

I grabbed my purse, digging out my keys. They were heavy in my hand. Keys. I turned them over, thinking. Keys. But whatever thought was on the edge of my brain, it was gone. Our dinner was all but forgotten. "Let's go see Tammy Nader," I said.

Chapter 29

"Meg may have tried to run down Ben, but that doesn't explain Sandra," Miguel said from the passenger seat of my car.

That was true, but I could only operate based on what I currently knew. Or thought I knew. I needed confirmation from Tammy that my thought process was on target. One thing at a time. I had a question I had to ask Tammy Nader. After that was answered I could move on to the Sandra conundrum.

It was only as we started out of Miguel's driveway that I realized I didn't actually know where Tammy and Ben Nader lived. Emmaline wasn't likely to give me the address without a full explanation of my reason. I wasn't ready to give her that quite yet. "Change of plans," I said, and I redirected the car inland.

A short while later, we arrived at Mercy Hospital.

"Ben," Miguel said.

"Ben," I agreed.

Up on the fourth floor, I knocked before we entered his room, but stopped short. Tammy sat in the same chair I had, facing the side of Ben's bed. Ben sat upright, casts on one arm and one leg, his face and what I could see of his arms black and blue. For as bad as his injuries looked, though, he looked better than he had the last time I'd seen him.

"What do you want?" Tammy demanded, standing with such force that her chair shot back and hit the wall.

I moved into the room, Miguel right behind me. "I'm really sorry to bother you," I said, and I was. "I won't be long. I just have a question for you both." Maybe two, I thought, but I wanted to keep it casual to start.

Tammy's face turned red. "Get out," she snarled, but Ben raised his good arm and said, "Tammy, stop." He sounded tired. Exhausted, in fact. "We need to stop."

"Mrs. Nader, I think I know who's behind this." I leveled my gaze at her. "But you do, too, don't you?"

The color drained from her face until she was pallid. She sank back onto her chair. "What do you know?" she asked, but the bite was gone from her voice.

"I know that your son's fiancée survived the accident that killed him. She was spared. Your grandson was spared."

"What are you talk—"

"Meg. I'm talking about Meg. She has a scar

above her lip, and another on her arm. I thought she was at Crosby House because she'd been battered like the other women," I said. "That she was escaping from some horrible situation. But it wasn't like that, was it?"

Tammy was as still as a statue. Not a muscle moved. But Ben answered. "No. It wasn't like that."

"Those scars, they're from the car accident that killed Grant, aren't they?"

This time Ben gave a nearly imperceptible nod.

Meg's situation became a little clearer. "Did you keep Kevin from her?" I asked, more horrified. She hadn't lost her son. Her child had been ripped away from her.

Ben cupped his hand over his forehead. "It was wrong," he said. "We never should have—"

He stopped when Tammy slowly stood and started for the door.

"Tammy, wait." Ben's voice rose above the beeping of the monitors he was hooked up to.

She stopped. "You're not going to take him from me." Her voice was low. Measured. But I sensed she was walking a fine line between control and an emotional break.

I shot Miguel a frantic glance, nodding to his phone. He understood exactly what I was trying to tell him. He angled his body so Tammy couldn't see, but from where I stood, I could see his fingers flying across the keyboard as he texted Emmaline. She and her cavalry would be here within minutes to stop Tammy from getting Kevin, wherever he was, and disappearing with him. I'd suspected Meg, but I hadn't understood what was behind the hit-and-run. Now I did. Meg had lost her fiancé and Tammy and Ben had kept her son from her. She'd been trapped in Ireland without him, probably with no proof of his birth, and with no money or recourse to fight for him. I didn't know why she'd waited ten years, but I wanted to give her the benefit of the doubt. She only wanted her child back.

I wanted that for her.

Another thought occurred to me. Ben had told Tammy about the ladder to the roof at Yeast of Eden's building. Tammy and Sandra had had a falling out. What if Sandra had figured out that Meg was back? What if she'd confronted Ben or Tammy about it? "What about Sandra?" I asked her.

She laughed, high and shrill and more than a little unhinged. "She got what she deserved."

The reason for their falling out, I thought. "She knew about Meg?"

Tammy glared at her husband. "You told her about everything. That Margaret was alive, but that we'd kept Kevin. You confessed your sins to her and then she tried to blackmail me. She said she'd tell everyone."

Ben choked out a sob. "Why didn't you tell me?"

"Because you were weak. You wanted to give Grant back!"

We all stared at Tammy, slack-jawed.

"You mean Kevin," Ben said quietly.

Tammy backed up, her arms flailing, looking like a trapped animal. "Wh-what do you mean?"

"Grant is dead, Tammy. And we were wrong to

take Kevin from his mother. Grant loved Margaret. He wanted to marry her—"

Tammy slammed her hands over her ears, violently shaking her head, but Ben continued, his voice low. "Did you kill Sandra?"

Tammy's eyes grew wide. Crazed. "Her death was like a gift. It was so much like a gift, like I was being told that I'd done the right thing because she couldn't hurt us. She couldn't take Grant away from us."

Oh my. The woman was truly losing her mind right in front of us.

"Kevin," Ben corrected.

"But Meg is the boy's mother—" I started.

"I am Grant's mother—"

"Tammy." The quiet voice came from Ben.

Tammy kept on. "I am his mother—"

"Grant is dead!" Ben's voice sounded with the force of a cannonball. "He loved Margaret. They were a family, and we took Kevin from her. *We* did this to her. We. Did. This. To. Her." He broke down into a sob. "To *them.*"

"Did you kill her?" I asked. I thought Tammy was unhinged enough to give me the truth.

"Not me. Not me." She wagged her finger at me. "I didn't kill her, but I wish I had."

That wasn't the confession I'd hoped for. I changed direction, turning to Ben, but keeping an eye on Tammy. "You volunteered at Crosby House and saw her there?"

"It was a true coincidence. I've volunteered at the shelter for years. Long before Margaret and her mother came into the picture there." His face paled and his voice dropped to a whisper.

"It was like seeing a ghost. She went by Meg, though. At first I wasn't sure. I thought my eyes were playing tricks on me, but—"

"Meg is a nickname for Margaret."

He dropped his chin to his chest. "It was like she walked out of my nightmares."

"I bet it was." She'd haunted him. I thought that was why he volunteered at Crosby House. To make amends.

Ben kept talking, cleansing his guilty soul. "She was there in the office one day when I went to talk to the director. Sitting there, plain as day. She didn't see me, and I ducked out. I tried to stay out of her way."

I thought back to when I'd asked Meg about Ben Nader the first time. She'd played me, I realized now, but I couldn't blame her. She had a lot at stake.

We heard rapid footsteps in the hallway. The cavalry, I thought. Tammy looked at the door, panicked. "You called the police?"

She grabbed the door handle like she was going to barge into the hallway. Instead, she let go, turned abruptly, and beelined for the bathroom. Emmaline rounded the corner into the room, her arm straight at her side, her gun in her hand pointed at the ground. A deputy slid in right behind her.

Tammy stopped cold.

"It's over, Tam," Ben said with a sob. "Thank God it's over."

Chapter 30

"Help me understand," Emmaline said to Meg. They sat in an interview room at the sheriff's station. Miguel and I stood on the other side of the one-way mirror, observing. "You were in the States on a tourist visa?"

"I was here on an H1-B visa as an international teacher, but it expired. Grant and I, we were engaged. We had Kevin. We left him here with Grant's parents while we went back to Ireland so I could . . . then we had the . . ."

"The accident," Em finished.

Meg swiped away a tear. "I almost died. My mam nursed me back, but by the time I was well, so much time had passed. I had to save money to come back—my mam and I, we're just ordinary people. And then I didn't know how to prove I was . . . that I am Kevin's mother."

I could see Em's blood boiling. It was as if the

stars had aligned against Meg reuniting with her son. "The Naders wouldn't help you?"

She scoffed through her tears. "Help me? They wouldn't even acknowledge me. They acted like they didn't know me. And then one day when I showed up at their house again, Grant's mother—Tammy—she . . . she threatened me."

"Threatened you how?"

Meg swallowed. Hard. Swiped at her tears. "She told me she would never let me take Kevin away from her. I b-believed her."

"What did you believe she'd do?" Em asked.

Em looked up. Down. Everywhere but at Emmaline. She tried to school her face, keeping more tears at bay. "Kill me? Hurt Kevin?" Her face collapsed. "I don't know. I was scared."

"What did you do?" Em asked quietly.

Meg wrung her hands. "I went home."

"To Ireland?" Emmaline asked.

She looked back up at Emmaline, the tears flowing now. "What else could I do?"

"And you came back when—"

"My mother and I, we saved enough money to come back."

Emmaline nodded. Paused, then changed directions. "Tell me about Sandra Mays."

"Is Kevin safe?" Meg asked. "Is he still with them?"

"Kevin is safe. He is with a foster family. Ben Nader does not want to press charges. With the extenuating circumstances, a judge will take that into consideration. He's safe, Meg. I want to get him back to you, but you need to help me."

Meg dragged her hands under her eyes and sniffed. "I didn't do it."

"Tell me about Sandra," Em said again.

"I don't know Sandra. I never met her."

Emmaline pressed. "Did you plan a meeting with her on the roof at Yeast of Eden?"

Meg shook her head emphatically. "No! Never. I did not do that to her. I did not kill her!"

Em took a breath. "Okay. Let's go back to the hit-and-run. Tell me about that."

"I didn't do it," Meg repeated. "It wasn't me."

"Meg, it was your car that hit him. We've had forensics go over it. We've compared it to the video we have. It was your car. You hit Ben Nader."

Meg had her elbows propped on the table and cradled her head in her hands. "But I didn't. You have to believe me. I didn't hit him."

Emmaline paused. Regrouped. I could see her patience wearing thin and I didn't blame her, but Meg was convincing. I kind of *did* believe her. Or at least I wanted to.

"Your car was in the shop, is that right?" Emmaline asked.

"Right. It needed a new bumper."

"And how did you get the damage to the bumper?"

Meg had been looking at the table, but she looked up suddenly, something in her eyes. Clarity? Understanding? "Oh no."

It hit me at the very same moment. That day at the shelter. The keys. "Oh my God."

Miguel turned to me. "What is it?"

"It wasn't Meg."

"What?" He stared, first at me, then through the mirror.

"It wasn't Meg. It wasn't Meg!" I backhanded his arm. "Let's go."

I pounded on the door of the interview room. I knew Emmaline would get there eventually with Meg, but I also suspected that the young woman would do what she could to hide the truth she'd just realized. Emmaline cracked open the door, looking more than a little irritated.

"We've got it wrong," I said. "We have to go to Crosby House."

Twenty minutes later, we arrived at Crosby House like a mini caravan. Two cruisers, Emmaline in her police SUV. Miguel and me in my pearl-white Fiat crossover.

We parked along the street, out of sight. Standing on the sidewalk, Emmaline put on her stern *I'm the sheriff* expression as she adjusted the wide black hairband that held back the tiny Z curls of her hair. "You need to wait. Don't be going all *Dirty Harry*."

I scoffed. It was only because Billy was a huge Clint Eastwood fan that she even knew about *Dirty Harry*. "You need to update your pop culture reference for vigilante," I said. "Maybe don't go all Walt Kowalski."

"That's Eastwood, too," Miguel said.

"And who the hell is Walt Kowalski?" Em asked.

"*Gran Torino*," I said.

"Still Clint Eastwood, so might as well be *Dirty Harry*—"

"Bryan Mills?" I interrupted. "Much more current."

They both looked at me, Em with perfectly arched raised eyebrows. "And who is that?"

"Liam Neeson? You know, in *Taken*?"

She rolled her eyes. "The point is, which I know you know, but to underscore it . . . Wait. For. Me."

"Yes, ma'am," I said.

And then I froze. Thought. *Ma'am. Or was it Mam?* "I'm so right, by the way."

One of the deputies handed Miguel and me each a Kevlar vest. "You want to come along to capture a murderer, you wear the gear," Em said.

Miguel was already putting his bulletproof vest on over his button-down shirt. "You won't get any arguments from me."

She waited while I put mine on. "No arguments from me, either."

"She does not have a gun," Meg said through her sobs, but I wondered if she could know that for certain. She fumbled as she put on her vest, barely holding it together.

Emmaline ordered Miguel and me to stand back as we all approached the building. Her team was at the front entrance to the shelter, guns drawn. She stood slightly off to the side with Meg next to her.

One of the deputies knocked on the door and called, "Vivian Cantrell!"

Miguel inched closer to me, edging his elbow slightly in front of mine. He was in protection mode. If either of our shoulders got shot, his would be first. "How'd you figure it out?" he asked, his voice low.

Finally, I got to explain. "It was all there from the beginning, but I wasn't connecting the dots. Vivian gave Meg a set of keys the first time I was here. I realized later that they had to be the keys to Meg's car."

"So she'd planned it?" Miguel mused, more to himself than as a question to me. "She made sure Meg took it to the shop, then Vivian went to get it, hoping the rest of the damage would pass as part of the first."

"Right. That's basically what the mechanic thought," I said, remembering what he'd said about it looking like someone had taken the car for a joyride.

"So it was revenge?"

"It makes sense. The Naders took her daughter's child."

"But how did you figure out Meg is her daughter? Since they have different last names?"

"It was one thing, actually. I remembered the first time I saw Meg and Vivian together. I couldn't hear their whole conversation, but I did hear Meg say, "Thank you, ma'am. I'd thought she was so polite, but that wasn't it. She called her *mam*, like *mom*. Her Irish accent came out more then. Vivian's got a little accent, too, but I couldn't place it. She worked hard to disguise it. Meg's ebbed and flowed."

Shouting came at us from the entrance of

Crosby House. Vivian Cantrell stood there with her arms up.

Miguel and I strode toward them. The stand-off had started and ended peacefully with Vivian standing stoically as Emmaline read Vivian her Miranda rights. She let Em take one arm down behind her back, then the other, cuffing them together.

Meg sobbed. "Why, Mam? Why?"

"Why? Margaret, I went to them on your behalf. That woman, she threatened to kill me if I didn't take you and leave here. When I went to Ben and told him what his wife had said he said he couldn't do anything. There was nothing they could do. She would never give Kevin up."

"Why Ben?" she asked. "He might have come around."

"*They* took your son from you. *They* took my grandson."

Vivian had gone from calling her daughter Meg to calling her by her given name. That simple act seemed to underscore the woman Meg used to be. The woman who'd lost everything thanks to the Naders.

"And Sandra Mays?" I asked, suddenly believing Tammy's declaration that she hadn't killed Sandra.

Vivian's face had collapsed, ten years of grief suddenly imprinted on her. "That woman was vile."

I thought about all Sandra's attitude and how difficult she'd been. I couldn't argue with Vivian's assessment, but being an awful person shouldn't lead to murder.

"She knew what the Naders did and she let it happen. She should have gone to the police," Vivian continued.

The reason for Tammy and Sandra's falling-out so many years ago.

Meg stared at her mother. "She knew they took Kevin?"

She was calm. Cool. Collected. She'd been on a mission. Only Tammy had been left.

"She knew everything."

"Did you try to blackmail Tammy and Ben?" I asked, suddenly putting another piece of the puzzle together.

"Me, blackmail? Pah! No. I confronted Ben one day outside the bread shop. Esmé—she was very helpful, letting me know the filming schedule," Vivian said. "I told him that I would take Kevin back. I was done waiting. He cried. He said he was trying to fix things, but his wife wouldn't agree. When I left, that woman . . . that Sandra Mays . . . she'd been there. She heard the whole thing. After the car . . . accident . . . she sent me a message telling me to meet her. To climb a ladder and meet her on the roof. Ridiculous, but what could I do? It was poetic, she said, because Ben had told her about the ladder and the roof. She was going to vindicate him there."

So Ben had told Sandra. I knew he had.

"Mam," Meg said through a sob. "You didn't . . ."

"She said she knew what I'd done to Ben. That she saw me in the car."

"You took the car from the shop?" Meg asked, sniffling. Trying to control the emotions crashing through her. On one level, she had to be destroyed by what her mother had done for her, but on another level, she knew she'd be getting her son back, and that was thanks to her mother. I didn't envy the poor woman . . . or Kevin.

"I picked it up from the shop. Ethan Bishop, he never saw me. I did that for several days, following Ben. Waiting for the right moment. And then there it was. He came out of the shop and crossed the street. There were no other cars in the way. I didn't even know for sure that I was going to do it, but my foot hit the pedal. I was outside of myself. I ran him over and drove the car straight back to the auto shop."

I wondered how this petite woman, who was slight and willowy, could have overpowered Sandra on top of the roof. As if she'd read my mind, Emmaline asked the question for me, but Vivian shrugged as if she didn't know the answer. Couldn't possibly explain it. "It just happened. I did not plan it. She threatened me and I pushed her. She fell and hit her head and was . . . was . . . gone. I didn't mean for her to die."

And there it was. The attempted murder of Ben and Sandra's accident were connected after all.

Chapter 31

"Yeast of Eden's Bread for Life program has been a resounding success. The inaugural cohort of women—one from Eritrea, one from Canada, one from Mexico, and one from Germany, have learned the basics of baking bread from the bread shop's founder and head baker, Olaya Solis. Born of tradition, the bread baked at Yeast of Eden follows the long rise, farm-to-table, every-loaf-by-hand philosophy, and those are exactly the principles Ms. Solis has taught to her first set of Bread for Life students.

"As part of our new show, entitled *America's Best Bakeries*, I had the pleasure of meeting the Bread for Life cohorts and seeing firsthand the impact this program and this establishment has and will continue to have on their lives."

Mack Hebron paused before saying, "Cut."

As Tae stopped filming, the women in the

bread shop's kitchen applauded. Mack had asked to come back to film. He wanted to feature additional footage on the cable station's online platform. "Additional content for our viewers," he said.

Claire was up. She was the quietest of the four women, and it showed. She looked down at her countertop rather than up at her audience—us—but once she got going, she seemed to forget that Tae was filming at all.

"Bannock," she said in her soft voice, "was called the bread of First Nations. Meaning the Squamish and Lil'wat Nations. There is no yeast in it. Only baking powder."

"So it is a simple leavened bread," Olaya interjected.

"It was originally made with cornmeal and flour that was made from ground-up turnip bulbs, then cooked like Esmé's Mexican bread over an open fire or in a pit."

"Heavy and flat, yes?" Olaya asked.

Claire nodded. "The Scottish made it, but with oats, and it was more like scones. When the Europeans introduced flour to our continent, bannock got better, but not by much. Nobody actually wanted it. But now? It has become . . . erm . . . glamorized," Claire said, warming up to her topic. "In Canada now, you can find it in farm-to-table bistros and bakeries. It's gotten fancy."

She took us through the making of the bread, warning us not to overwork the dough. "It must be light. Airy. It is different than the yeast breads we've made." We formed our lumpy rounds of dough and pushed our trays into Olaya's commercial ovens.

"You have all done it," Olaya said. Tae was still filming as Maggie came into the kitchen. She ushered in Meg, Kevin in tow. I waved at them all. Maggie grinned . . . at Tae.

Meg's smile was tempered by the reality of what her mother had done, but she had her son back, and that was amazing. I felt for her, but at the same time, I was thrilled that she'd been reunited with Kevin.

"You are incredible women," Olaya continued, her gaze taking in Meg. She gave her a nod, including her in the collective group. "Whatever you do from here on out, share your love of baking, of bread, and give of yourself to empower others."

Chapter 32

I was exhausted by the time it was all over, but I went home to freshen up, took Agatha to Mrs. Branford's, and headed back to Baptista's to meet Emmaline for dinner. She'd beaten me there and stood waiting under the awning at the entrance.

"Who hit your car?" she asked me.

So much had happened between the night I'd been followed and now that it seemed like a vague memory.

"Heather."

She gaped. "As in Luke's Heather?"

I nodded. "She went off the rails, but it's okay now." I didn't tell her about the breaking and entering, the theft of my electric toothbrush, or the phone calls. I was putting it behind me. Luke and Heather could have each other. I was done with both of them.

I hoped.

I looped my arm through Em's and we went

in to be seated for dinner. I stopped at the hostess station to say hello to Miguel's mother. She stood up from the stool she'd been perching on, came around the counter, and gave me a kiss on both cheeks. "*Mija*, you are well?"

"I am, thank you. You?"

She gave a slow, sage-looking nod. "*Bien, bien.* I cannot complain."

"We're celebrating Emmaline's upcoming wedding to my brother," I said, squeezing Em's arm tighter.

"And justice being served," Em said.

Señora Baptista clapped her hands to her cheeks. Her smile seemed to say that this was the best news she'd had in forever. "*Felicidades,*" she said. "Many, many congratulations."

As Emmaline thanked her, Miguel's mother summoned a host to seat us at a table on the back deck. She whispered something to him as he picked up menus. He nodded, then led us through the dining room. Miguel, with the help of Billy as his contractor, had replaced the restaurant's old Naugahyde booths and tread-worn floor with Aztec-patterned tiles, wood planks on the walls, enormous windows overlooking the pier and ocean, and a statement piece of a fireplace with cool graphic tiles stretching all the way up to the ceiling. He'd worked with a local glassblower to have custom fixtures created that looked like misshapen bubbles, one hanging above each dining table. The place was nothing short of spectacular.

The host led us through the dining room and past the long, sleek bar that housed hundreds of bottles of tequila and mezcal. It was Jorge's, the mezcal concierge's, domain. He'd taken Miguel, Billy, Emmaline, and me through a tasting just before their grand reopening. As a result, I had a new appreciation for the spirits. I waved at Jorge as we passed.

As the host seated us at a table overlooking the pier, the glow of lights from distant cliff houses were like romantic beacons reflecting off the water. The soft glow of patio lights outside created a sense of peace. The table was set with beautiful glass water goblets and heavy silverware. It was the perfect place to hear every last detail of Billy and Emmaline's wedding plans. The host handed each of us a distressed leather menu, the cover embossed with BAPTISTA'S CANTINA & GRILL. Beneath that, in smaller lettering, it read FINE MEXICAN DINING; and below that, Santa Sofia, California.

My stomach growled. Em arched an eyebrow at me. "A little excited for the *queso*?"

I flicked my own brows up in response, stifling my smile and staying focused on the menu. Inside were custom pages with a few select photographs from the collection I'd taken after the renovation, a list of wines, spirits, and specialty cocktails; appetizers, *ensaladas*, and *sopas*, and the entrée sections broken into beef, pork, chicken, seafood, and vegetarian. Desserts, I knew, were featured on a separate dessert menu card our server would bring us later.

When redoing the menu, Miguel had stayed true to the classic Mexican dishes we'd all grown up with, but he'd elevated them. There were so many new things to try. It would take a year to work my way through it all. Tonight was just one night. Did I want vegetarian or meat? Or . . . I narrowed one eye . . . did I really want seafood?

It ended being an easy choice. The prawn and lobster cast-iron skillet with avocado crema was calling my name. My stomach rumbled again.

A server I hadn't seen before approached the table with a chilled bottle of white wine. Her chestnut hair was pulled into a tight ponytail that hung like a mass of silk down her back. She wore the standard black slacks and sleek white blouse all Miguel's servers wore. "My name's Andrea. I'll be serving you tonight. I hear you're celebrating," she said as she placed a stemless glass in front of each of us. She turned to Em. "Congratulations!"

Em gave a little laugh and said thanks, but held up her hand. "Sorry, we didn't order—"

"Courtesy of Baptista's," Andrea said as she showed us the bottle of Monte Xanic sauvignon blanc.

Who were we to refuse a complimentary bottle of wine? "Thanks so much," I said, flicking my brows up at Em.

Andrea skillfully withdrew the cork and poured a splash in my glass. I was not a wine expert by any stretch of the imagination, but I swirled and smelled and tasted like I was a pro, giving a satisfied nod when I'd finished.

She poured Em's glass, filled mine, set the bottle down, and proceeded to tell us about the house specials for the evening. I was tempted by the sea bass and the scallops, but I couldn't do it. I stuck with the lobster and prawns. And, of course, the brisket *queso*. It was the one thing at Baptista's that I could not do without. The stuff was no ordinary *queso*. Layers of melt-in-your-mouth brisket topped with a savory barbecue sauce, three-cheese *queso blanco*, and a heavy dollop of perfectly pickled relish were served in a stone *molcajete*, which was a mortar—minus the pestle—and carried on a rustic wood slab piled high with the restaurant's thick homemade corn tortilla chips.

We placed our order with Andrea and sipped our wine. "We haven't done this in a while," I said. Being alone with Emmaline on a girls' night was a treat.

"Too long," she agreed.

We chitchatted for a little while before I finally leaned forward and begged her for the details of her wedding.

"Saturday, May twenty-third," she said. "Save the date."

"Like anything could keep me away."

I rapid-fired questions at her. "Where will it be held?"

"At Mission Santa Sofia in the rose pavilion."

"Time?"

"Ceremony at four, dinner to follow at a really cool venue we found. You'll love it. It's kind of rustic and earthy. Billy fell in love the second we stepped inside."

Even based on what little she'd just said, I could see why. Billy was a no-frills kind of guy, much like Miguel was. They both liked things simple, but at the same time, demanded character and charm. They liked the story that a place had to tell. As a contractor, Billy had gotten to the point where he worked mostly by referral. Part of his appeal was the keen sense of design and style he brought into his plans.

"Your parents must be so excited," I said. I'd known the Davis family since Emmaline and I were in elementary school together. Elijah and Elaine Davis were avid ballroom dancers who, if they went on *Dancing with the Stars*, would take home the whole shebang. They were down-to-earth people who had poise to spare and adored their only daughter with a fierce passion. Her being in law enforcement was not their first choice of career for her, but they accepted it. "Are they going to make you and Billy take dance lessons?"

She laughed. "You know it. Elaine already booked us an orientation appointment at the studio."

Em and I had always called our parents by their first names, to each other. It had given us a sense of power when we'd been kids. Now it was just a quirk based on the fact that they were our friends as much as they were our parents. "I cannot wait to see Billy do the tango!"

"Ha! Me too."

The brisket *queso* arrived and we dug in, but not before holding our wineglasses up in a toast. "To you and Billy," I said, my giddy excitement spilling into my voice. "You're so great together."

"Ivy," Em said after we'd devoured half the appetizer before us. "You're like my sister, you know that."

I did know. I was ginger-haired, lightly freckled, fair, and on the curvy side. Em had gorgeous black skin, had recently taken up having her hair braided, was petite, and had a body that was hard as a rock. We looked nothing alike, but we'd claimed each other as family long ago. I reached over and squeezed her hand, my way of saying that I felt the exact same way.

She looked sheepishly at me, not an expression she usually wore, and said, "Will you be my maid of honor?"

I'd been 98 percent sure she'd ask me, but still, my eyes welled and my lower lip trembled with the love I had for her. I put my hand on my heart, willing myself not to actually cry. "Emmaline Lorraine Davis, if you'd asked anyone else, I never would have forgiven you. Well, I would have forgiven you, but I would have been crushed. I will be the best maid of honor a bride has ever had."

She loaded up a tortilla chip with brisket, the cheese goo dripping off the sides. "Open up, sista," she said. I did. And as she plunged the chip into my mouth, we both burst out laughing.

Miguel came up to the table just as we scraped the last of the *queso* from the *molcajete*. He took the seat next to me, planted a kiss on my cheek, and gave us both a crooked grin. "You two are a mad team," he said. "Criminals better watch out."

We laughed again, simultaneously lifting and clinking our wineglasses.

"Has Meg been reunited with her son?" he asked.

"She has," Em answered. "They have a tough road ahead. Ten years is a long time."

It was very sobering. I hoped they'd find a way to be together.

We sat in a moment of silence before Miguel said, "You ladies did the brisket *queso* justice, I see."

Em threw up her hand and looked around. "Ivy's done. Check, please!"

I swatted at her arm. "I'm so not done. Lobster and prawns, baby."

Miguel draped his arm around me. "That's my Ivy. Nothing will stop her from a good meal."

I sipped my wine. "You better believe it."

"Thank you for the bottle," Em said, holding her glass up like a salute.

"I hear you have a wedding date set. That's a good reason to celebrate," he said, his gaze sliding over to me.

Emmaline, along with Mrs. Branford and Olaya, were convinced that Miguel and I would be next. I wasn't in a rush to settle down again, though. My marriage to Luke hadn't lasted. If—or when—I got married again, I had every intention of it being for the long haul. If that meant taking a little more time before Miguel and I made that commitment, I was okay with that. "It's the best reason to celebrate," I agreed. I lifted my glass. "Here's to Em and Billy."

Miguel stayed long enough to see our food delivered and to nod his approval at the plating. "I'll leave you to it. *Buen provecho*," he said. He gave me a kiss, then bent to kiss Em on her cheek. "And congratulations, Sheriff. I have no doubt that your wedding will be epic."

She glowed and I beamed. Miguel was charming and had a way of making a person feel incredibly special. "With Ivy as my maid of honor," she said, "you better believe it."

"My my, I think that is worth celebrating, too," he said, a twinkle in his eye. I had a sneaking suspicion Andrea would be delivering something else to our table before long, but for now, I dug into the lobster and prawns waiting for me on my plate.

Emmaline and I talked wedding dresses, bridesmaid dresses, and flowers for the next thirty-five minutes, our bellies bursting by the time we finished our meals. A young man, just as neatly dressed as Andrea, swept our dishes away before Andrea reappeared carrying two plates, one with an oval shaped baking dish in the center, the other with a decadent square of *tres leche* cake. Both were decorated with sliced strawberries and blueberries. "Oh my God," Em said, leaning back in her chair as Andrea set them in the middle of our table. "Your man is too much."

"Flan," she announced as she set down the first plate. She looked at me. "And *tres leche* cake. The boss said this is your favorite."

I felt my cheeks heat. "He's right."

She lifted her brows in a knowing way. "He

seems like a man in love," Andrea said as she set new napkins and dessert spoons out for us. "Enjoy."

"She's right, you know," Em said, taking up her spoon. "Miguel Baptista is most definitely a man in love."

I waved her comment away with a flick of my hand, but my insides were warm and as gooey as the layers of the *tres leche*.

Hembesha, East African Spiced Bread

Recipe credit, with permission, to Global Table Adventure (globaltableadventure.com/ recipe/eritrean-spiced-bread-hembesha-2/)

Makes one 12-inch hembesha

Ingredients:
1½ cups all-purpose flour
½ cup whole wheat flour
2 tsp instant dry yeast
1 tsp ground fenugreek
1 tsp ground coriander
1 tsp ground cardamom
1 tsp salt
1–2 cloves garlic, crushed
1 Tbsp vegetable oil
½ cup warm water (start with a little less)
1 large egg
Additional vegetable oil, for cooking

Directions:
First, mix all ingredients, save the additional vegetable oil, together by hand or with a mixer. Turn onto a floured surface and knead until smooth.

Cover and let rise in a warm spot for between 45 minutes and 1 hour, or until doubled in size. (Instant dry yeast works very quickly—but if you only have regular yeast this will take about 1 ½ hours.)

Roll out dough to about ⅓-inch thickness and put it in an oiled, 12-inch oven-safe pan or skillet. I used a paella pan. A round pan is best, but placing the round dough on a large cookie sheet is fine, too.

Immediately cut with a pastry wheel (a pizza cutter will also work)—first cut in wedges like a pizza, then create concentric circles about an inch apart. If the dough pulls with the cutter, try cutting toward the center.

Be sure to cut 99–100% of the way through—this is the only way your cuts won't "disappear" once baked.

Let rise 30–45 minutes—until puffed and doubled in size. Meanwhile, preheat the oven to 350º F.

Brush with oil and bake 15–20 minutes. Allow to cool in pan.

NOTE: Eritreans also like to cook their hembesha on the stovetop. Try over medium-low (flipping once after 10 minutes). This works better with a heavy-bottom pan as it cooks more evenly.

Rosemary Bread

Ingredients
1 Tbsp yeast
1 Tbsp sugar
1 cup warm water
2½ cups flour
1 tsp salt
2 Tbsp finely chopped fresh rosemary
2 Tbsp butter

Directions
Preheat oven to 375º F. Proof the yeast by adding to warm water and sugar. Let it rest for five or ten minutes until it becomes bubbly.

Mix in the butter, salt, and 2 cups of the flour. Add 1 Tbsp of the rosemary to the dough.

Knead for about 10 minutes by hand (or use the dough hook on a mixer) until smooth and elastic. Add more flour, as necessary.

Oil a metal or glass bowl, or proofing basket. Place dough into the bowl and cover with a towel. Leave in a warm, draft-free place until doubled, approximately one hour.

Punch down. Divide into two equal parts and let rise for an additional fifteen minutes. Shape each piece into 2 rounded oval loaves. Sprinkle additional tablespoon of rosemary on top of the loaves and lightly press it into the dough.

Spray a baking sheet with cooking spray or oil. Place prepared loaves on the baking sheet. Let rise for an additional 45–50 minutes.

Place in hot oven and bake 20 minutes or until brown.

After removing from the oven, brush lightly with butter or olive oil and lightly sprinkle with salt (optional).

Connect with

Visit us online at
KensingtonBooks.com
to read more from your favorite authors, see books
by series, view reading group guides, and more.